I0452931

Reality

The Arie Chronicles

Volume 1

By Dani Hart

ISBN-13: 978-0991601226
ISBN-10: 099160122X

Dedication

Without fate and encouragement this would have remained an unfinished story. Thank you to my family for being so supportive on my journey to realizing a forever dream, especially my sister-in-law, Nichole.

A special thank you to my husband and best friend who has been by my side for twenty years, supporting me in every way he can. He picks me up when I am down and knows when I need my space to create.

Thank you for understanding me!

I wish I could live in my dreams

and sleep in my reality.

re·al·i·ty

/rēˈalədē/

noun

The world or the state of things as they actually exist, as opposed to an idealistic or notional idea of them.

Chapter One

I always knew I was different. I just didn't realize *how* different. I guess at some point in everybody's lives, probably during the awkward high school years, we all feel it. While some of us spend a lot of the time trying to conform, I realized that I would never fit in so I never tried. As I stared at the plain white ceiling, trying to will myself asleep, my mind rebelled. It was so congested with memories, emotions, and random thoughts these days that insomnia was an understatement.

The first time I realized I wasn't like my friends was my seventh birthday. I could remember the day so clearly, and not because it was my birthday, but because of what happened that day. It was a day I would never forget.

The days leading up to my seventh birthday were shrouded in uneasiness in my mom. She seemed on edge more than normal, which if you knew my mom, you wouldn't think was possible. While others thought she was just overprotective because we were alone, I found it annoying sometimes. Although, if I'm being honest, most of the time I loved the attention.

In the months leading up to my seventh birthday, I could sense the change in the air. Our usually carefree lifestyle had become a little more strained. I used to be free to roam the meadow and the trails around the creek beds, but now my mom asked me to stay in the yard within eyeshot of the house. She rarely put restraints on me even when I was younger, so I didn't question her intentions. She always commented on how mature I was for my age and that I was never that child that wandered off. She was able to trust me, but something had changed, and I wasn't sure what. I couldn't think of anything that had happened that would agitate her so much.

The week before my birthday she spent a lot of time in the meadow meditating. I would watch her from the bay window in the kitchen. I remember thinking how peaceful and aesthetic she looked with the sun lighting up her milky skin, defining the contrast of her chocolate strands even more. When she wasn't meditating, she was gardening obsessively. The yard was free of all intrusive weeds, and every flower was perfectly manicured. Her routine repeated every day with perfect precision. The only time she sat still was during meditation. She even had me sit and meditate with her more than usual. I wanted to ask her what was wrong, but she was never one to keep secrets from me, so I didn't.

Her mood shift started making me nervous. I watched her carefully as if I was studying the veins on a leaf to see if their paths would lead to a secret world full of magic with enchanted creatures and lush forests boasting towering trees and oversized foliage. The night before my birthday was especially strange. She had woken me up before sunrise and led me down to the meadow.

"You need to sit with me, Arie," she said.

"Okay," I replied nervously.

I trusted my mom, so I sat across from her and closed my eyes, assuming we were going to meditate. She took my hands in hers and caressed them gently.

"Arie, I love you very much..."

Her voice trailed off, and my heart stopped beating. For the first time in my little life, I was terrified to hear the words my mother was going to speak. Her tone was unusual, and her actions even more unnerving. My throat started tightening. As much as I tried not to, I was going to cry and I didn't even know why yet. I just knew what I felt inside, and it was breaking my young heart. The first of many broken hearts.

I didn't expect what she said next.

"The world is yours, Arie. The ground you walk on, the dirt between your toes, the flowers that brush your skin, the butterflies that flutter past your nose, the dew in the air, the winds that rustle the trees, the creatures. They are all yours, Arie. You are unique and amazing, and the world waits for you. It waits for you to understand what you were meant for. It waits patiently until the day you see the light you already feel here." She touched my chest where my heart pounded. "One day this will all make sense, but I don't want you to be afraid. I never want you to be afraid of the world. Trust in it and it will never betray you. Trust your instincts above all. They will never lead you astray."

She brushed a few loose strands off my cheek and tucked them behind my ear. She didn't say anything else, and I was left in a state of confusion that all I could mutter was, "Okay, Mommy."

She smiled, but I could see through it and felt the pain within that small gesture meant to ease my little soul, but I knew better. I followed my instinct as she had instructed, and it was telling me that something wasn't right.

We watched as the sun rose above the horizon, slowly releasing the colors of brilliance that so many artists tried to replicate. They could never do this beauty justice. Meditation always seemed to transport me into a fairy-tale world. I imagined being Rapunzel with my hair blowing out the tower window as I watched the sun rise and set every day. As I reached out, the rays of the sun would find my fingertips and send a gentle tickle down my arm.

Meditation breathed life into my imagination and brought the world to life in a way that no one could ever imagine. Not even the best writer could dream up a world as enriched as the one that manifested around me. It was *my* world. One that only my mom shared with me to a degree, but my instinct told me not even she could feel and see the things the way I did. When butterflies flew by me, I could hear the quiet hum of their wings as they worked busily like the chains on my bike as I pushed my way to River's house. I wondered if their wings got as tired as my legs. The flowers were more vibrant in my fantasy world. Their colors glowed like the lightning bugs over the creek as they congregated together to dance and sing under the moonlight. The creatures were my friends and kept me company as I soaked in the energy and beauty of my life inside my head.

When I emerged from my secret world, the sun was high in the sky. I looked over to see my mom was still across from me. She smiled past me. I twisted around and saw a four-legged baby creature that looked like a mix between a dog and a raccoon approach us confidently.

"Mommy, is that a fox?" I had never seen one in real life. It was so cute. I reached out my hand as it got closer, and it playfully nuzzled its wet nose on my fingertips. It was cool to the touch. I looked to my mom for approval.

"It's okay, honey. You can pet him."

I looked back at the baby fox excitedly. I had witnessed creatures interact with my mom this way from time to time, but they rarely acknowledged me, and they definitely didn't pick me over her. I stroked the back of its head, which it took as an open invitation to jump onto my lap. He circled a couple of times and then curled into a ball and rested his muzzle on my leg. "How do you know it's a boy?"

"Because of the way he showed his affection for you. Females are a little less forthcoming with their trust with other females," she smiled. "He likes you."

"Can I keep him, Mom?" I pleaded.

"Creatures are not meant to be pets, honey, but I have a feeling this won't be the last time you see him. The world, including its creatures, will trust you as much as you trust them."

The fox glanced up at me longingly as if begging to be mine. The color of his eyes was unusual. They were a bright purple and reflected a protective demeanor. A moment later, he tucked his head into his body and closed his eyes.

We spent the rest of the day in the meadow. My mom seemed a little more at ease as she told me stories about the way of nature and about my dad. She loved talking about him, but I could also tell it hurt.

"We used to lie here for hours just soaking in the aura of nature. We felt the most connected to each other here. Butterflies seemed particularly attracted to this spot."

"Is that why you nicknamed it the butterfly circle?"

"Yes, it was our circle." She got lost in her thoughts for a moment. "Now it's our circle, Arie." She hugged me lovingly.

"I wish I got to meet him. You make him sound so wonderful."

"He was. No one could ever love with the intensity he did. He loved and respected everything and everyone. He was a remarkable man, and he would have made a perfect dad had he been given the chance."

A peace seemed to settle in my mom after that day in the meadow. We had spent many days together similar to this, but this was the first time she really talked about my dad. She made comments about him in passing, but she never elaborated. I felt like I got to know him a little better through the stories she told about their time together. It also made me miss him in a way I never had before. I was accustomed to growing up with just my mom, so I didn't really think about what it would have been like with him, but I couldn't stop imagining a life with him in it. I thought he would be like Ariel's dad in *The Little Mermaid*, strong, protective, and loving.

My mom had always kept my birthdays pretty low key, and this year was no exception. We only had each other, so it was usually just a few of my friends from school and my mom's best friend, Sierra, who was also River's mom. River was my best friend. We usually just BBQ'd in the backyard and ran around the yard. My favorite was grilled veggies on top of grilled pizza. We were vegetarians, so my mom was very inventive with food, and BBQing was one of her favorite ways of showing that creativity. She also loved to bake. We always had some sort of freshly baked goodie in the house, but today, she baked several different items. She made some mini vanilla cupcakes with vanilla frosting and sprinkles, one of my favorites. She also made Oreo cookie balls and apple crisp. Our house smelled delicious with the aromas of so many different foods swirling together in a tornado of salivating torture.

I never asked for anything special on my birthday. My mom had instilled in me to treat each day as if it were special, because life was a gift and something to celebrate daily. However, she couldn't resist adding a little spice on my birthday to make me feel extra special. I was excited to see what little surprise she had for me this year.

The next morning, my birthday, I woke up feeling different. My body buzzed with a foreign tingling sensation, and my heart raced with anticipation. When I wiggled my toes, the tingling turned to fireworks causing me to giggle. The new sensations were weird, but I liked it. I felt giddy and refreshed like I had never felt before. My mom told me that I had an innate ability to sense the world around me, but I never felt the physical sensations associated with it, until now. It was as if I could *feel* the sun rising rather than just seeing it.

Before I opened my eyes, I could hear the birds singing outside my window. A mother bird had made her nest on the perch of my window, and her babies must have finally hatched because I could hear them chirping their little hearts out. I lay still to listen to the birds break through the silence of the morning. When I opened my eyes, it was barely light out yet. I climbed out of my bed and quietly tiptoed to the window and very carefully pulled back the curtain so as not to scare the new hatchlings. The sun was fighting hard to break through the thick fog hanging onto the horizon. I peeked out the window and watched the mother bird feed her new babies. Their little heads bobbed quickly up and down to touch their mother's beak. It was the most beautiful thing I had ever seen. I was transfixed. Then, the strangest thing happened. The birds all turned and stared directly at me. They were so peacefully quiet like they didn't seem to mind that I was there. They almost looked fascinated, like I was the most beautiful thing *they* had ever seen. It was surreal, but as quickly as they had acknowledged my existence, they turned back to what they were doing as if I didn't exist.

"Arie? Are you awake, baby love?"

My mom, Ariana, peeked her head into the room. I had already made my way back into bed. It was a chilly morning since the fog was still blocking the sun's rays.

"I am."

"Well, good morning, birthday girl. How does it feel to be seven?"

She always asked me that on my birthday as if the answer would be out of the ordinary. When I was four, she told me she had been asking me that since I was born even though I was too young to respond. She sat on the edge of the bed and snuggled up to me.

"Well, actually, it feels great! My entire body was tingling when I woke up. The babies hatched this morning and were singing when I woke. I think they know it's my birthday. Maybe they were singing happy birthday! They even stopped to look at me when I was watching the mommy feed them. It was amazing," I exclaimed excitedly.

"That's great, love. They *must* have known it was your birthday." She collected me in her arms and gave me a kiss on the head and a gentle squeeze. She held me for a long time, and I could swear she was crying, but she got up too quickly for me to confirm my suspicion. It made me uneasy to think she could be crying. Why would she cry on my birthday? The only time I had seen her cry was when she mentioned Dad, and then she would change the subject quickly. She was a compassionate woman, but she liked to look stronger than I believed her to be.

"I put your clothes in the bathroom. I have breakfast cooking, so I'll see you downstairs in a few minutes." She rushed out of the room, closing the door behind her.

My mom was beautiful. Ethereal really! She had gorgeous long silky auburn hair and flawless milky fair skin. Her eyes were a piercing blue and almost spoke to you in the silence. I sometimes thought I could read her thoughts if I just stared into her eyes long enough. She was average height, but people always called her tiny. Actually, I heard some people call her frail. If they really knew her, they would know she was anything but frail. She was my hero. *She still is my hero.* Whenever I looked in the mirror, I imagined myself looking just like her when I grew up. Our similarities were striking. I had long dark hair, but mine was more espresso than her auburn locks. My eyes boasted the same blue brilliance as hers, and my frame was tiny like hers. We even shared the same curl of the bottom lip when we smiled.

I looked over to my bathroom door, which connected to my room. We lived in a pretty big house, and since it was only the two of us, I occupied the second master suite. My mom had inherited the house from an elderly couple when she was eighteen. She said they had tried to adopt her from the orphanage, but they were too sick to care for her. Despite this, they still loved her and visited her often. When they passed away, they left their estate to her.

The elderly couple was the closest she had to parents. When I thought about my mom growing up without parents, it made me sad.

My room was very girlie. My mom called it "shabby chic". She loved to create. It was the artist in her, and creating a beautiful space for me was no exception. It was decorated with pale purples and different hues of white. The valences had scallops on the bottom trim, and the curtains were white sheer with ruffled trim all around. They were lightweight and easily drifted in the wind when my windows were open. Above my bed, my mom had painted a grouping of solid brown colored butterflies. On every wall hung a hand painted whitewashed wooden word. Under the butterflies the letters spelled *DREAM. IMAGINE, BELIEVE,* and *FATE* adorned the other walls. In the corner of my room next to the window bench was a white wicker chair that my favorite purple teddy bear spent most of its time. It was a fairly large bear. My mom brought it home on my third birthday. It was bigger than me at the time. I had surpassed its height now, but it was still easily my favorite. My ceiling light was a beautiful candle chandelier with hanging crystals, my furniture was whitewashed with hints of brown, and my bedspread was a pillow quilt with different patchwork designs in the same purples and whites of the room. The trim of the bedspread was finished with a scalloped lace. I truly felt like a princess in this room.

One of my favorite fairy tales was *Beauty and the Beast*, and when I described Belle's room to my mom, she did her best to mimic my imagination. My mom thought the fairy tale was too scary for me, but I had picked it off a bookshelf at the store when I was three and never let it go. It was a board book meant for toddlers and mainly consisted of pictures, but it never revealed her bedroom, so I imagined it. The beast was a gentler version of that depicted in the older level editions, but my mom was always afraid it would give me nightmares. What drew me to the story was the beast. He was just another creature of nature albeit fantastical.

We lived far from others, so when I wasn't running around with River or hanging out with my mom, I spent a lot of time by myself in my room pretending I was a princess of a magical world where I had many friends and my dad. I thought if I meditated hard enough I could create the world of my imagination and make it real. Sometimes it even felt like I had, but then I would open my eyes, and I would be sitting in the same place on the floor in the center of my room. It still made me smile to think of the possibilities of other worlds created by little minds like mine.

I slipped out of bed, but instead of going to the bathroom to get dressed, I wanted to see the birds again. They piqued my curiosity. I wondered if they would look at me again. They weren't chirping anymore, so I assumed they were sleeping. I pulled back the curtain gently, but rather than seeing sleeping babies, they were all staring at me as if they knew I was coming. It was eerie at first, but then one of them sang softly to me. Did it want me to touch it? I was only seven, but I knew better than to touch babies in a nest. I had lived on the meadow since I was born, and my mom taught me everything there was to know about all the creatures and their ways. She wanted to make sure I respected them and their space. The bird chirped at me again. I put my hand on the window where the nest was resting. All three babies rubbed their heads on the glass where my hand was. At the time, I thought it was amazing. A better word would have been magical.

"Arie, five minutes!" my mom yelled from the kitchen.

I whispered to the babies, "I have to go, but I'll be back later." I ran to the bathroom where a simple purple skirt and a coordinating shirt hung. On the counter laid a matching headband and socks. Yesterday, we had gone to the boutique next door to the bookstore my mom owned to pick out a special birthday outfit. She had grown close to the owner of the shop over the years, and I played with her daughter who was the same age as me. We both got bored hanging out at the shops, so we spent a lot of time playing hide and seek in the untouched forest across the street. We also put on little story times at the bookstore for the kids under five. We had fun putting on puppet shows.

It surprised me when my mom picked out clothes for me. For someone who never wore anything but jeans and a t-shirt, she always seemed to pick out the perfect little outfits for me and they were always very girlie. She was always kidding with me that I was her little dress up doll. It made me giggle, and I didn't mind.

Chapter Two

Downstairs my mom was putting a bowl of fruit together next to a stack of pancakes. I ran over to the oversized calendar my mom had built. She had drawn a big heart around September twenty-third. Slashes through the days that had passed in the month stopped at that day. I smiled and took a marker and wrote "My Birthday" in the box with the heart.

"I made your favorite birthday breakfast."

"Thanks, Mom." I gave her a hug around her waist as she put my breakfast on the kitchen table. It was small and round with four chairs, and it faced a huge bay window with a reading nook that overlooked our backyard, which boasted miles of wildlife and forest. The sun was rising in a cloud-free sky. The fall was always so beautiful here. The mild heat made days in the yard playing with River last until sunset. I sat down in my chair that faced the forest. My mom had placed my plate on top of a birthday placemat we made together when I was five. It was more elaborate than I could have drawn on my own. She had asked me what I wanted to create, so I told her about my fairy-tale world of towering trees, luscious foliage, and beautiful butterflies of every color. She guided my lines and taught me how to make the perfect curves of butterfly wings. Even though I had my moments of frustration, she was always patient, and in the end, we had created the world of my daydreams. She had added the two of us off to the side with a tornado of butterflies swirling around us. When we finished it, we took it to a print shop and had it laminated.

I grazed on my pancakes as I looked out the window and watched the birds dance along the tree branches. If I were really lucky sometimes, I would catch a glimpse of deer rushing by on their way to the creek. I smiled widely. Today I was lucky. A family of three deer crossed the back lawn just outside the forest wall. They seemed in no rush as they strode easily pass the house. They walked so gracefully. Almost as if they were floating.

"Arie, you do need to get off to school at some point this morning."

The deer froze outside as if they heard my mom. I kept my gaze locked on them. All three of them turned in my direction. As quietly as I could, I whispered, "Mom, those deer are looking at us." My mom stopped cleaning up from breakfast and peered out the window. The deer turned away and kept walking as if nothing happened. "Did you see them?"

"Love bug, they were probably just startled by all the noise I was making with the dishes. Now, hurry up and finish eating. You don't want to be late on your birthday."

I glanced back at the deer and then continued to nibble on my breakfast. In the corner of my eye, I swore I saw my mom wipe away a tear.

I thought my day would go on as usual, and it did at first. Everyone sang happy birthday to me at snack time, and the teacher had brought in another one of my favorite desserts, frosted sugar cookies. She even made the frosting purple. After the cookies, we had extended play time on the playground. The breeze tickled my skin as my friends chased me in our daily game of hide and seek. For the next round, I went past the forest line and hid behind a wide oak tree. It was a silly place to hide since it was the most obvious, but most of the kids stayed inside the yard or just inside the first line of trees. I went in a little deeper. I giggled as I watched the kids searching wildly for me. I slid down the tree and sat on the ground, enjoying the warm breeze. I could hear my friends' voices off in the distance fading slowly as the sounds of the rustling leaves and the buzzing insects amplified around me. My skin started to prickle as the wind stroked it gently. The warm winds always put me in an especially giddy mood, but today it felt different, like a bolt of electricity flowing through me. My eyelids became heavy as the heat soaked in. I blinked slowly and watched the world around me begin to disappear. Just as I was closing my eyes for the last time, a dark shadow that could have been a figure, floated toward me. I felt calmly alarmed and fascinated at the same time, but I was too tired to make a move. It stopped just a few feet away and hovered. I couldn't keep my eyes open any longer. As they shut, I caught a glimpse of a man emerging from the darkness and then my eyes made their last attempt to stay open, but they failed and darkness overcame me.

I woke up in my bed at home. I looked out the window to discover it was still light out. I rolled off the bed, wiping the sleep from my eyes and descended the stairs. My mom was rushing up. When she saw me, she dropped the plastic glass of water in her hand, raced to the landing where I stood and pulled me into her arms tightly. This time I was sure she was crying as she sobbed loudly. She grabbed my cheeks in her hands and locked eyes with me as if studying the intentions of a lion on the prowl.

"Are you okay?" she asked seriously. "Are you hurt?"

The concern and sharp edge in her tone picked up the pace of my heart.

"I'm fine, Mommy. Why? What happened? Did I fall asleep? How did I get home?" The questions rushed together. The realization of the moment was quickly overcoming me, and I felt the persistence build for answers.

"Your teacher found you in the forest, sleeping. They called me just before they found you. What were you doing out there, Arie? You know better than to run off."

The tears streamed down her face, and her blue eyes deepened to a black. "We were playing hide and seek. I didn't go far. I'm sorry, Mommy. I just started feeling tired, and then I fell asleep."

"I just don't understand how you could be running around one minute and then sleeping the next, Arie."

Then, I remembered the shadow. "There was someone in the forest, Mommy. I wasn't alone. I think it was a man, though, but he was in a shadow so I couldn't really tell."

I didn't think it was possible, but my mom's milky skin turned stark white, and the frightened look in her eyes sunk my heart to the pit of my stomach. She grabbed me in a tight embrace again and wouldn't let go as she cried harder. I wanted to ask her what was wrong, but I was too scared, and she didn't tell me.

"Never run off like that again. You hear me?" she said sternly, a tone that was a rarity between us.

"Yes, Mommy," I replied without resistance.

She pulled away, but held onto my shoulders as she studied my eyes again. After a long moment, she broke the gaze, kissed me lightly on the forehead, and started to attend to cleaning up the spilled water. There was a knock at the door. She answered it, and River came running inside the house. He sensed something was wrong, so in the true nature of River, he shouted, "Let's go outside and play!"

My mom shot me a daring look. "Do not run off and stay inside the forest line. No creek."

"Okay, Mommy." I smiled hesitantly and then ran down the rest of the stairs, grabbed River's hand, and pulled him out back. There was nothing out of the ordinary in the yard, so I ran to my favorite spot, pulling River behind me to the back corner where the lawn met a patch of butterfly bushes. The flowers looked like purple trumpets, and I imagined an orchestra of flowers playing a beautiful chorus in the town square that filled the air with a beautiful string of notes and intoxicating scents. They were even more exquisite when they danced in the wind. I loved to watch the butterflies hop from one flower to the next as they drank from them. Sometimes I would even see a few chasing each other around in circles as if they were playing tag. There were days that I would run alongside them and stretch out my arms and wave them as gracefully as possible as if I was flying with them, but today, I slipped off my shoes and socks and lay down on my back. I closed my eyes and listened to the music of the swaying flowers around me. It was so peaceful.

"Arie."

A whisper filled my ears. I opened my eyes and saw my best friend, River, standing above me. My mom said River and I had known each other since birth. He was a few months younger than me and lived next door. Of course, next door was a mile away. It was a long walk, so we usually rode our bikes between the two. Our moms only started letting us do the ride alone in the last six months, so we played together more now.

"How many have you seen today?" He carefully lay down next to me. He loved watching the butterflies almost as much as I did.

"None, yet. I just got here." I closed my eyes again, and we lay silent for what seemed like forever. I thought I fell asleep. A quiet swishing sound just above me made me open my eyes. What must have been almost a hundred butterflies were twirling around in a corkscrew direction above me. I gasped. I looked to my side and shook River's arm softly. He opened his eyes and looked at the butterflies in amazement. It seemed like the world had turned into a kaleidoscope, the multitude of colors mixing and combining endlessly. Neither of us dared to move as the butterflies continued to flutter inches above our heads. After a minute, I sat up slowly, expecting the butterflies to fly away, but they didn't.

Instead, they broke their tornado pattern and started circling around River and me like a funnel of water finding freedom. They looked like they were playing tag, only they never quite touched each other. They were in a perfectly rhythmic flight pattern unaffected by the world around them. River sat up slowly too and faced me. I was the first to break the silence. "Is this really happening? Are we dreaming?"

"This is awesome," he whispered.

Our eyes locked, and this was the first time we both realized we would be together forever. I wouldn't be as bold to say that this was the first moment we knew we loved each other because what seven-year-old knew what love was? But we definitely had a pivotal moment inside the shelter of the butterfly circle. It was like the moment a butterfly breaks through its chrysalis and stretches its wings for the first time. It's reborn into a life with endless possibilities.

I didn't experience a moment like that again until the day my life changed forever. The day the world I knew and loved turned dark. The sunshine that filled my heart burned out, and an ecliptic moon had taken its place. It no longer breathed life into my lungs. I no longer felt the breeze that used to send shivers through the fine hairs on my bare skin. I no longer celebrated my birth, but instead, was lost in the memories of the smile my mom engraved in my soul. Flowers of condolences and tears replaced colorful balloon bouquets and friends. From that day forward, I spent my birthdays from sunrise to sunset alone, staring at a gravestone in the meadow next to the butterfly circle.

Here lies a beloved mother, Ariana Belle.

My only request for the gravestone was an engraved butterfly. Every time I saw a butterfly I would imagine it was my mom's soul watching over me.

As my eighteenth birthday quickly approached, the memories of my mom magnified, as they did last year before my seventeenth. I was sixteen when she died. The courts didn't know what to do with me since I had no known relatives. We weren't wealthy, but we had money and a home, so I was emancipated under the supervision of River's parents. I was sixteen and living alone with only the forest creatures to keep me company. River's parents handled the finances, and River helped me around the house. They visited often, and we always had dinner together either at my house or theirs. They were the closest I had to family, and they took care to remind me of that every day. The time between school and dinner was hard. I filled the hours immersing myself in other worlds within the pages of fiction. It was invigorating how minutes turned into hours in a blink of an eye when I traveled into the minds of the characters.

The hardest time was after dinner lying in bed in an empty house. I was alone with my thoughts, dreams, and nightmares. It took several weeks for the reality of my mom's erasure from existence to sink in. When it did, I didn't think I would make it. I felt like I couldn't breathe, and there was a gaping hole in my heart. The tears would come so fast and hard I could barely sit up. She was my everything, and now I had nothing. No one.

With her death came the stark realization what death was and what it meant. I wasn't sure what was harder to grasp, that my mom was gone or that death existed. That one day I too would vanish and be nothing. No one I knew had died, and we didn't have pets, so I never really had that emotional connection to death. My life was sheltered, and I was far removed from grief. I had a happy and uneventful, peaceful childhood. *I was naïve*. Now, I had so many questions about death.

I don't think my mom was faithless, but she definitely didn't discuss God or heaven and hell. She believed in the purity of nature and that everything was made in nature's eyes and we all would one day return to nature. It made her death that more unbelievable. Returning to nature seemed so natural and peaceful, but what she didn't tell me was the emptiness it left behind.

I was so deep in despair after she died that I threw myself into religious studies. We had a pretty good collection of religious books at the store. I spent hours, sometimes days, dissecting the literature and taking notes, even cross-referencing and comparing similarities and differences among religions. There was a lot of cross over, which led me to believe there was one ultimate source and just many different translations and interpretations of that source. It created a necessary distraction, but was also my attempt at some sort of clarity and peace for my mom's death. What I discovered was that faith can't be taught and that most people turned to a God to keep from going insane and killing themselves when the realization of death took hold of them. Without some sort of faith in a higher being or afterlife, you were forced to face that death was inevitable and THE end. Whereas, if you convinced yourself to believe in an afterlife, you could live this life in peace knowing that when it was over, you and your loved ones will continue in another place. My mother believed that. She believed once we all returned to nature we would be reunited. I wanted to believe that. *I needed to believe.* It was just enough to get me through my darkest moments.

I wasn't sure where I stood. It made me feel better thinking my mom wasn't gone forever and that she was somewhere waiting for me. It helped me breathe when a moment socked me in the gut and took me down. Was that faith enough? Was that cheating? Was that fair to those who truly believed? If I was being honest, I didn't care. If it got me through the day, then I would take it, whether it was real or not. So, now I prayed. To whom? I don't know. To God? Sometimes to my mom. My prayers were ramblings of a shattered heart and an empty soul, begging for a break from the pain. Pleading for answers to why she died. Sometimes I even asked for the same fate to set me free.

I prayed at night when I was alone in bed and thoughts of my mom overwhelmed me. I prayed in the morning when the sun's warmth was cold and dark. I prayed in the meadow where the butterflies had once touched my soul and taken me to another place. I prayed that they would come back and do it again, so I could remember what it was like to feel happy. *To feel anything*. Now, I was just numb as I lay in bed waiting to live in my dreams and sleep in my reality.

Chapter Three

I must have finally drifted off because the sun was now warming my face. These days I kept the curtains open. I felt too enclosed with all the light shut out. Waking to the light gave me a false sense of happiness. Once I opened my eyes and my mind registered where I was, that all disappeared. I wished I could sleep longer. I wished I could sleep forever, but sleep was almost a distant memory. My body was starved for it, but was only fulfilled with two or three hours at a time. It was deprived of one of the most essential elements it needed to survive. *Good*, I thought. My usual crankiness settled in as I became more coherent.

The phone rang loudly in my ear. "What?" I snapped to the empty room. Seriously, who could be calling this early? I snatched my cell off the end table before the obnoxious second ring. "Hello?" I didn't have to try hard to sound annoyed.

"Are you okay, Arie?" River asked.

"Oh, hey. Yeah, I'm okay. Just waking up. Isn't it kind of early for you?"

"I wanted to be the first to say happy birthday. Starling didn't beat me to it, did she?"

"No, you're safe. Star rarely wakes before noon." Their passive competition for my friendship was irritatingly cute. I was lucky to have them. They kept me going.

"I know this day is not the easiest, but it's your eighteenth birthday, and that should signify something important."

I stayed silent while I tried to fight back the tears. I tried all week to not think about what today was. I flashed back to the calendar that still hung in the kitchen downstairs. My mom had made it a ritual to put a heart around the number twenty-three. September was written in large cursive at the top. To follow her ritual I had my own. I would write my birthday in the square. I hadn't changed it since my sixteenth birthday, so my birthday still had a heart around it, but the day of the week had changed. River's voice brought me back to the conversation.

"Well, I was hoping you would go to a show with me tonight. One of your favorite bands is playing."

He sounded unsure of my answer, and why shouldn't he? I had slowly shut down after my mom's death, which included shutting him out. "Sure, I guess. It's been a while."

"Great," sounding more confident now.

"Yeah, okay, but I have a lot to do today, so I'll just meet you there." I planned on clearing weeds from my mom's gravestone out in the meadow as I had done last year. Then, I would just sit there and remember. Remember her voice, the way she walked, the way she felt.

"It's at The Pinnacle."

"Okay, I'll see you tonight."

"The doors open..."

I hung up the phone.

I managed to stay in bed for a few more hours. I tried not to think by examining my room for the millionth time. I hadn't changed anything after my mom's death. Right before my sixteenth birthday, my mom had surprised me with the idea of updating my room from the little girl room it was to a room that was better suited for a young adult. And, yes, she did say *young adult*. I was so proud that I had that title. We picked out everything together and even painted the walls ourselves.

My curtains were a deep purple and hung absently from a curtain rod. Maybe if I closed my curtains I could sleep past sunrise. My sheets were a simple black, but my favorite and most cherished possession was the blanket my mom had personalized for me and I slept with every night. It was a plush zebra print minky fabric on one side and a smooth deep purple minky on the other side. She personalized it with embroidery on the purple side.

Nature speaks if you listen.

Those words were embedded in the deepest parts of my soul. The soft whisper of her voice still echoed in my head when I read it.

I kept my furniture because it was still in great shape, and I liked it. It kept memories alive in the room. I hadn't done much shopping in the last couple of years. My mom was the shopper. She always knew how to put outfits together. I never put much thought into the trends. I was simple with my jeans, t-shirts, and sweatshirts. *Just like her.* I guess like my mom I was OCD about cleanliness, so needless to say, my room was always spotless. I wished I could say the same for my life.

It was time to get up. I remembered when I used to look forward to waking up and starting a new day. I would be so full of anticipation I would skip breakfast. How times have changed! I peeled off the sheets, and the chill hit me like a snowstorm on a summer's day. *I should have picked my sweats to sleep in rather than the boxers and tank.* I ran to my closet and grabbed the black velour robe hanging on the door hook and threw it on as quickly as humanly possible. As I tied it around me, I hugged it longingly, inhaling deeply hoping to catch a faded scent of my mother. I had taken the robe from her room after she died. Other than that, her room remained untouched and unchanged.

How could it be so cold? Had winter overtaken fall already? The thought made me even sadder, as if that were possible. I loved the fall. Every year the season seemed to get shorter and shorter. The summer heat lasted longer than should be normal, and the winter barged in before fall even had a chance to say hello.

My mom said I was too thin, and that's why I was always cold. Not enough meat around my bones to keep me warm. Of course, like every teenage girl, I never thought I was thin enough. Now I did. I had lost a lot of weight that I couldn't afford to lose after my mom died, and I just couldn't seem to gain it back. I had managed to eat better, but I was still thinner than my mom would have preferred. I missed her.

I peered out my window to see a cloudless day ahead of me. I dared to open the window, fearing it would make the room colder, but it was surprisingly warm outside. So much so that it served as a heater for my room. I opened it all the way and let it work its magic on my chilled bones.

A lot had changed over the past two years. Aside from the weight loss, my grades had slipped. I went from being an "A" student to barely hanging on to a "C" average. It was hard to focus when my scarred heart weighted so heavily on me. I just didn't care anymore. Grades seemed pale in comparison to life and death. At this point, I just wanted to get through. I was almost done.

Now, warm enough, I pulled off my robe and hung it back on the hook. I made my bed methodically, gently petted the zebra blanket, and headed to the bathroom. One glance in the mirror made me regret it. My brown hair was a knotted mess. My mom would say it looked like my hair was a handful of espresso beans after meeting their fate in the grinder. I had my mother's hair and fair skin, but unlike her, I could stand in the sun without getting third degree sunburn. My eyes were bloodshot, which was a shame, because it hid my piercingly blue eyes, which also had an uncanny resemblance to my mom's. The sadness that resided in them now betrayed the happiness that my mom's always reflected.

I looked so much like my mom that it would be impossible for someone to look at a picture and identify if it was my mom or me when she was my age. My mom used to tell me there was something extraordinary about me. She said it was in my eyes. She believed that eyes were the windows into the soul, as many do, but she said mine disclosed much more. I never really understood what she meant. They looked as blank as I felt these days. I turned on the shower just as the phone rang. "Hello?"

"Hey, we got disconnected. Sorry my cell service sucks."

It was River again. *Poor guy was trying so hard*. How I must be hurting him. I didn't realize that I hadn't said anything until he interrupted my thoughts.

"So, doors open at 7:30. I'll swing by and leave the ticket for you."

"Okay, thanks. I'll see you tonight." There was a time when I pictured being married to him. I had loved him my whole life. It was always he and I. What's that saying? Thick as thieves.

I imagined us having two kids, a boy and a girl, growing up in this house and running around the very meadow we chased about in. I would sit on River's lap on the back porch watching our perfect little kids giggle as they chased the butterflies like I did when I was young and carefree. At least that was what I thought married life would look like. That was how it looked in the books I read that had a happily ever after ending. *It was a good dream.*

While some may speculate that we fell in love with each other at our first kiss, I knew better. We were soul mates from birth. We shared our first kiss in the meadow on the day of my sixteenth birthday before my mom died. We lay on the grass as we had done that first time the butterflies blessed us with their magnificence on my seventh birthday. We did this on my birthday every year in hopes they would return. My birthday not only signified being a year older, but it was also *our* day. Every year River and I shared a private ritual and a hidden connection, until that kiss when the secret was exposed and our hearts were bound beyond platonic feelings. My mom's death broke this ritual and the dream of a perfectly unflawed life together.

"Sixteen is a big one, you know." He smiled softly.

"I know." I looked over at him as he lay there with his eyes closed. He was beautiful. I knew handsome was the preferred word when describing the male species, but not for him. His face looked like it was chiseled by the most talented of sculptors. His hair was a sandy blond, and while it wasn't long, it definitely couldn't be called short. It had soft waves that fell perfectly around his face. His eyes were as blue as the sky, and his skin was fair like mine. His lips were full and, as soft as they looked, I wished for the first time that I could feel how soft they were against my own lips. His body was perfect. For someone whose only workout consisted of running a few times a week, he had a flawless physique. The football team was always trying to recruit him because he fit the mold of a jock. I asked him once why he didn't participate in sports, and he just responded that they didn't hold his interest. He liked his freedom and independence.

My body began to tingle all over. A light breeze sent shivers down my spine. I wanted to touch him, but not in the playful way we touched when we horsed around. I wanted to embrace him. I reached out my hand to touch his when the fluttering of wings filled my ears. I pulled my hand away quickly.

"River?"

He opened his eyes and stared at the return of the prodigal butterflies.

"Wow, they're as beautiful as I remember them," he whispered.

We sat up slowly and faced each other as we had done on my seventh birthday. Their return was a mystery. They circled around us, leaving us in the eye of the swarm. There were hundreds of them displaying every color imaginable on their wings. Some had stripes while others had splatters. Even the most talented artist could never capture the true brilliance of these magical creatures. They were flying so swiftly around us that the color of their wings looked like fresh paint being swirled in a can with a multitude of colors to make that perfect color combination.

I saw River staring at me as I watched the butterflies. I turned to him and got caught within the depths of his eyes. His stare bore deep into my soul. We sat like that for what seemed an eternity. My body burned from the inside out. My heart raced. My mind was anticipating what my body wanted. I couldn't think. All I could do was stare into his eyes, begging for him to feel the same way. The butterflies continued to circle around us, but they seemed to be fluttering faster as if they were anticipating the moment, too. Right at the moment I thought my body was going to explode if something didn't happen, he took his hand and grazed the side of my face. His touch sent electric shocks through my cheek and down my body. His hand followed my jawline, and his thumb outlined my lips on its way to my neck. He gripped the back of my neck gently and leaned into me as he pulled my face toward his. He paused and looked into my eyes as if waiting for me to say no. I didn't think I could wait any longer. My heart was pounding so hard I could barely breathe. The eternal pause ended, and his lips brushed mine. I thought I was going to pass out as I inhaled him. *How can one moment be so intense?* He brushed his lips against mine for a few agonizing moments as if, again, waiting for me to protest. I couldn't handle it anymore. I pressed my lips against his, and he responded. I felt like that kissed lasted for hours. It was soft and slow and perfect.

I wish I could say the moments after that kiss were just as perfect, but they weren't. I thought that moment would change my life forever, but it was the moments after that would. I would never be the same. I would never be that innocent little girl in the meadow again.

The mirrors in the bathroom were covered with a thick film of steam from the shower. *How long had I been dazing?* The past was clever at sucking me in. There had been times when I would get lost in my memories for so long that day would turn into night. I swiped my hand across the mirror in front of me and looked at my reflection pathetically. Tears had fallen during my walk down memory lane. *Traitor!* I hadn't even noticed I was crying. I wiped them away harshly and jumped into the shower.

Chapter Four

I dried off and threw on a pair of jeans and a t-shirt. *Today was going to be rough.* I wondered if it was going to be as bad as last year. *Would it ever get easier?* How could it? If it did, then that meant I was forgetting her. I could never let that happen! I would never let go of her. I ran a brush through my long wet hair and tied it back. No sense in making a fuss over my hair just to pull weeds. I glanced at myself quickly in the mirror and poked at my rib cage that was evident through my tight-fitting shirt. *My mom would hate what I was doing to myself!*

I softly sighed and headed to the hallway. This was always the hardest walk of the day. I had to pass the walls covered in picture frames of my mom and me at various stages of our lives. In fact, I hadn't changed anything in the house. I couldn't. I tried once with River's encouragement, but it cut like glass against my heart when I tried. I promised myself I would never try it again, at least not until I was truly ready. And then there was her room that I had to pass to get to the stairs. I kept the door closed. It was just easier that way.

I spent the first few months after her death hidden beneath her sheets. I missed a lot of school in the beginning, but I was at risk of losing my emancipation rights, so I attended half-heartedly and did just enough to get by and pass. River hovered over me to make sure I would be okay. I had successfully assured him I would never do anything to risk my life. I attended weekly therapy sessions known as grief counseling and overall mental health monitoring. It was part of the emancipation agreement. I also got bi-monthly visits from the department of social services. My final visit was last week. Now that I was of legal age, I was officially on my own. *I was an adult.* I still didn't know what that meant.

Everything in my mom's room smelled like her, so I stayed there until River pried me from the hold it had on me. He saved me from myself. He was my guardian angel during the hardest of days, and I pushed him away. *Jerk!*

I stood outside her door and rested my hand on it. *Could I do this?* It had been so long. I hesitated as I put my other hand on the doorknob. *Screw it!* I turned the knob and pushed the door open carefully as if I was afraid something might grab hold of me and trap me in the room again. I held my breath, but nothing happened. I was being ridiculous. *Or was I?* The room smelled stale from lack of inhabitance. River was kind enough to come every month and clean the room, so it wouldn't get dusty. *I really owed him.*

The house had double masters. I had one, and my mom had the other. My mom's taste could be described as traditional vintage. She loved antiques. The room had a four-poster bed made of beautiful whitewashed hand-carved wood. It was accompanied by a matching set of nightstands and a dresser. She was excited the day she found this set at a garage sale. I have to admit, although it was not my style, it was gorgeous. Her bedding was a pale iridescent blue mixed with cream undertones. A ceiling fan took the place of table lamps, and the walls were decorated with old world beach scenes painted by her to match the overall theme of the room. There was an adjoining master bathroom that was as miraculous as the size of the room. My mom was simple, so there weren't many knick-knacks lying around. It made it easy for cleaning. I took a deep breath in hopes of filling my lungs with her familiar scent. *Failure.* Any traces of my mom's scent had long since disappeared. I could feel the disappointment register on my face. I was left with only the memory of her comforting aroma.

It was dreary in the room, so I went over to the curtains and pulled them open. This room had the most breathtaking views of the sunset that engulfed the valley. We spent a lot of time on her bed watching the sun go to sleep. I hadn't seen the sunset from up here in a long time. Maybe I would tonight before I went to the show. *Maybe not.* I sighed deeply. It was time to clear the weeds around my mom's gravestone in the meadow. As I was closing the curtains, I noticed a misplaced shadow down below near the path that lead to Deer Creek. I tried to break the trance I was under, but the sight of the shadow held tight and squeezed the life out of my muscles, paralyzing me. A blinding pain stabbed behind my eyes and forced me to the carpet. The intensity caused beads of sweat to form on my forehead. I tried to scream out in agony, but it was lost in my throat. An unfamiliar dark face flashed through my head. The sight of it summoned fear and hate and made me want to lash out on it like swatting at a blood-thirsty mosquito. I couldn't make out his features clearly, but I could feel the evil that resonated in his soul. The pain in my head deepened as a frighteningly familiar voice that I couldn't quite place hissed from one ear to the other. "Arrrriiiieeee." I wanted to take a fork and stab him in the eye to make the throbbing in my temples stop. And just like that, I was standing at the window like nothing happened. My headache gone, the beads of sweat dried, and my sanity in question. *Was I hallucinating?* Or was that just another nightmare to add to the stack? If I was dreaming, then how was I still standing here? I searched the yard for proof that I wasn't going crazy, but the attempt was futile. I didn't find anything out of the ordinary, and it *felt* the same as it had before the...vision? Was it a vision? *Well, damn.* No wonder my mom's stories from her visions were so real. That was about as real as they came. I could accept the abnormality of having visions or dreams or whatever, but the voice that accompanied this one had me shaken. I didn't know the voice, but it *felt* familiar and that scared the crap out of me.

I went downstairs into the three-car garage. My mom was very organized. The garage had floor-to-ceiling cabinets on two walls, and one wall was devoted to tools hanging on hooks. A workbench with drawers occupied the last wall. My gardening gloves were in one of the drawers. I also took a weed digger off one of the hanging hooks and grabbed a brown paper bag for the weeds. I went out the garage door into the yard and made my way down to the meadow.

The meadow wasn't as picturesque as it used to be. I neglected it a lot. In the spring, beautiful California poppies in all colors occupied the meadow. It was one of the most magnificent sights, or at least it was when my mom was around. She loved the meadow even more than I did. She would spend every weekend out here pulling weeds and humming like there wasn't anything better to do. When I asked her why she loved it so much, she said, "It's my time alone with my thoughts and feelings and that of the world around me." What was funny was I didn't have to ask her because I knew. I felt the same way about being in the meadow.

I stood at the edge of the meadow closest to the house. I inhaled a deep, cleansing breath under the bright sunshine. It was a comfortable temperature, but winter was quickly approaching. River promised to come by this week to mow if I got the weeds under control first. At the far end of the meadow against the bank of trees was my mom's grave. I could barely see it hidden beneath the overgrown grass. *What a disgrace!* She was the most amazing person that anyone ever had the pleasure to come into contact with and look what I had let come of a place that represented her honor. I needed to do better by her. I made a new promise to myself I would never let her grave become suffocated by weeds again and that I would plant her favorite flowers, butterfly flowers, around it. *Maybe this was a sign of better days to come*. River would call it progress. I walked cautiously to her gravestone, and without looking at it, I started to absently clear away the weeds.

After a few hours, I was proud to see that I had cleared away most of the shrubs around her gravestone and the meadow surrounding it. I was drenched in sweat from the heat. The sun had already passed overhead and was making its way down the horizon. This was why I was so skinny. I hadn't stopped to eat lunch. In fact, I skipped breakfast, too. My stomach immediately started to growl as if it heard what I was thinking. As I was wiping the sweat from my forehead with the back of my glove, I heard a rustling come from the spot that my mom had named the butterfly circle, the place where the swarm of butterflies had so magically appeared twice since I was seven. I felt a cool breeze blow across my shoulder blades as I moved closer to the circle. A handful of butterflies were flying around with no apparent rhyme or reason. I walked over to my usual spot and plopped down. I watched the butterflies for a few moments and then lay down and closed my eyes. I envisioned my mom lying next to me meditating. After all, wasn't meditation blind faith? How was this any different? Belief that she was with me. The hissing sound of the voice from earlier haunted my pleasant thoughts. Whose voice was that, and how did it get into my head?

A noise startled me awake. I sat up quickly and noticed the sun was setting. I looked in the direction of where I thought the noise originated, but didn't see anything. I listened for another minute, and when I was content that I must have imagined it, I stood up and went back to the house. *Damn, I was on edge.*

I peeled off my gardening gloves and left everything on the back porch. I went inside to the kitchen, washed my hands, and made myself a peanut butter and jelly sandwich. I washed it down with a large glass of water and stared out into the meadow as I nibbled on a strawberry. Dusk and dawn always made the meadow look like another world the way it lit up the plants and trees. My mom said it was because the light was reflecting off the creek that was just on the other side of the meadow. She believed that at those times the sun kissed the meadow and filled it with magic.

That's why I would spend so much time in the meadow at sunrise and sunset. I believed her, and I always felt a little more alive and safe. I wished I still felt that way. I could never truly feel safe again. Just then, I caught a glimpse of an owl in the tree closest to the house. I always thought their hoots were mesmerizing and calming. The sound came flowing out of them like it was being carried on a soft breeze. As it was putting me into a trance with its rhythmic call to the world, it stopped suddenly and looked toward the meadow. I followed its line of sight and saw something flash across the meadow past my mom's grave and disappear.

Was it another owl? That was a pretty big one if it was. The owl started hooting eerily. I shielded my ears and scrunched in discomfort. The sound penetrated the walls of the house and violated the tender fibers of my eardrums. I had never heard an owl make those sounds. These were the creepy moments when I regretted telling River and his parents to stop coming over for dinner because I needed space. It made me nauseous once I had made the decision to tell them. That night at dinner I nervously pushed my food around my plate until the courage rose within me. The looks on their faces when I told them made me ashamed for saying it, but they were supportive. They would send River over with dinner instead. It was sweet how they could never completely let me go.

Just as quickly as the owl started screaming, it froze and stared at me. I released my hands from my ears. This was the first time since my mom died that I felt like the world knew I was still here. But why now? Why had the world ignored me when I needed it the most? It shut me out and now it tried to breathe life back into an almost vacant soul.

The familiar sound of a text message broke through the noise in my head. It reminded me that I would be responsible for my own finances now, including my cell phone bill, which I was less than thrilled about. *Can't wait.* I wasn't really sure what that meant, so I needed to talk with River's mom, Sierra, about it soon.

The sun had been quickly replaced by a rising full moon. How long had I been stuck in my head this time? I looked at my phone and saw a text from River.

Where are you?

Shoot, it was already eight o'clock. The Pinnacle was at least a twenty-minute drive into the city. *Whatever.* It was my birthday. I could be late if I wanted to be. I ran upstairs for another shower.

This time I thought I should probably dry my hair and try to look somewhat presentable. It was my birthday after all, and I hadn't felt like this in a long time. Although I still felt weighed down by the darkness that was thrust upon me, I somehow felt a little lighter today. I felt it creep up on me when I woke up, and it peaked during the owl incident. *I might actually smile for River again.* He was such an incredible person, and I could tell he was still waiting for me to return to the love that we once shared, back to the feeling of utter and complete bliss with the electricity flowing through our bodies every time we accidentally touched. I wanted to feel that way again, too. I wanted to be a part of something that filled the cavernous hole deep inside me, not to forget why it was there, but to take the edge off and make life worth walking through again. I picked out a tight-fitting black V-neck tee, a pair of nice skinny jeans, and black leather boots with just enough heel to make a statement. I took a quick glance in the mirror at my almost non-existent makeup and looked deep into my own eyes. I swore I could see my mom staring back at me. It was uncanny that two people could look so much alike. We really did share the same eyes. I hadn't decided if I liked seeing so much of my mom in me every day. It did, however, solidify the fact that I could never forget her even if I wanted to. With that thought, a faint smile sparked a fire in my eyes. *I can do this.*

Chapter Five

I pulled up to a packed parking lot in front of The Pinnacle. The arm gate was lowered, and the sign indicated it was full. I drove past the entrance and parked about a block away on a residential street. I checked the time on my phone. It was almost ten p.m. I saw the text message notification and ignored it. I knew it was River. He probably thought I was flaking again. It wouldn't be a first, that's for sure. I knew I should respond, but I wanted a moment to myself in the club before I met up with him. I wanted the freedom that I loved and needed when the music consumed every fiber of my body.

I glanced in the rearview mirror and stared at my reflection. I froze for a moment, lost in my own eyes. A car alarm a few cars down the street jerked me out of my daze. *Deep breaths. I can do this.* It's been long enough. I stepped out of my car and tried hopelessly to lock the car with the alarm button. My car was a modest silvery gray Toyota Corolla. My mom had bought it off a used car lot for my sixteenth birthday. After several attempts with the alarm, I gave up and just locked it manually. It's not like I went out enough to need an alarm, so why bother with a new key battery.

I looked down the street and could see The Pinnacle at the end. I could hear the vibrations of the music oozing from the walls. There were people littering the street out front smoking cigarettes and talking loudly. The building glowed against the dimly lit streets. It really had been a long time since I went anywhere outside of school, the bookstore, and the house. I just graduated a few months ago and had been burying myself in books from the bookstore my mom owned in town. Reading allowed me to fill the void and escape reality.

By default, the bookstore became mine when my mom died. We mainly dealt in used books, but we obtained some new ones and maintained the children's section. My mom and I had conducted story time the first Saturday of every month. I recently added an electronic section with e-readers and tablets to accommodate the new technology taking the place of paperbacks. This also ensured that we didn't isolate our market, but allowed us the freedom from turning into just another "giant" bookseller. Our store was unique and intimate, and I wanted to keep it that way. It was my mom's vision, and I inherited it with the store.

River's parents helped me run it. Sierra mainly. She was there from open to close every day. I would go after school and hide in the couch chair in the corner of the store and read. We didn't have a lot of foot traffic at once, so Sierra managed most of the customers. I tried to run story time as I always had, but I couldn't mimic the enjoyment needed anymore. My heart just wasn't in it anymore. It was a hard decision, especially because there was this one little girl in particular that would come every month and sit quietly in the back of the group. She was very shy. She started coming when she was a toddler. Something about her fascinated me. I was drawn to her. I tried to talk to her once, but she hid behind her mom's leg and then stopped coming altogether. I felt awful, and I kind of missed seeing her there. I would wait in knotted anticipation every month, hoping she would return, but she still hadn't. I didn't even know her name, but for whatever reason, story time felt incomplete without her presence. Her light lifted me.

Sierra had slowly started training me on the administrative side of the business over the past year. She gave me my time to grieve, but today marked the day it was legitimately mine. I hated all the questions about where I was going to attend college and what I was going to do with my life. Really?! Who the hell knew? And who the hell cared? I liked the bookstore. Couldn't that be enough? *Again, deep breaths.*

I walked quickly down the street. As I passed the smokers out front, I couldn't help but make a gagging noise. I hated that people smoked, and even more, I hated that they felt it was their right to surround me with their clouds. It was kind of bitchy, but I didn't care. A girl dressed in cheetah print tights, a mini skirt, and a skin-tight half top that barely covered her breasts shot me a glare. I returned it with a fake smile and went to the front door. A female and a male bouncer were guarding the entrance.

"Ticket?" the male bouncer asked.

I pulled the ticket out of my back pocket and showed it to him. He scanned it and pointed to the woman. I walked over to her and without a word she scanned me with a wand.

"Turn around."

I did a little spin for her.

"You can go in." I managed a smile after the cold space invasion.

I walked into the club and was immediately smacked in the face with the loud music, the humidity, and the crowd. My heart started to accelerate a little as I examined the room. I didn't know whom I was kidding. This place was vast and packed. If I had any hope of finding River, it was going to be by text message. I decided to push through the crowd that was sandwiched like sardines just so they could get closer to the band on stage, their sweat combining to form a musty concoction of body odor and perfume.

I used to love this scene. I was a little young for it, but after my mom died, I escaped to it. River thought it would help to get me out of the house. He was right in a way. The music drowned out the endless words that filled my thoughts and scratched at my heart. For the first few months afterward, going to shows was the only way I could breathe without choking. I would close my eyes and just let the beats, vibration, and words take over. I danced for hours next to hundreds of people, but always felt like it was just me.

Tonight my favorite band, Equinox, was playing. It was an indie rock band with a girl singer who had the most enchanting voice. It was a strange coincidence that I was also born on the autumnal equinox. Maybe that's why I liked them so much. They had the best stage presence. You couldn't help but get into their show and drift off to another world. They started playing one of my favorite songs. I decided to enjoy a few songs before texting River, so I could lose myself like I had for so many months.

I stepped to the back of the crowd and left a few feet distance to give myself some space. I closed my eyes and let the music envelop me and slowly enter every pore of my body. It invaded my soul and erased my thoughts. I started to move with the music, letting myself go, including letting go of the pain. I could feel the energy around me grow more powerful as the chorus began. Bodies started rubbing up against me, but I kept my eyes closed and focused on the energy building inside me, the feeling of release and freedom. I allowed myself a quick glance at the crowd. They all seemed to be in the same place as me, unleashing everything outside of the walls that were trapping us together.

As I was about to rejoin them, I caught a glimpse of a guy lurking in a corner next to where I was standing. He was staring at me. You would think he would look away when I caught him, but he held strong. His eyes became more intense when they locked with mine. They seemed to harness the energy of the room. I felt a penetrating pull pass between us that I could only describe as euphoric. Just looking at him made my body sizzle with intensity.

He was the complete physical opposite of River. He was tall and skinnier than River. He had dark chestnut brown hair and a ruggedly square jawline. He looked like a model for rock attire. He definitely had an edge about him that screamed rebel. *I bet he rode a motorcycle, too.* He never broke his gaze as I studied him. This feeling was foreign to me, but not unfamiliar. It was a feeling I used to get when River would come around. An arm suddenly wrapped around my shoulder that dissipated the energy exchanged between us. I jumped a little being shocked out of my trance. I knew it was River's arm around me. I didn't even have to look at his face. His touch had its own special signature that always felt safe and comforting.

"Were you planning on hanging with me tonight or just by yourself?" he kidded as he squeezed my shoulder gently.

"Yes, sorry. The song just took over for a minute." I glanced back at the corner, but *he* was gone.

"What are you looking at?" River had followed my line of sight to the corner. Thank goodness *he* wasn't there anymore. I didn't want River to get the wrong idea and get his feelings hurt. I had already hurt him enough the past couple of years. His insecurity in our relationship had elevated, and if I didn't change something soon, it would implode and this wasn't the time or place I wanted it to happen. He had never been the jealous type, but my lack of attention and affection increased his protective nature. He checked in on me at the store at least once a day, drove me home, and popped in on the weekends. He tried to get us to reconnect once about a year ago, but I wasn't ready and I wasn't sure that's what I wanted anymore. In an opportune moment when he found me in the meadow one evening under the stars, he had tried to kiss me. I let him for a second, but I pulled away and broke any sense of security he had about us.

"I thought I saw somebody from school." Okay, so I guess the trail of lies started now.

"Really? Because you were staring pretty intensely."

I could hear a hint of jealousy in his tone. "I was squinting. Are you seriously going to give me a hard time on my birthday?" I shifted my stance and scratched my arm nervously, something I always did when I felt uncomfortable or stressed. I thought it was hives, but I never got bumps or a rash. It was a phantom itch that attacked me relentlessly in any time of unease. I had to wear long sleeves and pants for several months after the funeral or else I would have permanently damaged any exposed skin.

Screaming over the music was starting to give me a headache. "Can we talk after the show?" That came out bitchier than I wanted. He took his arm off my shoulder and settled for our bodies just barely grazing skin. I tried to focus on the band instead of the weird tension between us. There were a bassist, guitarist, drummer, and singer. The singer was the only girl. I wondered if they fought for her attention, or if they just saw her as one of the guys. She was awkwardly beautiful, which is how I would describe myself. There was nothing traditional about the features of our face. I'm not sure what her natural hair color was, but today, she was a redhead. Her wild and graceful movements to the music offset her tiny frame; otherwise, she would have been lost on the stage among all the equipment.

As the band continued, I couldn't help but glance around. I swear I could feel *him* close by. I was captivated by him. I wanted to know more about him. Who was he? Where was he from? Why was he staring at me when there was a room full of half-naked gorgeous girls dancing around me? And more importantly, where did he go? It was hard to accept this as a coincidence. It was my birthday, and strange things seemed to happen on my birthdays, although usually subtle. This birthday was taking weird to a completely different level. When I was younger, it mainly had to do with creatures being friendlier than normal with the exception of my seventh birthday when I was visited by the shadow person. I tried not to think about that day because it scared my mom and me, and it had changed the carefree nature of our lives. My mom had restricted my freedoms. I couldn't go past the forest line or visit Deer Creek without some sort of supervision. This included going to River's house. My mom kept a watchful eye on me whenever she could, but she tried to hide it. She was sheltering me so I could remain blissfully innocent for as long as childhood would allow me, but I knew anyway. She carried the weight of worry with her from that time forward.

I gave up looking for the mysterious guy with the energy of hurricane force winds when I felt River watching me. I closed my eyes and tried to let the music overtake me again, but it wasn't the same with River next to me. The energy was off. It had been off between us for a long time. I wanted so badly to force it. I promised myself that tonight I would try with all the heart I had left. I owed it to him. He saved my life, and in return, I felt I owed him mine, whether it was true or not. River had brought me back from a black hole of depression that was slowly sucking the life force out of me. The control it had on me was unnatural and threatened the last thread of sanity I had left. The haunting reverberate of the singer's voice infiltrated my thoughts. Her voice hung in the air for a few seconds after she stopped singing and then faded. The crowd hollered and clapped, but the lights shot on, signaling the end of the show and enlisting boos from the crowd. I squinted until my eyes adjusted.

"Did you have fun?"

When my eyes focused, I saw the hope in his gaze. He really wanted to make me happy. "I did. Thank you." I gave him a sweet peck on the cheek, making his face light up.

"Do you want to go watch the meteor shower?"

"Sure." What I really wanted to say was I was tired and just wanted to crawl into bed and cry myself to sleep, but I didn't. *I was trying.*

We waited another awkward minute until the crowd thinned and then started heading toward the exit. River was a few steps in front of me. The energy in the room shifted suddenly, and I could feel *him again*. I looked over my shoulder, and there he was standing by the bar across the room watching me. I shyly looked away. I felt like I was caught looking at a boy crush in school. A hand laced through my fingers and pulled me outside. I glanced back, but he was gone again. The cold air took my breath away. River protectively put his arms around me, and I instinctively snuggled into the warmth of his chest. I inhaled the essence of his being. He always smelled like heaven, if heaven existed and had a smell.

"Where are you parked?"

"Down the street a few blocks. You don't need to walk me there. I can meet you at the park. Same place, right?"

"Um, yeah, but I would feel more comfortable at least walking you to your car." He squeezed me tighter.

"Seriously, River, it's not a big deal. There are crowds of people walking in the same direction. I'll be fine. Better yet, why don't you go get your car and meet me at my car, and we'll follow each other there, okay?" He seemed to resign to that because he lightened his grip around me.

"I know there's no point in arguing with you, so I won't." He bent down and kissed me on the head. "I'll see you in a minute." He walked up the street and turned the corner.

The street was becoming deserted quickly. It was cold out, and people were trying to escape the frosty chill in the neighboring bars. Some were brave enough to make the trek to their cars in hopes of an immediate rush of warmth from their heaters.

I moved briskly toward my car. It felt like my mere presence had scared off everybody. There were only a few people walking in the same direction as me now, and they were well ahead. I didn't normally scare easily, but things had been a little unusual today. The universe had definitely been speaking to me, and I would be stupid to ignore it.

River would be at my car before me at this rate. I picked up the pace, but stopped short when I saw a shadow lurking at the back of my car. I looked around, but I was alone now. That was when it hit me. Like a lake of fire, the energy coming from my car consumed my body and filled my soul with an intense burning. I choked down my breaths as I clawed at my throat to get air. I frantically looked around for help as I felt life seeping out of every viable organ of my body. Headlights lit up the street and crept up behind me. I suddenly had control over my breathing again as I fell to the concrete. I gasped sharply and quickly as I tried to gain composure.

I made this huge deal about being a big girl, and I didn't want River to see me having an anxiety attack, if that's what it was. I had many attacks right after my mom died, but this just didn't feel the same. Either way, I didn't want River to start treating me like a child again. His role in my life changed from a boyfriend to a parental figure. I think that was part of the reason why my romantic feelings and dreams about a future with him dissipated. I closed my eyes and let the air enter my lungs in slow even breaths. The cold felt like shards of glass against the inside of my throat.

"Arie, why aren't you at your car yet?" River was rolling down the window and drifting up to me.

"It's right there. I was just petting a stray cat." *Ugh!* I hated lying to him. We valued truth in my family and that carried over to River and his parents. Lying to him *felt* wrong.

"Okay, well, in case you didn't notice, it's freezing out. Maybe a little less petting and a little more walking."

"Funny." I stuck my tongue out at him and looked over to my car. The shadow or whatever or whomever it was had disappeared. I crossed the street in front of River's truck and quickly unlocked the door and got inside. I couldn't turn on the engine fast enough. I checked out the backseat like a paranoid freak and then gave River the headlight signal that I was ready to follow him. He passed by me, and I turned my car in his direction and followed.

Chapter Six

I couldn't help but feel anxious when we reached the park. It had been so long since River and I had been alone together, and I wasn't sure what he expected from tonight. Two years ago today we shared our first and last kiss, with the exception of the stolen kiss last year, and I could only imagine he was hoping to break the silence of intimacy.

This park held many captivating memories for us. At least once a week we would come here at sunset and watch as the sun melted into the darkness and the moon lit up the sky. Our passion for each other was always strong but restrained. We both knew our limits and never tested them. The first time we did, the universe lashed out and took away any hopes of eternal happiness again. A quick flash of my mom's lifeless body crossed my thoughts.

I pulled into a spot next to River's car. I watched as he swiftly hopped out of his car and raced over to open my door. It was kind of funny how old-fashioned he was. In fact, his parents were, too. They were the family living in the wrong century. River smiled as he opened my door.

"I hope you brought blankets," I said.

"Of course, I did. Have I ever forgotten?"

I shot him an accusing glance. "Um, yes, you have."

"You are never going to let me live that down, are you?"

He walked over to his truck and dug out two blankets and a backpack. His truck was a black older model Ford. His taste was always reserved although we both knew he could afford whatever he wanted. He was never one for drawing attention to himself. He showed me his stash. "Well, this time I am more than prepared."

Why did that not comfort me? My stomach started feeling queasy, and my palms started sweating. Shivers rushed through my body like a tidal wave swallowing a sandy beach. *I can't believe I didn't bring a jacket!*

"Are you coming?" he asked as he started to walk to our spot.

"Just go ahead. I'm going to see if I can find a jacket."

"Good luck! I've seen your car on its best days."

"Ha-ha." *Always a comedian.* He was right, though. Not that my car was dirty, but I tended to leave a lot of books and papers in it. It was stuff I was constantly carting from the house to the store, so I finally gave up and just called it my mobile storage unit. I was sure I would have at least one jacket intermingled in the piles. I crawled halfway into the back of my four-door. I could only imagine how ridiculous I looked with my legs hanging out the front door and my head in the backseat! The chill was rapidly sucking the heat out of my car. I swiftly pushed books around and grabbed a jacket from beneath a box full of papers. I tugged at the sleeve trying not to knock over the box. Unsuccessful! I yanked a little too hard, and the contents of the box spilled all over the ground. "Dammit!" I grabbed the jacket and scooted back into the front seat. As I sat up, I saw a person standing by the tree in the shadows only a few feet in front of my car. I nearly jumped into the backseat I was so surprised. I scanned around frantically for River, but he was probably already at our spot. I looked back at the tree, but the person had disappeared.

"What... Seriously, could things get any weirder?"

"Are you talking to yourself again?" River had snuck up on me, so naturally my reaction was to scream louder than any normal person should. I jumped out of the car and started beating up on him.

"What the hell, River?" He blocked my sad attempts at punching him while laughing at me.

"Did I really scare you?"

He had managed to pin my arms around my ribs in a bear hug. My back sunk into the safety of his chest, and I relinquished my fight. "Honestly, I kind of feel like I'm going crazy lately." He squeezed me a little tighter in a hold that longed for more. Something my mind and body weren't rejecting. We might have drifted apart and things might be different between us, but down to the very essence of my being, I loved this man. He was both the heart and soul of my world. The warmth of our bodies made me sizzle. I didn't know what it was about today, if it was because it was my "big" birthday, but I was starting to feel alive again. It reminded me of the days of discovery and exploration of new and uncharted love that we once shared. Just the brush of his thumb on my shoulder or a whisper into my ear made me shiver. The nervous butterflies in my stomach right before I saw him drove me crazy. So much lost before it was found.

Today my body was responding in ways it never had before, so I let him hold me for what seemed like an eternity. Time turned into hours rather than minutes, and my breathing became irregular. My vision turned crisp and clear among the darkness and shadows of night. River turned me around and touched my face gently. His fingertips caused pulsating waves of energy to pass over my skin. I closed my eyes and let the chill of the night be consumed by the heat generating between us as his thumb brushed over my bottom lip, making me crave a distant kiss.

Elevated sounds of nature distracted me from River. All my senses seemed to be heightened, and I was enjoying every moment of it. I could hear the creatures of the night dancing across the broken fall leaves on the ground and the hoots of owls that filled the tree lines. I swear I could even hear the whisper of baby birds being tucked into their nests.

Traces of lunar energy building as the full moon served as a source of renewed peace within my soul as it traveled down the rays that met my bare skin. As I inhaled deeply, I took in the fragrances of the sap dripping from the elm trees in the forest and the flowers that draped elegantly off their leaves. There was a creek nearby, and its inhabitants made themselves heard by their splashes as they swam upstream. A chorus of howls signaled that the hunters found their prey.

The air swayed softly through my hair, lifting it off my skin and leaving my neck exposed. A soft pressure took advantage of its vulnerability. River cautiously kissed my neck, carving a path upward and across my jawline to the corner of my lips. He paused momentarily, and when I didn't reject, he took in my lips with his. The sweet taste of River was exactly as I remembered it. *I missed this.* I missed him, and now I craved more. The tingle on my lips erupted into explosions as I responded desperately. The energy between us rose by the second as if our bodies had been waiting an eternity for us to kiss again. His hands crawled down my back, increasing the intensity of the moment. My hands had become limp in the embrace, but now came alive and found his face and locks of hair. I hadn't felt this alive since my mom died, and I wasn't going to back down so easily now that the veil had been lifted.

River pushed me up against the car as the desperation in our kiss deepened. Like a mother being reunited with a lost child, neither one of us was willing to let go again. I saw how life was when we were apart, and this reminded me of what our future could be like if I just held on tight enough. And then it was quiet! The rustling of the leaves stopped, the owls went silent, and the quiet whispers of the birds ceased. Instinctively, I stiffened and stood still.

"What's wrong?" River pulled his lips from mine.

"Do you hear that?" I looked around. Not only had it gotten quiet, but also the breeze had stopped. The world seemed to be frozen.

"Hear what? I don't hear anything," he said with a concerned look on his face.

"Exactly. Why is it so quiet all of a sudden?" The sound started to slowly come back, and the breeze kicked up again, but not to the heightened level I had just experienced.

"It's midnight, Arie. Of course, it's going to be quiet." He rubbed my back gently, responding to my shivers.

"For a moment it seemed unnaturally quiet." The chill was penetrating my bones. I couldn't stop trembling.

"Let's get to the blankets and warm you up. The shower is going to start soon."

He rubbed my back briskly now. With his foot, he slammed my car door shut careful not to release his hold on me. The sensations that overtook my body had seeped out and dissolved into the air around me. My body felt numb. River softly pushed me forward. My legs responded, and we walked onto the curb and across the park. My senses had returned to normal, but something was still off. I spotted the blanket ahead and just past that was the most picturesque view of a desolate valley filled with the light of the midnight stars. Our cars had climbed what seemed like a mountain as they wound in and out of the hills to get to the naturally preserved park. It was obvious from this view why it was protected. It was serene and filled with all sorts of extraordinary creatures. To lose this little piece of heaven would have been a shame. This was *our* spot. The spot no one else seemed to know about. It held the essence of our past together like a diary. It was secret, sacred, and it was ours.

River led me to the blanket. I plopped down, and he quickly wrapped both of us in the other blanket he had brought. *He really was prepared.* He put his arm around me quietly as we stared into the valley, admiring the backdrop of the stars and ignoring the moment we had just shared at my car. It seemed like we were floating on clouds we were so high up. As a shooting star shot across the horizon, I rested my head on his shoulder. It felt nice to be physically close to someone again. His embrace made me feel safe. Something I had lost with my mom.

"Are you going to make a wish?" He avoided looking at me.

"What's the point?" I shrugged my arms as I fell into a complacent state of mind. A familiar dull ache surfaced in my chest, knowing I could never reclaim what was once mine. The laughter that filled a room when my mom was being silly, the security her words brought when I was scared to sleep in my room alone, the comfort I felt in her embrace when I had gotten hurt, and the love I needed to be strong.

"The only thing I would ever wish for isn't possible. Nothing else is worth my breath." With that, we both silently watched as the sky was filled with shooting stars. It was the most naturally alluring creation the universe could ever display for the world to experience. Every once in a while there would be so many that the sky would light up as bright as daylight. All I could think about was how much my mom loved these moments. She loved anything that nature had created. I could never appreciate the universe as much as she did. Life was everywhere and in everything, and it seemed to respond to my mom's presence. If it were hot, a light breeze would kick up when she worked in the garden. If it were raining, it would pause long enough for us to make it inside the house before getting soaked. Birds would eat seeds from the palm of her hand as she held it out for them. Butterflies would follow her around the meadow and even rest on her shoulders from time to time. Flowers never died in our yard, and weeds never grew. Her connection with nature was a divine intervention. Only a few times had it recognized me as a part of her, carrying the same affinity for nature. The baby fox, the butterflies in the meadow, and then the owl today. I never saw the fox after its first visit. I waited for him every day for months, but his memory faded with time.

A butterfly suddenly landed on the blanket in front of us. I was stunned and rightfully so. I had never seen a butterfly at night. They normally hang from the underside of leaves or find a crevice to slip into so they can rest. They don't sleep per se. They just become inactive, but that was certainly not the case with this little guy. "That's odd." River turned his attention from the show to see me reaching for it. I spread my hand out on the blanket. It hopped onto it. I moved it closer and showed River. "This is a little strange, right?" I looked at River for an answer. He didn't look as shocked as me.

"I would say that nothing that happens around you shocks me anymore."

That was a fair statement. Peculiar things tended to follow me around like a lost puppy looking for a home. Its wings were beautiful colors of red and orange with an outline of black. It hopped to the tip of my finger and froze. It could have been asleep with how still it was being. Just then, my focus was broken as another butterfly landed on the blanket. And then another and another. Butterflies covered every inch of the free space on the blanket in a matter of seconds. River and I stayed as motionless as we possibly could.

"There are so many," I said in amazement. The butterfly on my finger suddenly flew off, and as if they were summoned to another place, all the butterflies followed obediently. The space in front of us was clouded by hundreds of them fluttering around. They spiraled around us and disappeared amongst the shooting stars. I watched as the last couple flew out of sight. That's when I caught a glimpse of a shadow flash from one tree to another. At some point, I should have probably told River that someone was following me, but for some reason, I didn't feel like I was in danger. I tried to track the shadow across the park, but it had vanished amongst the canopy of the trees.

"Butterflies really seem to like you, Arie." He put his arm around me and pulled me in close to him and whispered into my ear, sending chills down my spine. "It's nature's birthday gift to you. Happy birthday, Arie." He kissed my earlobe before he pulled away.

"Yeah, I guess." I was still distracted by the person shadowing me.

"Hey, Arie, I know things have been off, but I just want you to know that I'm never going to leave you, and I'm never going to give up on us. I'll wait as long as it takes."

I could feel a panic attack starting to rise in my chest. I had been avoiding this conversation for so long. I was afraid of what I might say or what I might not say. I stumbled to get words out. "I, uh, umm…" He put his lips on mine so fast I could barely compose myself enough to respond, but his lips persisted, and mine refused to reject another taste of him. I reciprocated with a harder kiss and let the energy swelling inside me encase my thoughts. My other senses took over. This feeling was so raw and new, I would do anything for it to last forever. Was River the source of this? Was the long since past passion between us returning, or was I just really good at fooling myself into believing it? Who wouldn't want River wrapped around them and walking by their side for eternity? He was perfect! Beautiful, sweet, and protective.

As the meteor shower continued above us, the moment of anticipation increased. River's lips parted from mine carefully. He held my face in his hands and studied my eyes, looking for permission. I brushed my fingers through his golden hair as I searched for an answer to an unspoken question stalling the moment. I grabbed his locks and pulled him close to my face so our cheeks were just barely touching. I lingered with my lips and warm breath by his temple, and my fingers remained intertwined in his hair. I wanted this. *Dammit, I needed this.* River's lips made their way back to mine before I could make a sensible decision.

I could feel everything! I could feel the roughness of his jeans on mine. I could feel his heartbeat race as his anticipation rose with mine. His warm breath sent goose bumps down my spine. My body felt exposed as if it was searching out the sensations and saving them for later. The breeze crawled through the space between us teasing us further. I shivered, so River pulled the blanket over us without skipping a beat. He was being careful and safe and keeping to the innocence of our past relationship. He pulled me in and kissed me again, this time with purpose rather than wild passion. It was a kiss of unconditional love.

My thoughts invaded the sensations as a virus would invade cells. Should I be doing this? Was I being selfish because I would do anything to not feel numb anymore? Was this fair to River? I loved him, but was I *in* love with him? All great questions that I didn't have answers for. Not yet.

All of a sudden, the park came alive with screams from all the creatures that inhabited it. River jumped over me protectively. He looked around desperately as I covered my ears. The sound was deafening. A sharp pain started pounding in my head. Between the ear-piercing screams and the concentrated lightning bolts of pain shooting through my head, I thought I was going to pass out. River shifted his attention to me.

"Arie, what's wrong? Why are you screaming?"

I was screaming? How could I not know I was screaming? The sounds of nature were so loud, and my head felt like it was going to explode. My heart was racing as if being chased, but by what? I could feel tears running down my face, but couldn't tell where they were coming from. Why wouldn't it stop? I tried to open my eyes, but immediately regretted it. I shut them quickly and scrunched into a ball, trying to block out the chaos around me.

"Arie, the noise is gone. Arie."

I could hear River pleading with me, but his voice was so distant that I couldn't make out what he was saying. Then, everything went black.

Chapter Seven

My body felt stiff, my eyelids were heavy, and I felt disoriented and nauseous. I was scared to open my eyes, fearing the pain that would be associated with it, so I kept them closed. Everything was quiet except for faint whispers, among them a woman's voice.

"I think it's time she knows. It's starting, and you know it's only going to get worse," the woman's voice stated anxiously.

Was that River's mom? Tell me what? What could get any worse? Because I can't imagine how things could. I tried to move my body, but it wouldn't respond. I hoped it responded soon or else I was going to vomit all over myself. I tried to focus on the conversation.

"I know. I just don't know how."

I had never heard River sound so anguished. What could be so bad to make him fear telling me something? He never kept secrets, or at least I didn't think he did. I guess I wasn't the only one lying these days. Now I was scared. This was not helping my stomach. I finally was able to move my fingers. The tingling in my toes was a sign of my legs returning to life. My mouth felt dry, and my lips were cracked. I needed water. Now! I tried to make a coherent sentence, but I couldn't seem to do anything. I must have made a noise, though, because I could hear shoes shuffling toward me.

"Arie, are you awake?" River touched my hand lightly and softly stroked my forehead with his other hand.

I opened my eyes to a squint and tried to focus on him. I could see a blurry shadow standing behind him, which I could only assume was his mom.

"Water." My voice was almost inaudible.

"I'll get it, sweetie." Sierra went out of focus as she retreated for my water. She was stunning. Her silky blonde hair was wavy and long and framed her gorgeous milky skin. Her frame was tiny, but curvy in all the right places. She was taller than me, but not quite as tall as River.

"Welcome back." He bent down and kissed my forehead faintly.

I wanted to ask him a million questions, but I just couldn't get anything out. I squeezed his hand gently to let him know I was all right. Sierra made it back with a glass of water and a straw. River took the glass and carefully put the straw into my mouth. The cold rushing waves against my tongue and down my throat were the instant relief I needed. Why was I so thirsty? How long was I out? Even after I guzzled the entire glass, I wanted more.

"That's enough for now. I don't want you to throw up all over me," he teased. It was as if he read my mind.

I started to wiggle my toes. That was when I realized I wasn't wearing socks or shoes. In fact, all I had on was a t-shirt and my undies. Thank goodness a blanket covered me. I shifted my body around to recapture some movement. I was in River's bed! I was wearing River's shirt! *What the hell happened?* I opened my eyes wider and focused on him. I tried hopelessly to sit up in bed as River leaned over and helped me. "Thank you," was all I could say. I looked around the room. The light of the day filtered through the curtains. River watched me as I took inventory of my surroundings.

"It's afternoon." He sounded concerned.

"Oh, how long have I been asleep?"

He shifted nervously on the bed. "Today is day five."

"What!" I jumped up, which was stupid, because my body was not ready for the drastic movement. I screamed as a pain shot down my back, bringing on a wave of dizziness and nausea. Sierra came barreling into the room and ran over to the bedside opposite of River.

"Are you okay, sweetie?" She sat on the bed and rubbed my back as I scrunched over to my knees in pain. "What can I do?"

There was nothing she could do for me right now. I appreciated her help, but having her as a substitute for my own mom was almost too much to bear. To make it worse, she was partaking in keeping something from me, which fractured my trust in her now. I burst into tears. The pain was too much, physically and emotionally. "Can I please be alone?" No one moved. "Please," I demanded harsher than I meant, but I needed to be alone. I felt both of them get off the bed. The door closed, and it was quiet except for my sobs that filled the room.

I was so dehydrated that the tears dried up, leaving me with only dry whimpers. The pain in my back was subsiding, but the pain in my heart had increased exponentially. The partially healed wound from the day I found my mother lying on the ground near the back porch had been ripped open. The moment I bent over her and realized she was gone haunted me endlessly. *How can it hurt this much again?* It was like time never passed. I uncurled from the damp sheets I had balled up into and gazed out the window. The sun no longer penetrated the room. I wiped away the last of the tears rolling down my face and slowly got up. Little shards of pain flashed through my body, but I was determined. I took a deep breath and went over to the window and pulled back the curtains. The night sky was filled with stars, and the moon was now at its first quarter phase. I couldn't believe five days had passed! What the hell happened to me? I still felt stiff from lying motionless for so long. The night looked so perfectly calm. The window was slightly cracked, so I pushed it open to get some much needed fresh air. The air was cool, but not as cold as it had been the other night. The chill served as an ice pack on my hot cheeks. My body was drenched in sweat from my emotional outburst, so when the brisk air tickled my skin, it sent a clammy burst of quivers throughout me. And again, there was the shadow. I couldn't handle much more. I yelled out the window, "Seriously? Didn't anyone teach you that lurking around is creepy?" The person stood motionless across the dirt path in the shadow of the night. The door creaked open. I turned from the window to find River emerge from the hallway. He walked over to me.

"Who are you talking to?" he asked suspiciously as he took his protective stance next to me.

He had slightly pushed me out of the way to get a better look. I peeked passed him out to the street, but the shadow was gone. This was getting ridiculous! "No one apparently." I tried to brush it off. I really didn't want to deal with explaining this right now. Even though I slept for days, I was exhausted. I honestly just wanted to crawl back into bed and hide under the sheets. River grabbed a blanket off the couch chair and wrapped it around my shoulders. It was my mom's blanket.

"I thought you might want it."

"Thank you."

He held me tightly while resting his chin on my head. We both stared out at the view in a relaxed silence.

"Not as spectacular as the other night." He kissed my head.

"Nope. That it is not. I'm sorry I ruined it for you." He immediately turned me around and held my face gently in his hands. He looked me directly in the eyes, forcing me to see the purity of heart in his blue eyes.

"Stop it! You didn't ruin anything. It was perfect." He softly brushed his lips up against mine. He only lingered there for a second, but my body was already reacting to the energy his touch put into me. He pulled away slowly.

"I love you, Arie, and what happened the other night before you passed out was the most amazing night of my life. I have missed you so much, and that night I felt like I had my Arie back."

My heart sank at the sincerity of his words and the heartbreak that I may one day inflict on him. How could I do this to him? Because I was selfish and I wanted him any way I could have him, because, let's face it, he was all I had left and I did love him. I didn't want to be eternally alone. A shiver rushed through me and shook my body at the prospect of losing him. "Why didn't you take me to the hospital?"

"Your breathing normalized quickly after you passed out, and you know how far away it is. There were no symptoms that warranted it. Besides, you know my mom has a nursing background. She would have told me to bring you if she thought you were in a medical emergency. I think that's enough fresh air tonight." He closed the window.

"Can you tell your mom I'm sorry? I didn't mean to yell. I just..."

"You don't have to explain. It's been a hard week for everyone." His voice cracked as he led me back to the bed.

His devotion to me would have left him a broken man had something happened to me. He was never shy about making it clear that I was his reason for living. "I actually think I want to take a shower if that's okay."

"I was going to suggest that." A sheepish grin painted his face, and he waved his hand in front of his nose as if he were trying to fan away a bad smell.

"Gee, thanks!" I nudged him playfully as I walked passed him to the adjoining bathroom.

"I brought some of your things over from your house. They're on the sink." He closed the door as he left the room.

Wow, I was a sad sight! The mirror reflected an image of a girl who looked beaten by life. My hair was a rat's nest, my skin was paler than normal, which I didn't think was possible, and my eyes were gray. It seemed like all my color had faded from the lack of life over the last week. How did I survive without food or water? I looked at my arm and noticed puncture wounds from where needles had been penetrating the skin. A deep bruise was darkening around the area. I clasped my other hand over it and looked pathetically at my reflection again. *They were taking care of me.* His mom was a nurse and had minimal supplies at the house in case of emergencies since the hospital was so far away. It took at least forty-five minutes to get there. I felt bad that I had used her one bag of fluids.

They had been taking care of me for so long, and I didn't know if I could ever repay them for that. I hated being a pity party. All my senses had returned to normal since my episode, maybe even lessened. I just felt numb again. My mind had expelled all the dark thoughts swirling around in it during my breakdown, and my body had given up after the beating it took while balled up for so long in the bed. I was back to where I started. I sighed sadly and turned on the shower.

When I finished my desperately needed deep cleaning and got dressed, I ventured into the dark hallway. I could smell the aromas coming from the kitchen. Sierra had always been a wonderful cook. My stomach growled viciously at the smell. When I walked into the kitchen, I was surprised to see River manning the stove. He was turning off the burners and starting to plate the Italian feast he had just labored over. My favorite! He was too good to me. I didn't deserve it.

He turned around. "Hungry?"

"Are you kidding me? If there was an animal living in my stomach, it would have scratched its way out by now." I made my way to a barstool at the island.

"Okay, well, sit and eat then." He placed a very full plate of spaghetti and garlic bread in front of me.

"Where's your mom?" I asked through a mouthful of noodles. Classy, I know, but I was starving.

"She and my dad were out of town when this happened. She came home to help, but I told her I could handle it now." He walked over with his plate and sat next to me.

"Where did they go?" I took a healthy bite of the garlic bread.

"They're doing some volunteer work."

His parents had generous hearts. They were always volunteering for some organization. Sierra wasn't a practicing nurse anymore, but instead, helped Hudson run a nonprofit organization. Hudson was River's dad. I didn't know where they got all their money. I asked River once, and he said his mom had inherited a large sum of money when her parents passed. I didn't pry further than that, and he didn't offer up any more information.

"How are you feeling?" He stared at me cautiously as he picked at his food.

"Well, I'm awake, so better I guess. Aren't you going to eat?"

"I ate a little earlier, so I'm not that hungry." He looked down at his plate and pushed around the noodles, only taking a few bites.

We sat in silence while I finished my whole plate and polished off the bread. I washed it down with a glass of ice water. The silence was starting to get uncomfortable. I knew he had a lot on his mind, and I knew I had a lot of questions I wanted to ask about what I heard, but neither one of us mustered the courage to say anything. I got up to clear my dishes.

"I got it." He grabbed both of our plates and started to clean up from dinner.

I walked over to the back door and hesitated for a moment. "Would you mind if I sat outside for a little bit?"

"Not if you at least take a blanket with you."

"Deal." I had brought my mom's blanket out from the bedroom with me and thrown it onto the couch, so I wrapped myself in it. I walked out onto the porch and sat on the swing. Like I said before, old-fashioned. I pulled my knees into my chest and rested my chin on them. The only light came from the half moon and the stars above. We lived outside of town against the forest, and my house was the nearest, which was almost a mile away. My mom loved nature and instilled a deep inner love inside me for it as well. I needed it. I felt nervous and out of place in the city and around too many people. This was where I felt like myself the most. It was also the closest I felt to my mom.

She always said that when it was her time she would be all around me in anything that nature created. She promised I would never be alone as long as I held onto that belief. That was the only thing I held onto these days, and it was the only thing that kept me going.

I sat quietly and listened to the night awaken from its daytime sleep. I closed my eyes so I could focus on the sounds. It was beautiful. I heard the calls of a distant coyote and the leaves rustling in the breeze. I could hear frogs croaking and the trickling of water over the rocks in the creek. *Why would anyone want to live in the city?* They had no idea what they were missing.

The sounds started to get crisper and louder. I shot open my eyes and there was the shadow, only a few feet from me. My heart stopped for a moment, and I gasped to take a breath. I could feel a panic attack rising. The sounds became louder, and then everything went quiet. The shadow remained motionless. I looked around as I tried to gain composure and assess the situation. I could get up and run. I could scream for River, or I could do what I knew I wanted to do. I got up and took a step toward the shadow.

The energy pulling me toward it was hard to resist. I was scared, but elated. I took in slow, deep breaths as I took another step in its path. The energy between us lit up like fireflies in the night. I could now see what I felt. Specks of light between the shadow and me pulled me in closer. My body started to tingle and heat up. I closed my eyes as my body soaked up the heat that penetrated into my soul. *I felt free!* I slowly opened my eyes. I felt like I was floating on air, and there was nothing but the shadow and me. Was this what true happiness felt like? I reached out. A hand emerged from the shadow and reached for mine. Sparks erupted in the space between our hands. It was the most magnificent sight I had ever seen. Just as I tried to touch the hand, the sparks extinguished and the "fireflies" faded. The sounds of the night returned, and the shadow disappeared. I glanced around desperately, wanting the feeling back, but it was gone. All that remained was the sorrow. A tear rolled down my cheek.

"Hey, going for a walk without me?" River had joined me on the patio.

"No." I peered into the darkness hopelessly and then turned back to the house. "I'm done." He had no idea what that one statement really meant to me. I was done with the sadness, with the unfulfilled hope, with this life. It needed to change before I was permanently sentenced to a wasted half-life. I walked past him and went back into the house. He stood on the patio for a minute before he followed me.

Chapter Eight

As much as I appreciated River taking care of me, I needed to get back to the bookstore. River had mentioned that he had put an *out of town* sign in the window, but I had never been closed more than a day at a time and even that was rare. My mom loved that bookstore, and I poured my heart into it making sure it stayed afloat for her. It had a loyal customer following, but since it was small and specialized in used and unique books, it was manageable on my own, especially since I didn't have anything else. I had graduated in the spring, and I wasn't really close to anyone at school, besides my best friend Starling, and River, of course.

I left River a note on the island while he was out running. I knew he would try to make me rest a few more days, and I wanted to save us both the verbal warfare. I grabbed my bag of things and headed outside. The sun was hot for a late fall day. I squinted at the brightness and made my way to my car. Sierra had driven it over from the park the night that left me unconscious. I wished they had been home. I missed his parents. It made me regret sending them away when all they were trying to do was be there for me. I knew they understood my need to heal on my own, but I secretly wished they had fought me a little harder.

The day was beautiful. Birds were singing, and dragonflies were buzzing. I got in and rolled down the windows. I let the wind brush through my hair as I made the short drive to the store. I was anxious to check on it. It had become my obsession since my mom died. It was a pivotal piece of her that helped keep her present in my life in some fashion. Maybe it was unnatural and some would say it kept me from letting go and moving forward, but it was my choice, and I had no intention of letting her go. Ever.

As I drove past a nursery farm, I thought about the conversation I overheard between River and Sierra. I never had a chance to ask him about it, and to be honest, I was kind of scared to. Did I want to know what was wrong with me, especially if it was going to get worst? I just didn't think I could handle any more bad news right now. As hard as it was to live, I wasn't ready to give up, but I did need answers soon. Things were changing in me that I didn't understand, and if it was going to kill me, I was going to put up a good fight.

I pulled up to the curb in front of the store. It was at the edge of the town strip mall and basically deserted. I liked being on the end because I hated the idea of being trapped in between other stores, but it definitely affected the amount of foot traffic. It was lacking. I got out of the car and looked up at the sign that read, *Books and Butterflies*. There was a butterfly carved on the wooden sign in the top left corner. When my mom bought the store, it had a generic name, *Used Books*. She hated it and wanted to make it her own. *Books and Butterflies* was the perfect name for her shop. It encompassed the life we believed so strongly in. Butterflies being the source of life's essence and books bringing to life the worlds of nature's imagination through the life of the author. It felt good to be back.

I opened the shop. All the blinds were pulled down, so it was dark. We were fortunate enough to have windows on two sides of the store since we were on the end. That's why my mom picked this spot. She rarely used the blinds, saying it shut out the natural beauty the light brought inside the store. I, on the other hand, liked my privacy, so I compromised, and while the blinds were always down, I left them cracked open.

River must have closed them when he came by. I could barely see through to the back of the shop. I kept the closed sign on the door for the moment and made my way carefully to the light switch in the back. I flipped it on and was stunned to see it filled with butterflies. They had been resting on the ceiling like bats in the day until the light startled them out of their slumber. They fluttered around madly looking for their way out.

"Oh my God!" It was beautiful. There were hundreds of them. I put my arms out and watched in astonishment as they landed on me, sending shocks of energy that raised the hairs on my skin like static electricity after a lightning storm. It felt intoxicating. I closed my eyes and giggled in elation. My mom always said that if you listened hard enough that you could hear nature talk to you. In my case, I could *feel* it. The sensation coursing through my veins felt like nothing I had ever experienced before. Suddenly, the front door swung open, and the butterflies rushed outside. Starling stood in the door and ducked as they fluttered by her head frantically.

"What the hell?" She rushed inside the door and slammed it closed after the last butterfly had found freedom. "Seriously, what was that? I just had flashbacks of that movie *The Birds.*"

"I don't know." I tried to divert the attention from the spectacle. "Guess what? Today's my first official day as sole owner." Starling had a good point, though. How had all those butterflies gotten in here? "What's up, Star?" Starling worked at the boutique next door and had also become my best friend after my mom died. She was an aspiring model. I wouldn't doubt it if she was discovered soon. She was tall, skinny, had long blond hair, and was absolutely perfect. I liked her. She was sassy, but real, and always told me like it was. I needed that. She handed me a pile of mail. I threw it behind the counter to deal with later.

"There has been a guy staking out your shop all week. Cute too. Where did you pick him up?" She leaned up against the wall with her hands crossed and wearing a devious smile. She was practically drooling.

A guy? What was she talking about? "I have no idea what you're talking about, but didn't it strike you as odd that someone was staking me out?"

She scooted up on the counter and made herself comfortable. "He was too cute to be dangerous. Anyway, where have you been? I have been dying of boredom all week without you."

"Funny because I don't remember receiving a phone call or text message on my birthday."

"Well played. Sorry. Would you hate me if I admitted that I forgot, but right when I remembered, I tried?"

"I'm shocked. The illustrious Starling forgot my eighteenth birthday," I said sarcastically. I was a little hurt that she forgot, but so much had happened this week that it paled in comparison.

"I'm really sorry. My mom was pretty sick, and we were at the hospital that day, so I was just really preoccupied."

My heart stopped. "Is she all right?" I panicked slightly, feeling my mom's death slither to the surface.

"She's fine now. It was just a scary moment. She had a really bad case of the flu that led to pneumonia. She's at home now. I was staying with her until she got better."

We were so similar. Her dad left when she was a baby, leaving her essentially fatherless like me. Her mom was all she had.

It was odd that we hadn't become closer sooner because her mom had owned the boutique next door ever since we were little, and we used to put on story times together. It took a tragedy for us to really develop a true friendship. We were pretty opposite in high school. If our looks weren't enough of a reason, she was also super sporty. I was not popular or into sports, so our paths didn't cross much. She never treated me badly, though. No one really did. It was almost like I didn't exist. I knew that she had always had a crush on River, but so did every girl in town. I think it drove people nuts that none of them were even a blip on his radar, especially when I was around, which was almost always.

"Hello? Arie?" She waved her hand in front of my face.

"Sorry. I was really sick. The flu. Still kind of out of it. Recovery mode," I said shortly as I walked over to the blinds and started cracking them.

"Must be going around. So, where's your better half? I haven't seen him around lately."

"I don't know. It's not like I'm his keeper."

"Well, why not? Every girl would kill to be his keeper."

"Including you." She turned away bashfully when I called her out on it.

"Well, if we're being honest, yes." She jumped off the counter and walked over and hugged me. "Happy eighteenth, bestie."

Her embrace was comforting. We grew impossibly close in a short time, and I loved her like a sister. It was hard for me to admit that because I was so terrified of losing anyone else I loved, but I did love her. I returned her hug. "Thanks."

"Lunch is on me, birthday girl."

With that, she left and the silence engulfed me. *Music.* I went to the counter and switched on the radio. The sound filled the shop as it poured through the overhead speakers. The song playing was one of my favorites, "Misguided Ghosts," by Paramore. It encompassed my life now. I was a misguided ghost just floating through life, aimlessly trying to accept this life and the pain that came with it. I took in my mom's paintings adorning the walls of the store. She had made this store her own in so many ways, and her artwork was the most profound. She used to sell it right off the walls, but I couldn't bring myself to sell a single piece after she passed. They were mine.

I only had a half hour before the store was officially open for the day, and I had a lot to catch up on. I switched on the computer behind the counter and rifled through the mail. Bill, bill, another bill, junk mail, coupon book, magazine, and then an envelope caught my eye. It was handwritten and had no address on it, which meant it was dropped off. The writing was in script. It was beautiful. My writing was awful, so I always admired the beauty in the curves of script writing. I tore it open carefully and pulled out a single note-sized paper.

Happy Birthday, Arie. I am sorry Hudson and I couldn't be here today, but we love you and are so proud to be able to turn the store over to you. Your mom would be so proud, too.

A teardrop fell onto the paper.

Ignore any bills you receive. Your mom had a trust set up especially for the shop, so we will continue to take care of them per your mom's wishes. This is your time now. Enjoy it, but be cautious, and if you need anything, we are always here for you.

Love, Sierra and Hudson

I took a deep breath as I folded the paper carefully and put it back inside the envelope. That's when I noticed the ring. I dumped it out into my hand and stared at in disbelief. It was a modest oval-shaped opal outlined with small diamonds. It was my mom's ring. I thought it was lost. I looked for it endlessly for the months after her death and was distraught that I couldn't find it.

My mom believed in the power of gems. The mythical meaning behind the opal was that it amplified sensations and buried emotions and desires and also aided in visualization, imagination, dreams, and healing. It was said to be a powerful gem, because it could take on the power of any gem represented in the color spectrum of the opal. It also possessed the power of recalling past lives and memories and seeing other planes of existence. The diamond was believed to amplify the thoughts of others and expose the strengths and weaknesses of other gems and those who wore them.

She said my dad had given it to her before he disappeared. She never took it off, so I found it strange that it wasn't on her the day she died. Even stranger that Sierra had it and didn't feel it necessary to mention it in the note.

I slipped it onto my ring finger of my left hand. Each gem had a specific place on the hand to release its maximum energy. Both the opal and diamond were recommended to be on the ring finger, and for women, on the left hand. I caressed it gently as another tear fell onto the desk. *I needed this.* I needed a piece of her with me right now. Things had been weird lately, and I was feeling confused and alone. This brought me some much-needed comfort, albeit minor. I closed my eyes and brought the ring close to my heart. I could feel its energy. *I could feel my mom.* Her words of comfort repeated in my head. "Everything's going to be okay, Arie. I will always be with you. I will never leave you, even if my physical time here expires." She spoke those words the night before my sixteenth birthday. I remember thinking it was odd, but now it made me suspicious that she knew her days were numbered.

I opened my eyes, and I was no longer in the bookstore. I was in my backyard. I could see the swirl of butterflies in the meadow above River's head and mine as we were experiencing our first kiss. *How was this possible?* I was in my own memory, but as an outsider looking in. An eerily familiar and terrifying scream filled the air, and I saw River and me jump up. Oh no. This can't be happening! I can't live through this again. I closed my eyes and pleaded with myself, "Please wake up." I opened my eyes again, but I was still there, only a few feet away from the back porch.

My other self came running from the meadow to find my mom lying on the ground. River just behind me. "Mom? Mom!" I bent down and started shaking her to wake up. My heart stopped, and tears flooded my eyes and poured down my face. "Mom, wake up. River, what's wrong with her?" He had bent over her across from me with a defeated look on his face. "Don't you dare, River! Don't you give up on her!" My voice was shaking, and the tears were choking me. "Mom, please wake up. What is happening?" I put my head on her chest in anguish. She was so still. No movement came from her chest and no breath from her lungs. *She can't be gone. She can't be.* I cried uncontrollably on her. River tried to pull me off her. I beat his chest with my fist as hard as I could. "Don't touch me! She's not gone. We have to do something." My voice was starting to betray my heart as I quietly repeated, "We have to do something. She can't be gone." My voice was less convincing by the second. River took me into his arms firmly and held me as I cried the first of many tears to come.

As I relived that moment, all the feelings rushed through me as fresh as they were that day, tears rolling down my face and an aching in my stomach that had me curled on the ground. I covered my ears and closed my eyes to block out the vision. I rocked back and forth methodically until everything went quiet. I cautiously opened my eyes. My other self was still in River's arms next to my mom's lifeless body. That's when I saw it, a shadow flash across the yard and disappear into the forest line. *Oh my God!* Someone was here when she died.

Everything went black, and then I woke up. I was back in the bookstore. My head was resting on the desk. Was I dreaming?

"Hello, sleepy head."

Starling was standing on the other side of the counter holding lunch. Panic set in as I realized I had lost almost four hours. I looked at my phone. It was 12:30 p.m.

"Are you okay?" She came around the counter and set down the food bags.

"Yeah." I tried to quickly recover from my step down memory hell.

"Are you sure? You don't look okay." She started pulling salads out of the bags.

"Yeah, I must still be tired from the flu." I got up. "I'll be right back." I darted for the bathroom. I closed the door quickly, turned on the water, and immediately started to dry heave into the sink. My stomach was in knots. I could barely breathe, and my heart felt ripped through. I turned from the mirror and crunched down to the floor holding myself tightly. I couldn't gain control. I was losing it. A lot of time must have passed, because an urgent knock on the door prompted me to pull out of it.

"Arie, are you all right?" River's voice penetrated the door.

Was it that bad that Starling felt she needed to call River? "Yes, I'm still alive. Just give me a minute, okay?" I was pleading. How pathetic was I? All because of a dream. *Pathetic.*

"Fine, but if you're in there much longer, I'm going to knock down the door."

"I'm coming. I promise." I pulled myself up from the floor and turned off the water. I looked at myself in the mirror and tried to rub off the terror. I straightened my clothes and opened the door to face River. He looked me over and assessed the emotional damage. Without a word, he pulled me into his arms and held me. It took everything in me to not breakdown. I focused on the warmth his body generated and the sweet smell of his own personal cologne. I focused on those two things to maintain grounded in the moments that passed. "Where did Star go?"

"She left when I got here. I guess she figured you wouldn't want an audience."

River pulled me away from him slightly and forced me to look at him.

"What happened?"

"I'm not sure. One moment I was reading a letter from your mom and the next I was dreaming about the day my mom died, and then four hours later, I woke up to Starling standing over me with lunch." That summed it up pretty well.

"I'm sorry, Arie. I was hoping the nightmares had passed for the most part."

"That's just the thing. It wasn't a nightmare. I was there, River. It was like I was watching a movie, only it was my life. It was my darkest memory. I saw us at the meadow and then us at my mom's side. I saw it. I felt it all. And we weren't alone." His grip tightened on my arms, and his stare harshened.

"What do you mean 'we weren't alone'?"

He sounded upset. Angry even.

"I saw a shadow cross the yard."

He looked at me quizzically and then let go.

"It was just a dream, Arie. There was no one else there but us." He started to rock nervously on the balls of his feet.

"I don't know, River. It seemed so real. I felt everything the way I felt it that day, and we wouldn't have seen the shadow, because we were too wrapped up in our own grief. I just can't ignore what I saw. It was just too real, and we don't know what happened to my mom. One minute she was cooking in the kitchen and the next she was..." I couldn't say it, not even now. I walked up to him and touched his arm. "What if someone killed her?" The thought made my head spin. Everyone loved my mom. She couldn't make an enemy even if she tried. *What if this was what they were whispering about?* "River, you have to promise me that if you know anything you will tell me."

He pulled me back into him and held onto me so tightly that I could barely breathe. "We'll figure this out, Arie. I promise." He kissed the top of my head and rocked me gently.

Chapter Nine

I felt like a butterfly with broken wings, and River was trying to mend me back together. However, after a butterfly's wings were broken, it was destined to live a life without flight, and fate's destiny for me was not to fly. I would never soar above the sorrow and be free from the guilt of those surrounding me whom I would drown in sorrow.

River had stayed with me at the shop until closing and followed me home. He didn't leave until I was safe in my bed. He fought me on being alone, but I didn't want to seem weak. I didn't want him to feel like he had to take care of me. I didn't want to lose the connection we were fighting so hard to regain.

I tried to sleep, but I couldn't. The vision had made me restless and uneasy. What if someone did kill my mom? What was their reasoning? And more importantly, who did it? I was ashamed at how close I let the shadow get to me the other night at River's house. I saw a shadow flashing from my mom's body. Could it be the same person who was following me, and if it was, was I next? That vision made me realize that I wasn't ready to give up. I wasn't ready to die. I wanted to avenge my mother's death if someone had taken her from me. I was ready to fight until I had nothing left in me, and then I would still fight. A determination rose within me that I had never felt before, and it felt good. It gave me purpose, something I had lost with my mom. It lit a fire inside me that only the truth could extinguish.

I turned over and stared outside. I had left the curtains open to let the breeze come through the cracked window. Tonight was an unusually warm fall night. One of my favorite things about the weather in Southern California was the seasons never manifested into much. One day it could be freezing and the next the warm winds could tear through the valley. There was something about the warm winds that electrified me when they crashed against my body. It was hard to enjoy the breeze tonight after what had happened.

After tossing and turning for a while, I gave up and got out of bed. I walked to the window and sat on the sill. I opened the window wider and closed my eyes. I let the breeze blow through me and around me, trying to let it consume the dark turn of events that had occurred this week. When I opened my eyes, I was face to face with a crow on the ledge just outside my window. It was so still I could have sworn it was a stuffed replica, but the black beady eyes glared at me accusingly. I froze, too. It let out a big squawk, startling the crap out of me and then swooped down the side of the house just missing the ground when it gracefully headed back up to a tree and landed.

It kept its eyes on me. If it wasn't so damn creepy, I would say it was beautiful. Everything in nature had a purpose and was to be respected in its own right, but not all things were enchanting.

The crow shook its head violently from side to side and then burst into a ball of blinding light. The residual sparks looked like fireworks as they shot out from all angles and fell into the darkness below. I was paralyzed with fear. *Holy crap!* Did that just happen? As the last spark touched the ground, I saw her.

Only it wasn't actually her.

It was the glowing essence my mom told me lives on after our bodies die out. She looked beautiful. She was wearing a white dress that hugged her chest and hips and then flared out and flowed to the ground. She turned and walked toward the meadow.

I jumped off the sill and ran out back. The trees and bushes were alive in the breeze, and it whipped my hair around. The grass tickled my bare feet as I ran after her. She was standing in the butterfly circle facing me. I slowed down as I got within only a few feet from her. She was even more beautiful up close. Tears welled up in my eyes. I wanted to reach out and touch her. Her lips started moving, but no sound came out. The wind was gusting through the forest and stirring up the leaves around us. They swirled in a twister formation.

I screamed hysterically over the wind blasts. I knew this wouldn't last long, and I needed to hear her voice again. "Mom, I can't hear you."

Her lips kept moving calmly. My heart started to race and ache. She was unaffected by the wind as she continued to mouth words that I couldn't hear. My eyes had been holding back the tears like a dam holds back a river, but that dam broke, and tears covered my cheeks.

She reached out her hands to me, and I took a longing step forward. I extended my hands to touch hers. Our fingertips were only inches away from each other when my sorrow started to dissolve. Her lips stopped moving and were replaced by an ethereal smile that could light up the world. When her fingertips touched mine, all my pain disappeared. I took this opportunity to tell her everything I hadn't been able to because her life was stolen abruptly. "I can't be here without you, Mom. I can't breathe. I need you. I love you." She started to fade and panic set in. "No. No, don't go. Please, not yet." Then quietly, travelling over the breeze to my ears, I finally heard the dim whisper of her voice.

"The ring will lead you back to me."

Then she faded, and hundreds of fireflies replaced her aura and flew away. I looked down at the ring as it pulsed with light and then returned to normal. I dropped to the ground and wept. It was bittersweet to see her again no matter if this was a dream. I closed my eyes tightly, trying to block the tears from flowing. I breathed hard as I tried to gain control of myself. I squeezed my fists so firmly that I could feel my nails causing damage to my hands as they dug in. The choking started to subside as I took in slower breaths. As my body stopped convulsing, I noticed the wind was no longer whipping around me. I opened my eyes and lifted my head slowly. I was curled in a ball on the windowsill looking out into the dark meadow.

I was dreaming.

I raised my hand and admired the ring. Was it possible that deep within it held a piece of my mom's essence? Ever since I put it on my finger, I felt closer to her and that was enough for me.

At some point, I finally crawled into bed and fell into a deep sleep. Something magical was happening to me. I didn't know if it was the ring or if it was triggered by something else, but things had definitely become surreal. I had always believed in fairytales when I was younger, but that faded as I grew older and died altogether with my mom. Sometimes it was hard for me to buy into the stuff my mom said about nature being alive. The interactions with the creatures were strange from the butterflies to the over-friendly fox, but never seemed abnormally so that I would think I had some magical allure. However, my mom believed there was something hidden inside me that called out to them and that one day I would understand why and to not ignore it. I never asked many questions about it. I just trusted in what she said.

It was Sunday already. This was the only day the store wasn't open. I lay in bed for a little longer and tried to hold onto the image of my mom as she looked like an angel floating in the meadow. As I stared at the ceiling, I imagined her in the space between watching over me. Even alive she looked like an angel without wings. For the first time in a long time I thought about my dad. Not that there was anything to think about. I never met him. He left right before my mom found out she was pregnant. Or should I say he disappeared? My mom believed that he loved her and would never have left without a good reason. I tried not to be angry with him. I tried to believe he loved my mom. I wanted to believe he would have loved me if he knew I existed, but it still hurt to grow up without a father. Being raised by a single parent, I wasn't alone, but somehow that was not much of a comfort. It was nature's beast within us to want what we didn't have, and this was no exception.

I rolled over and stared out the window. It was another beautiful fall day. Very few of these days were left before winter officially took over. My mom spoke about my dad often. She said I looked like him and that his essence was strong in me. Like I said before, she was very ethereal, not only in presence but also in her mindset, but not to the point where people thought she was a weird hippy. Just her presence made people smile. I peeled myself out of bed. I couldn't sit around my house all day. Not today. I needed to get out, and I knew just the place.

I arrived at the preserved park as the sun rose to the center of the sky. I parked in the same spot as last week when *things* started happening. I was hesitant to get out not knowing if the person I thought I saw the last time I was here when I passed out would be here again. I looked to the trees where I last saw him. Or her. Or it. I really had no idea what I saw. This was ridiculous. To fear something that could just be a figment of my imagination.

I grabbed the bag on the passenger seat that I had packed, got out, and walked to my spot. I laid out a blanket under the cover of a large tree and sat down. I unpacked a bottle of water, a book, and a shoebox. While I frequented this park with River in the past, I came here every Sunday by myself. This was my escape. Normally, I would just read a book, but the recent events had prompted me to bring along the small shoebox. I removed the lid, revealing pictures and letters.

They were my favorite memories. The picture on top was one of my mom when she was very pregnant. Sierra took it. She was sitting in the meadow reaching for a butterfly flower. It was captivating. I stared at it for a long while, taking in the innocence of that day. Looking more closely at the picture, I saw a shadow in the meadow in the distance. I had never noticed it before, but then again, I hadn't looked at this picture since my mom died.

With all the strange things happening, I was definitely more aware of everything. I brought the picture closer, trying to get a better look at the shadow. Maybe it was just a tree. All of a sudden, my breath caught in my throat, and I couldn't breathe. I dropped the picture and clutched my neck. I couldn't catch a breath as hard as I tried. I looked around frantically knowing that there was no one to help me. My vision started to blur, and I started to panic. I was rendered helpless and genuinely frightened.

As I was on the edge of losing consciousness, a figure came into sight and put its hands on my cheeks. I could hear muffled sounds coming from the voice, but couldn't make out what they were. Just then, a large breath rushed through my lungs. I inhaled deeply and coughed as my body remembered how to breathe. My vision returned, and the person who saved me came into focus. It was the guy from the club! His skin was sun-kissed, and his eyes were a lustrous shade of amber. He was tall, and I could see his muscle definition through the fitted t-shirt he wore. His jeans were a dark blue and hugged him perfectly.

"Are you okay?" He bent down to me again.

I was dazed. What was he doing here?

"I am now. What did you do?"

His expression was blank. "Nothing. I think you were having a panic attack or something."

I could have been. Anytime I thought about my mom I tended to have one, but this felt like that night outside the club. It just didn't feel the same. "Where did you come from?"

"Third degree and we haven't even exchanged pleasantries yet." He stood up. "Hi, I'm Ashe."

"I'm Arie."

"It's nice to meet you, Arie. If you're okay now, I need to be going." He stood up. He was even more handsome in the sunlight. He picked up the picture of my mom and looked at it. The thought of someone else admiring her bothered me.

"She's beautiful." He handed me the picture.

"Yes, she was." I took the picture from him and stared at it.

"Oh, I'm sorry. Was she your mom?"

"Yes," I said sadly.

"You look like her, especially your eyes." He penetrated my gaze. The hairs on my skin started to rise, and my body began to warm. My heart raced, and I quietly relished in the sensation his stare was triggering. What was it about him that made me feel like this? It's like he attracted every molecule in my body. I couldn't resist the pull. It was powerful and filled me with comfort. He looked away, and the sensation faded. What was he doing here now? Was it just a coincidence that he was here at the right time to save me? I gasped. What if he was the one here that night? My heart started beating like a bass drum at a rock concert, and my breathing quickened once again as I thought of the possibilities. I looked around instinctively for an escape.

"You were at the show the other night."

"Is that a question?" he asked smoothly.

"No, I saw you at the club. You were watching me," I stated uncomfortably.

He smiled. "It's hard not to watch someone who dances as beautifully as you."

My cheeks betrayed me as I blushed. "You know it's a little creepy having someone watch you in an intimate moment."

I flinched as he bent down and whispered into my ear, "That's why I was watching."

His breath on my neck was warm and sweet and aroused a primal feeling of desire. It was a profound feeling burning in my chest that hungered for a taste of something it never knew it needed until now. I should have been scared since he was a perfect stranger, but I was intrigued. I was drawn to him. I didn't want him to leave. He pulled away slowly and stood up and started to walk away.

"Wait. You didn't answer my question. Where did you come from?"

His smile touched me down to my toes. "I was out for a walk."

With that, he disappeared around a bend. I waited while my body cooled down and my heartbeat normalized. He had conjured feelings in me I didn't know I had. He made me feel more than alive. And that was just from one look! I could only imagine if it was more. The guilt immediately set in as River entered my thoughts. It had only been a week since I shared this spot with him. The feeling Ashe had just exposed me to was on a different level. It was primal as if it had been buried deep within my DNA, and he had finally released it from the confines of its cage. I could still feel it scratching at the bars wanting out again. *I wanted to let it out.*

I sat in my spot as the sun fell behind the hills and cast a pink and orange glow across the sky. There was no other place in the world that could compare to the sunsets that I witnessed here. I didn't want to leave. There were days that I would stay until well past the time the moon rose in the sky, and the stars twinkled under its gravitational pull. I had forgotten to bring a flashlight tonight, so I packed up my stuff and headed back to the car.

Headlights raced up the hill, and River's car pulled into the spot next to my car. *What was he doing here?* I felt the day's events fill me with shame as a smile plastered his face when he saw me. He jumped out of his car and ran over to me grabbing my things.

"You found me," I teased sarcastically. I wasn't surprised.

He threw my stuff into my car. "I know this is your Sunday hideaway, but when you didn't answer my text message or the phone, I got a little worried."

"Oh, sorry. I think I left my phone at home." *So stupid.* I didn't have that much need for it, since I could count on one hand the number of people who had the number, but with my shadow stalker, I should probably have it with me.

"It's useless to have one if you aren't going to keep it with you, you know." He had placed his hands gently on my shoulders to gain all my attention.

"I know," I said guiltily like I was being punished for running away. River responded by pulling me in and snuggling his neck into my hair. I could never resist the way he smelled and the protective nature of his embrace. He placed his hand under my chin and lifted my eyes to his. I could see the hazel specks hidden amongst the blue. River had a stare that would have any woman groveling at his feet and any man begging for mercy. Starling was just another innocent victim of River's natural attraction. I joked with her about how she blushed and acted silly whenever he was around, but it did kind of bother me that she saw him in more than a friendly way. I trusted them, but I didn't trust the laws of attraction. Nature was stronger than nurture and no matter how much they loved me, if nature wanted them together, they would lose the right versus wrong battle. Nature would always win.

"How about we go get something to eat?" He stroked my chin lovingly.

"Sounds good." I brushed off the jealousy. I hadn't eaten since this morning, and I was starving.

He held my chin in his hand and slowly lowered his lips to mine. I could feel the anticipation tingling on his lips. It spread to mine, and I reacted quickly by kissing him back. I lost myself in the moment until Ashe flashed into my thoughts, causing the sensation to flee as if it were being chased away by a rabid dog. I backed away from River abruptly.

"What's wrong?" He looked confused.

"Nothing, I just...my emotions have been left unchecked lately, and I really need to get a grip on things before... I'm sorry." I put my head down shamelessly.

River raised my chin. "Don't ever be sorry with me, Arie. I meant what I said. However long it takes." He kissed my forehead lightly. "Let's go get something to eat."

Chapter Ten

As I sat across from River, all I could think about was asking him about what I overheard the other night. We went to a burger shack in town for dinner. I loved this place because it made the best food, and the outdoor seating bordered a meadow of daisies. It always seemed so peaceful and scenic sitting outside. No matter what star-rated establishment it was, I would always give it a five star if it had outdoor seating. I would even sit out in the rain with the only coverage being an umbrella to keep my food from getting soiled. I always found restaurants to be loud and chaotic, filling me with anxiety every time a server dropped silverware or a busboy loudly cleared a table, not to mention all the people's voices that elevated to talk over the table next to them.

I swirled a french fry into a cup of ranch as I contemplated how to bring it up.

"Are you going to put that fry out of its misery or just keep drowning it?"

I stuck the fry into my mouth.

"What's on your mind?" He put down his burger and gave me his undivided attention.

"A lot." I picked at the bun enclosing my veggie burger.

"I can see that. Care to share?"

"What, are you Dr. Seuss now? There's a wocket in my pocket." I gave him a sarcastic smile.

"You're funny and great at diverting the conversation."

"It's always been one of my better skills." Kidding aside, what he didn't know was that I was petrified to ask him. I didn't know if I was ready to find out what was wrong with me. What if that wasn't what they were whispering about? I looked down at my plate and bit at my lip. I didn't know how to start the conversation. "I was thinking about the other day when I woke up from my week long dream vacation."

"Okay, I'm game. What about it?" He studied me warily.

"When I was coming out of it, I heard you and your mom whispering." I looked up into his eyes. He had a great poker face, but I could tell he was uncomfortable with where this conversation was heading.

"What exactly did you hear?" he asked as he shifted in his seat and took a bite of his burger.

"Me needing to know something before things got worse. What was she talking about, and why would you keep secrets from me?" I was hurt. I could feel my chest tighten as I held back tears. I didn't realize how betrayed I felt until I said it aloud. He got up and moved to the seat beside me, putting his arm around me and squeezing tight.

"I don't really know much. My mom mentioned a few things to me when you were unconscious. I could tell she was leaving a lot out, though, so I really think you should talk to her about this."

Not good enough! I pushed him aside and glared. "What did she tell you?" He tried to grab my hand, but I pulled it away. "Seriously, River, tell me what you know."

"Your mom had similar things happen to her."

"'Similar things?'"

"You know, like communicating with nature, and I guess she had visions, too. That's all she told me. She said they got pretty bad before she died. My mom figured that's what killed her." He looked down at his feet.

"And now she's afraid I will meet the same fate." I let that swirl around in my head. So, I was going crazy, and it was going to kill me. *Awesome!* "I need to talk to your mom."

"They don't get service where they are. She said she would check in when she got to an area with a signal. I can tell her to call you."

Of course. How convenient. "When is she coming home?"

"In a few days."

I got up from the table and started walking away.

"Where are you going?"

He followed behind me and grabbed my arm to stop me. I tried to get away fast enough, so he didn't have to see me cry yet again, but it was too late. I yanked my arm from his grip and turned to him. "Home, River." That's all I could say. That's all I wanted to say. I saw him in the rearview mirror as he watched me drive off. It hurt to see him standing there as if I had crushed all his hope of us reconciling. *Jerk.* I was a selfish jerk, but he lied to me, and it ached. Actually, it stung. The thought of losing the one solid thing in my life burned like hell.

I pulled up to my house and ran inside with the shoebox, locking the door behind me. I scrambled to the kitchen table and dumped the contents out of the box. Letters, pictures, and a few mementos littered the table. I quickly spread them out. I couldn't believe my mom would keep the visions a secret. I knew she had a way with nature, but I had no idea that she experienced the same thing I was starting to experience. It wasn't like her to keep secrets from me. All we had was each other, so we shared everything, or at least I thought we did. She was probably just trying to protect me, but look at me now. I needed to know more about her visions.

I sorted the mess into piles: mementos in one, letters in another, and then pictures. There was also a small journal. It was a simple black faux leather journal that was small enough to put into a purse, but big enough to write a substantial amount of stuff inside. It was my mom's diary.

She didn't catalogue her daily events, but instead, wrote what I thought were poems and stories because they were so unrealistic, but now I wasn't so sure. I petted the cover slowly and took a deep breath. This was going to be hard. I hadn't read this since right after the funeral. I grabbed her blanket off the chaise and headed out to the back porch, flipping the light switch on my way out. Unlike River's house, the porch was adorned with an oversized couch bench and two large cushioned chairs with ottomans.

This was my mom's favorite place, so she wanted it to be comfortable. When I was little, I would sit on her lap, and she would read me stories out of this journal. They were both beautiful and dark at the same time. They had fairies and angels, talking animals, and of course, my dad.

I sat on the large couch and stretched out across it. As soon as I was comfortable, I hesitantly opened the journal. On the inside cover, my mom had signed her name in her elegant script writing. She tried to show me how to write like her, but I just couldn't seem to grasp the delicate curves of the lines. I rubbed my fingers across her name. I admired the ring I now wore that was hers. I vowed to never take it off. On the front page, she had drawn three intricate butterflies with our names etched on the wings: *Ariana, Arie,* and *Tivon*.

I always thought my dad had a peculiar name. When my mom referred to him, she called him Teve. She said his name meant *nature lover*. She had a thing about names. Ariana, Arie for short, meant holy one and someone who needs to be surrounded by nature. I have to admit they do have beautiful meanings although I was not so sure about me being a holy one. I had never stepped foot into a church, and my faith in religion was lacking to say the least. I wish I had inherited my mother's beautiful writing and artistry. I turned the page. My mom always dated her stories. The first one was dated shortly after I was born, November 1995.

I walked through the meadow to the butterfly circle where hundreds of fireflies were twisting around a figure under the shade of the night sky. I couldn't see the figure clearly, but I knew it was him. I could feel him. How I had missed his touch, his warmth, his beauty. I wanted to tell him we had a baby girl. I wanted him to smell her sweet scent and see how much she looked like him. More importantly, I wanted her to know him. He reached his hand through the veil of the fireflies. I came closer and touched my hand to his. The energy flowing through us brought me to tears. I couldn't hear him, but I knew he still loved me by the tingles he sent shooting through my body. He slipped a ring onto my finger as he started to fade. I didn't want him to go. My heart was breaking all over again. Suddenly, the fireflies twisted manically around him, and he was lost in their whirlwind. They floated into the sky and disappeared in the light of the full moon taking him with them. I fell to the ground and pounded it as tears filled my world. Once I gained control, I focused on the ring he had placed onto my wedding finger. We were supposed to get married just before he disappeared. It was beautiful. It was a snow white oval-shaped opal encircled by diamonds. The opal was glowing softly, or was it the moon's reflection? It was hard to tell. I was too weak to walk back to the house, so I spread out on the grass and let the moon absorb my sorrow and the wind dry my tears. At some point, the twinkling stars lulled me to sleep.

The story ended there. I always assumed these were dreams she recorded, but now with my first vision experience, I wasn't so sure. Were hers and mine just elaborate dreams, or were we having visions of some kind? I moved onto the next story. It was dated on my first birthday, September 23rd.

I could feel a pull from the forest line, so I didn't resist. I wanted to see Teve again. I knew it was him who was calling for me. I ran barefoot through the grass in my nightgown. Sierra stayed the night after the small birthday celebration, so I wasn't worried about Arie. She was in good hands. I started to breathe heavily as my pace quickened. I halted to a sudden stop when I saw a shadow at the edge of the forest. It didn't feel right. It felt dark and cold.

Could this be the same shadow that was following me? If so, then maybe I needed to fear it. Some of the interactions seemed almost protective in nature, while others frightened me. This made me conclude there had to be more than one shadow following me. What were the shadows? Were they just nature's essence expelling both emotional spectrums when my mom and I came in contact with them? My brain was hurting. It was obvious I still had a lot to learn about myself, but my mom never got the chance to teach it all to me. Now, I was left to figure it out on my own. My emotions were mixed like frozen yogurt swirled with anguish, annoyance, betrayal, and love. I was a mess. I focused back on the journal.

Then the warmth enveloped me and carried me away from the darkness. Teve's arms wrapped around my body from behind, blanketing me from harm. His arms illuminated with a soft glow. I caressed them longingly. His breath warmed my neck as his lips grazed my ear. He whispered, "The ring will always lead you back to me." He kissed my neck, and my body filled with the energy of a thousand moons and then it went limp.

All her stories ended similarly. I looked out into the forest line where my mom's story took place. I wondered if the shadow in this story was the same one that was there when she died. Her stories left me with too many questions. Here I was hoping they would shed some light on them. My attention diverted to the yard where I saw something emerge from the forest line. Not just something, but several things. They started their way toward me. It was a family of deer. There were a mom and two fawns. As they moved closer, I noticed them staring at me. Not through me, but at me. It was amazing!

I put down the journal and walked down the porch steps slowly and quietly, stopping at the last step. They walked right up to me, the mom in the front and the fawns behind her safely. The mom looked at me and stuck out her nose toward me. She was only a foot away now. I reached out my hand and carefully touched the fur just above her nose. I had never petted a deer before. Her fur was coarse but smooth. She never took her eyes off me. As I stroked her nose, she came closer and nuzzled my cheek. Then she stepped away and let the fawns approach me. Their fur was much softer. They were breathtaking! They licked my hand and nuzzled up to me. A loud noise from the forest startled all of us, and they ran in the opposite direction, leaving me alone in the darkness.

I looked to where the noise came from, but it was quiet now. *Maybe it was just a tree falling.* It made me uneasy, though, so I scooped up my blanket and the journal and went back into the house. I locked the door and took another look out into the forest through the glass. I didn't see anything, so I turned off the light, satisfied. I snuggled up on the chaise in the TV room to read more when a light knock on the front door interrupted me. *Not cool!* I hesitated, contemplating whether I should get it. I was certain it was either River or Starling. Just to make sure, I got up and grabbed my phone off the island and texted River.

That better be you out front because if it's not then you better get over here quickly.

I waited for a second. No response. I started to panic a little. Maybe it was Starling. I'll try her, too. Just then a text came in.

If you really have to ask that then we seriously need to talk about what's been going on lately.

Oh my God, really? Can't he just answer the damn question!

That doesn't sound like a yes to me!

Yes, it's me. Can you open the door now?

A frustrated breath found its way out of me. I slammed down my phone, probably harder than I should have, annoyed with him. I was honestly spooked! I walked to the door and let him in and walked away without saying a word.

"I was just being polite knocking, you know? I could have just used my key." He closed the door and started to follow me.

"Can you lock it, please?" I was still frustrated with him. He did and then followed me into the TV room. I plopped back on the chaise and covered myself with the blanket. River sat on the couch across from me. The awkward silence filled the room.

"Look, I know you're still upset. I promise I was going to talk to you about things, but it just never seemed like the right time. I don't want to lose you again. You were almost back, Arie, and then this all happened, and you started distancing yourself again. I didn't want to add to it."

He leaned forward, pleading with his body language for me to forgive him. I knew I couldn't stay mad at him.

"I'm not mad at you. I'm just confused. I don't understand why my mom didn't tell me about her visions, especially if she thought I might get them. And now there's a chance someone killed her. I don't know how to feel." The panic started to fill my lungs and drown me. "I don't know what to think anymore." My lips betrayed my thoughts, and I couldn't say any more.

River got up and made me scoot over to let him squeeze in next to me. I sucked the body warmth from his body and relented to snuggling up to him. He put his arms around me and scooped me up onto his lap. In the process, his hair teased my neck and made me shiver with elation. The past several years I had looked upon River as a brother figure because of the way he looked after me, but in the last week, my body was refusing that label and wanted more from him.

He put the blanket over me, misreading my shaking. I anticipated every small movement he made, hoping he would touch me and kiss me. I felt the embers inside my body spread and ignite into flames. River nuzzled his now scruffy chin against my cheek, causing a firestorm to erupt. I closed my eyes and laid my head back on his shoulder. He kissed my exposed neck, taking this as an open invitation.

Before his lips touched me, I could feel his hot breath travel down my spine, touching every vertebrae. My breathing became restless as his lips connected with my neck. I couldn't resist reaching my arm back and gripping the back of his neck and pulling him into me. I wanted the safety of his presence. I wanted a break from my manic thoughts. I wanted the heightened sensations and feelings that were rushing me like a windstorm lately to linger and leave me with a nice after buzz. I turned around on his lap and looked deeply into his soul. He returned the gesture with his lips on mine.

The journal fell to the ground, forgotten in the moment. I gave into the mindless affection and reciprocated his kiss with a determined passion. Unbeknownst of me, a war raged inside, and my mind smashed through the barriers. I broke free and inhaled sharply. *What was I doing?* It was clear that my intentions did not mean the same as his. This wasn't fair to either one of us. I looked into his questioning eyes.

"I'm sorry. I shouldn't have started this." I removed myself from him and stood up.

"Did I do something..." He tried to reach out for me.

"No, you didn't do anything wrong." I was so aggravated with myself. Only hours ago someone else was sending my world spinning out of control, and here I was ready to lay it all out there for River without a second thought. I fell back on the couch where River had been and threw my face into my hands. I peeked up. "I want to... everything in my body wants to, but with everything... I just can't right now." I felt defeated and hid myself within what little security my hands could provide for the moment.

"I don't want to rush it or force it for that matter. When you're ready, Arie. You're it for me. There's no one else. I will love you even after the day my life here is over."

He stood up, walked over, kissed my head, and left.

I cried uncontrollably. This wasn't healthy. I couldn't keep doing this to us.

Chapter Eleven

I needed to understand what was happening to me and what had happened to my mom and how she actually died. Her autopsy was inconclusive, giving me no closure. My mom always carried a sadness in her heart that no one could mend besides my dad. I decided her broken heart finally gave up trying. I always imagined it was peaceful. That she just walked outside to let us know that the food was ready and then she collapsed without warning, but then there was her scream. The disturbing idea planted in my head that my mom might have not gone so quietly upset me to the very core of my being. She had such an infectious light inside her that for her to meet a violent death would be cruelty in its worst form.

I wanted to get to the store a little early, so I could look through my mom's journal more and do some more research on this ring. I knew we had books about gems and mythology, so I was hoping it would shed some light on it. I always assumed it was a promise ring and carried no other significance, but with there being two visions directly related to it, I would be naïve to think there wasn't more. I rushed down the stairs and grabbed the journal that was now hidden beneath the couch from my encounter with River the previous night.

My stomach churned as I thought about it. I knew it was wrong to lead him on, but I couldn't help it. So much was stirring inside me lately that it was hard to control my emotions, and the sensations were unbelievable and mind numbing. I couldn't avoid him, though, and I didn't want to.

I snatched my phone off the island. There were two text notifications, one from River and one from Starling. I chose to ignore both for now. I slid it into the back pocket of my jeans, retrieved my keys, and headed out the door.

When I pulled up to the bookstore, Starling was waiting for me out front with a bag in one hand and a tray holding two coffees in the other. She was so good to me and yet how had I been a good friend to her? I had just been someone to listen to sassy banter but not more than that. She had been my back up to River, especially when things were really dark and I needed distance from his family. Being around their happiness and love for each other stung like a snakebite, and it suffocated me with pain.

Starling stepped in at the perfect time. *Almost too perfect.* I sometimes wondered if River put her up to it, and considering she would do anything for that man, I was sure it wasn't hard to convince her. Fortunately, what might have started as contrived turned into one of the most beautiful friendships a person could hope for. She knew her place in my heart and knew where River's was and always knew when I needed him. She never held it against me and never got jealous. She was an unconditional friend that I would cherish for the rest of my days.

Her gleaming smile was over the top, and I knew she was trying to pretend the other day didn't happen. That was sweet. I wasn't much of a talker, and I loved that she accepted that about me. I got out of the car.

"Aw, honey, you shouldn't have!" I grabbed the coffees out of her hand.

"Oh, I'm so embarrassed. You think this is for you? I was actually waiting for River." She winked playfully.

"Well, then you will be waiting for a long time." I opened the shop.

"Ain't that the truth? That boy sees nothing beyond you, girl." She followed me inside.

"What's in the bag?" I put down the coffee tray onto the counter and pulled out our coffees and handed her one.

She shook it in front of me. "Donuts, of course. It's Manilicious Monday, remember?"

I rolled my eyes at her. "You seriously kill me sometimes. Why don't you just ask Dan out already? You have been hitting up that donut shop every Monday since he bought that place."

"Well, little missy, unlike some of us who seem to have men swoon over them, I am waiting for him to see that I am swoon-worthy and ask me out." She grabbed her coffee and took a sip.

"He's crazy if he doesn't soon." I rifled through the bag and pulled out my favorite donut, a maple bar, and took a big bite. I walked around the counter and stiffened. A book was on the desk by my computer. I didn't put that there, and the shop had been closed since my meltdown on Saturday. Resting on the book was the most brilliant butterfly flower I had ever seen. It was called the Butterfly Clerodendrum because of its striking resemblance to butterflies. The stamen that darted out from the center of the flower looked like an antenna, four petals were shaped like the wings, and the fifth petal shaped the tail of the back wings. Several of these blooms adorned the stalk in a circle of magnificence. Their tails were a deep purple while the wings were a lighter lavender. I could hear Starling's voice in the background, but I was drawn to the flower and terrified by the book's magical appearance. The room got deathly quiet.

"There better be something good over there. I don't think you've heard a word I said."

She walked around the counter to join me. I hadn't moved a muscle. Her silence spoke volumes to the beauty of the flower.

"Wow, that's gorgeous! It looks like three butterflies holding hands in a circle. Have you ever seen anything like it, Arie?" She bent down and picked up the stalk and sniffed the flowers. "Oh my God, they smell as amazing as they look! We need to get this in water before it dies."

She walked with the flower to the back of the shop. I still couldn't move. How did these things get here? I heard the faucet in the bathroom turn on. I moved closer to the book and reached out for it. The ring immediately started to glow faintly. As I moved my hand closer to the book, the glow deepened and I could feel an energy poking at my skin, prickling it like static electricity. I was only an inch from touching the book, and the energy that was building between us was escalating.

"What are you doing?"

I tugged my hand back quickly, startled by Starling's sudden reappearance.

"You look like you're trying to touch a ferocious lion. It's just a book, Arie. It won't bite. I promise." She picked it up like nothing and read the title.

"*Spirits of Nature*. That sounds like a tantalizing read." She giggled at herself and put it back down on the desk.

I couldn't keep my eyes off of it. Starling touching it didn't have the same effect it had on me. Not that I should have been surprised with everything that had been happening lately, but everything that was happening had no place in the forefront of common sense thinking. This stuff didn't happen in real life. It was trapped in the thoughts of authors, dreams, and nightmares, and in the worlds of fairytales and mythology. Except here it was in my reality, teasing me at every corner I turned, and either I was going to accept it as truth or let it drive me insane. I preferred my sanity, so for now, I would accept the weirdness that had become my beautiful nightmare.

"Okay, since that book seems to be more interesting than me, I'll see ya later," she said frustrated and started to walk out.

"I'm sorry, Star. I just have a lot on my mind right now. I'm a little distracted. I don't mean to be a terrible friend." I felt awful. This was one of those times where I didn't feel like I deserved her friendship.

She walked back over to me and grabbed my hands. "You could never be a terrible friend. Whether you know it or not, you saved me from myself when we became friends. I was lost and soul-less. Your friendship showed me what real life was about and how much meaning there is out there in the world, so don't ever say you're a terrible friend again. I'm here when you're ready to share your secrets, okay, hon?" She pulled me in and gave me a soothing hug.

Her love surrounded me in a protective shield, and I felt safe for a moment. As her hold released, so did my comfort. I hugged her again. "Thank you."

"You're welcome," she whispered. "I'll see ya later, okay? I'll be next door if you need anything."

She put the flower, now soaking in a cup of water, down onto the counter and walked out the door. The store instantly filled with the chill of the night before. I didn't feel the chill earlier. I rubbed my arms, trying to warm them and walked over to the window to bathe in the sun that was filling the corner of the room. I could feel the energy it harnessed fill me with an intense rush of heat as I stole as much as I could. Satisfied with my body temperature and my obvious diversion from the book, I sighed in defeat and shuffled back to the desk and carefully reached for it. Nothing happened this time as if Starling touching it took the essence right out of it.

The front door slowly creaked open, and the little girl that used to come to story time walked inside dragging her mom by the hand. She looked to be around four years old now. Her soft long brown curls framed her olive skin and bright pink cheeks and were offset by a bright aqua blue sundress. She was beautiful and a spitting image of her mom. It made my heart ache. I stood up and walked around the counter. I was careful as I approached her, not wanting to scare her away again. "Hi, may I help you find anything?"

"Oh, no, thank you. I promised my daughter a book if she started sleeping in her own bed."

I bent down to the little girl's level. "You know what that means, right? That you're a big girl now." I gave her a warm smile. She unexpectedly offered me a quick hug and ran giggling to the children's section.

"Wow, you really have a way with kids. I've never seen her do that. Ever since her dad died, she's been very introverted."

The words stabbed at my heart as I remembered what it was like growing up without a dad, but this poor girl had one and then lost him.

"Are you still doing story time?" she asked.

I stood up. "I haven't in a while."

"I'm sorry for your loss. We stopped coming a few months before. My daughter wasn't quite ready for it."

"Thank you. It was two years ago this week," I shifted uncomfortably. I wasn't sure what to say. She gently reached out and squeezed my arm.

"Your mom was a remarkable person. The world mourns the loss of such a beautiful soul." She walked to the children's corner to join her daughter, leaving a small crevice in my heart.

I went back to the counter to look through the mysteriously appearing book, but it was gone and in its place was the cup with the flower in it.

What the hell? I looked around the desk, but the book was nowhere to be found. I picked up the cup cautiously as if it would bite me and put it back onto the counter where Starling had put it. I noticed my ring change between several colors and then return to the milky opal color. *If only rings could talk.*

The little girl ran up to me, holding a book. It was the book that was on my desk. She grinned at me.

"I found this on the floor."

She shoved it toward me. I took it hesitantly. "Thank you."

Her mom joined her. "Yeah, it was sitting on the floor and, of course, the fairies caught my daughter's eye. It's her favorite thing right now."

"Oh, that's weird. Sorry about that." I smiled and looked down at the girl. "You know this was my favorite book when I was your age? My mom would read it to me every night." Her face brightened as I handed it back to her. Her mom gave me the money for it, took her daughter's hand, and strutted out the door. The little girl hugged the book with her other arm just like I did when my mom let me pick out my first book, and I chose that one. In fact, I still had it somewhere in the house. It was out of print and that lucky little girl just bought the last one, but what was it doing on my desk and then on the floor? And really I should be asking how the hell it moved.

A few customers started filtering in, so for now, I had to try to put it out of my mind. I walked around to help people. There was a farmer's market today, which usually meant more business for all the shops. A steady flow of people filled the store throughout the day.

I couldn't stop thinking about the book. Who left it for me and who knew about it? The more questions I asked the more sprang up. My life was so much simpler when I was just going through the motions and getting by. All this purpose and answer seeking was tiring and wearing on me, but what choice did I have? If it meant I could find out what really happened to my mom, then I would do whatever it took. It was hard for me to hold back tears, but I was getting better at it. Better at hardening the layers of sediment settling surface deep, drying up the tears before they betrayed me.

Hopefully, in the process, I would find out what was happening to me too, what significance it had to my eighteenth birthday, who or what the shadow was and why it was following me, make sense of the visions that connected my mom and me, and where all these heightened sensations were coming from. There were also the weird animal encounters, but that had been happening since I was seven, so it didn't seem that out of the ordinary to me. Like I said, a lot of questions. Questions that weren't going to come easy, and at times would probably be painful, but they would come, and I would finally know who I was outside the sorrow that suffocated me.

Chapter Twelve

My only mission as I was closing up the shop was to get home and find my copy of that book. There was a reason it was floating, literally, around my store, and I had a feeling it would make things that were happening to me clearer. I turned off the lights and locked up. Outside, the sun was beginning to tuck itself into bed for the night, and the breeze was warm and inviting. *God, how I loved these nights!* The breeze crawled around my exposed skin on my neck, kissing it as it made its way to my ears. I closed my eyes and took a deep breath, enjoying the tranquility it brought.

"Arie," the breeze whispered to me.

I shot my eyes open to see *him* across the street, leaning on a tree. *Ashe.* My heart fluttered. I didn't know how to react to his sudden appearance. He was gorgeous, and my attraction to him seemed to go deeper than a few brief meetings. He was wearing a fitted black plain t-shirt that showed off his perfectly sculpted abs, a pair of dark denim jeans that looked like they were tailored just for him, and a pair of black DC skate shoes. Nothing else existed as I soaked in his presence. He stared at me with such intensity I thought I would pass out. As he crossed the street, my body started to heat up. I could feel my milky cheeks turning red. The closer he got to me the weaker I got. My vision started to blur. *Oh God, I was going to pass out!* As my legs gave out, I saw his silhouette speed up toward me. Then I was floating, and then there was nothing.

I woke up in my bed with a humongous headache. *What happened?* The last thing I remembered was Ashe setting my body on fire. I sat up quickly and looked around. Was he still here? The pain in my head was killing me. I rubbed my temples gently trying to will the pain away as I jumped out of bed. Thank God, I was still wearing the same clothes! It was dark outside, so I knew some time passed, I just didn't know how much. I went to my window and looked out. Under the night's glow, I saw someone lying down in the meadow in the butterfly circle. Why was River here? He must have come by to check on me, but what happened to Ashe? I had to admit that my heart ached a little at the thought of not getting to spend any time with him. I went to join River at the circle.

The warm breeze confirmed that only a few hours had passed. It wrapped around me and guided me to the meadow. As I approached the circle, I realized it wasn't River lying down in our circle. It was Ashe. I paused. My breath caught in my chest, and my heart pumped excitement through my veins. A faint smile lit up my eyes.

"Are you just going to stand there, or are you going to come sit down with me?"

He spoke to me completely unmoved or unfazed. It was hard to find the words. What do you say to someone you barely know who makes your heart skip beats and you seem to fall apart in front of them every time they're around? "Ummm, yeah." I guess that's what you say. *Lame.* I slowly walked up behind him and lay down, leaving only a few inches between us. I was scared to look at him, so I didn't. I swear he could feel my body vibrating the ground as I shook nervously. We lay there in a complete meditative silence watching the stars twinkle and the flying creatures of the night pass by.

"Aren't you going to ask what happened?" He turned his head to mine and looked into the depths of my soul.

"No." He said it so sweetly and matter-of-factly.

When I looked into his golden eyes, I felt like I knew everything I needed to know about him. He felt safe. He felt like home. The silence filled the space between us again. I wanted to touch him, but I couldn't.

"Why do I feel so safe around you? I barely know you." I watched his eyes for some sign of untruthfulness as if I could read his mind.

"I don't know, but I like it."

His words went straight through me like a bullet blazing through the air. My heart began racing at the anticipation of what could happen tonight in this meadow. It filled my body with sensations of dancing flames burning as they hopscotched on my skin. I wanted him to touch me. Even a little graze of his hand on mine would send me over the edge, but he kept his distance. I wondered if he was feeling the energy building between us, or if I was just imagining it. He looked back up at the sky.

"Look."

He pointed to a few fireflies flying above us. They were so close that if I reached my hand up I could touch one. A few more joined, and they started flying in circles around us. "I've never seen them so close up before. They're magnificent." I lifted my hand, and they immediately changed course and began to circle around it. I let out an childish giggle.

"I guess I'm not the only one attracted to you."

I could feel his eyes watching me. Did he really just say that? Oh my God, this was too much. If something didn't happen soon, I was going to make it happen. "You don't think it's weird that fireflies are circling around my hand?"

"No, should I?"

Well, actually, yes. He should think it was weird. There were only a few people who knew my unnatural attraction with nature, and as far as I knew, he wasn't on that very short list. The fireflies glowed brighter and began to circle around Ashe and me, urging us to sit up, so we obeyed. This took me back to my first kiss with River. *Oh no, River!* What was I doing? What was happening? Why was I so naturally attracted to this complete stranger? I couldn't deny the power his energy had over me, though. We were still staring into the distance in front of us, coexisting in our own worlds as comfortable as if we had known each other our whole lives. I couldn't take it anymore. I reached out my hand and touched his. Instantly, I felt like I was transported to another plane of existence. I felt incredible. All the years of pain disappeared and were replaced with unconditional love and happiness. My body felt invincible. And then just like that I was lying on the ground shrouded in darkness. The fireflies had disappeared, and Ashe had created a bigger distance between us. "What happened?"

"I don't know. We were sitting here and then you passed out."

I sat back up. "When I touched you… I… it was…"

"Arie, I think I should be going now." He stood up. "I just didn't want you to be alone when you woke up." He started to walk away, leaving me alone with the night breeze and stars.

"Wait, really? You're just going to leave?" I couldn't make myself leave the safety and warmth of the butterfly circle. He didn't respond and faded as the shadows of the night enveloped him and took him from me. All I could do was stand there in complete dismay and wonder. I wanted to believe he was a positive light signifying a new era for me, but I was also hesitant. Something had been stalking me, and he appeared at the same time. I would be stupid not to be cautious and maybe a little bit scared.

I went to sleep that night with a heavy heart. I didn't know what to think with Ashe leaving the way he did or the way he made me feel when I touched him. Then there was

River. It had always been just him. My mom would have wanted it to be River, but the way Ashe made me feel was almost indescribable. I couldn't stop thinking about him. When would I see him again? He seemed to just pop up whenever he felt like it. He was the definition of mysterious.

Last night had sidetracked my mission to find the faery book, but I was not going to let anything distract me today. I jumped out of bed and threw on some sweats. I had thirty minutes before I had to start getting ready for the day. I went into my mom's closet and pulled on the tether hanging from the ceiling. A set of collapsible stairs descended, allowing access to the attic. I turned on the light switch and climbed up. I was so glad my mom had the sense to have electrical installed up here or else I would be crawling around with who knows what while trying to hold a flashlight.

Along with electrical, my mom had the attic finished, so I didn't have to worry about falling through the rafters. The attic was full of boxes, old paintings, and unused décor that my mom couldn't seem to part with. Most of it was mine when I was little that my mom became sentimentally attached to, which was funny, because she hated junk in the house. I guess that's why it was tucked out of sight out of mind, but still close by.

I felt a little overwhelmed, like a looking for a needle in a haystack moment. I couldn't even imagine where it could be. I grabbed a box randomly. I let out a sigh of relief when I noticed my mom had taken the initiative to label the boxes. This one was marked *baby clothes*. Chances were pretty good that the book wasn't in there. I came across another box that read *canvases*. I didn't realize my mom had saved all of these. She sold her work in a small gallery in the city and did pretty well with it. I just assumed all of her work was gone aside from the ones in the bookstore. I would have to go through this box later and hang them around the house. After discarding a few more boxes, I finally came across a box marked *Arie's favorites.* I dragged it into a clearing in the middle and peeled off the tape. I opened it to find a few of my favorite stuffed animals, my first sad attempts at drawing, my snuggie blanket, and the faery book. I dug it out and made myself comfortable on the floor. The binding was worn and the edges tattered, but it still made my heart smile.

I didn't know why I always referred to it as the faery book. The figures on the front had a wispy quality to them and a faint lining of what could be wings I guess. The title read *Spirits of Nature.* I remember when my mom unpacked this book from the supplier at the bookstore. I instantly fell in love with it. I was drawn to it. It was just after my fourth birthday, so my mom let me have it as a gift. I literally made her read it to me every night until I was old enough to read it to myself. Oddly enough, it prepared me for the day the creatures started treating me like their own on my seventh birthday.

Most kids would have freaked out, but in my fictitious reality, that was normal and natural. It never fazed me. It only amazed me. It still amazed me. The book was a normal-sized children's book with only fifteen pages. The cover looked like an oil painting with two spirits in the foreground of a beautiful blend of purple hues background. One of the spirits was a woman and the other a male. Randomly surrounding them were butterflies of all different colors. Even now the book cover awed me. It was beautiful.

My mom made a replica of the cover for me, which now lived inside the same box this book resided in. A shame, really. I placed my hand on the cover and closed my eyes, trying to force memories from a happier time. I could feel my mom's arms wrap around me protectively as I sat on her lap while she read to me. She always added more details to the story, constantly surprising me with her relentless creativity. I relished in the memory for a moment and then opened my eyes. I just knew there was something about this book that had to do with what was happening. I opened the cover. There was a hand-scripted note from my mom on the cover that I had never seen before.

My precious Arie,

I don't know when you will find this, but I want you to hold onto the bond we have shared, not only as mother and daughter, but also as two spirits of nature. We will always be together because the essence we are made of will live forever in the world around us. Close your eyes and find me within, and then we will be together again forever and always. Remember all the unwritten stories I told you. They will help you discover your true self and find your way back to me. I love you, sweet Arie, and I hold onto the moment when we will be reunited.

Love,

Mommy

Tears betrayed me once again and rolled down my cheeks. I wiped them away harshly. My eyes were so blurry that I couldn't focus on the words, so I just looked at the images as I flipped through the book slowly. There were only a handful of words on each page that simply described the pictures, which was why my mom added more. My heart was aching as the stitches started ripping apart with every memory and flip of the page.

The images showed figures similar to the ones on the book cover living amongst the forest and creatures. There was a little girl who was outlined with a beautiful pinkish white glow interacting with the different creatures and surrounded by beautiful butterflies with her dad close by. A little boy also appeared in several images, playing with her.

It all looked so surreal and peaceful. How I longed to live in the world within the confines of these pages.

It was hard for me to turn to the last page. It always was. I would beg my mom to skip it so I could believe it ended with happily ever after like all the princess books, but it didn't. The last page was shrouded in darkness and sadness that now occupied my soul. I hesitantly flipped the page. The background was filled with blended colors of dark blues and grays and in the foreground lay the little girl, her glow faded and her dad standing above her with his hand on her cheek with his face full of despair. The little boy stood close by mourning the loss of his playmate, but the mom was nowhere to be seen.

This was when my mom taught me about the essence of life, and that while it looked like an unhappy moment, it was actually a rebirth in a different form for the little girl. I tried to hold onto that, but it still made me sad because no matter what form her rebirth took she would never be with her dad, mom, or playmate again. Chills rushed through my body as I imagined her all alone. I turned the last page over, and on the back cover, my mom had drawn her ring. It was also surrounded by a faint glow. Underneath it was written *The ring will always bring you back to me.*

This was the third reference to the ring. I just didn't understand how it could bring me back to my mom. She was gone, and she was never coming back. I closed the book hard and hugged it tight against my heart like I did the first day it found me. I rocked back and forth with it, letting the tears wash away the images of my mom's body lying on the ground, lifeless. The sounds of my sobs were absorbed by the insulation of the attic walls, giving me free reign to cry out as loud as I wanted.

After a few minutes passed, I let rational thoughts start to penetrate the pain. I needed to understand the importance of this ring, and the only person I could think of asking was Sierra. If she wasn't home yet, I would do this by phone, but either way, I needed to talk to her. She had the ring last, and she was my mom's best friend. She had to know something. This gave my life purpose again, so I threw all the stuff back into the box, keeping the book with me, and sealed in the secrets of the attic once again.

Chapter Thirteen

As I pulled up to River's house, I noticed his truck was missing. I hadn't talked to him since the other night, which was strange, because he always checked up on me one way or another. *Maybe he was just giving me space.* I parked on the gravel in front and made my way to the front door. He said his parents were coming home in a few days, so I was hoping that would be today. I knocked, but no one answered. I knocked again and waited. I tried the knob. It was unlocked. I could just go in, but what was the point? I needed to talk to Sierra, and she was obviously not home. I knew I was like a daughter to them, but I still didn't feel comfortable just walking into their house uninvited. Besides, I really needed to get to the store. I would just try to call her on the way. I hopped back into the car and grabbed my phone from the center console. I was hoping to see a missed call or text from River, but there was nothing. I was disappointed, but did I have a right to be? I knew we weren't officially together, but my emotions were playing a dangerous game with my mind and leaving me full of guilt and shame. I looked up Sierra's number and called it. Straight to voicemail. I debated leaving a message, but in the end, decided not to. I pulled out of the driveway and headed to the shop.

Driving along, I noticed the weather was taking a turn for the worse. Dark clouds were starting to make their way toward town, and the wind was kicking up. Most shops on the strip closed on days like these. The perks of living in a small town and opening and closing whenever you wanted. I still liked to stay open. Mainly because I had nowhere else to go, especially since River was MIA. Maybe Starling was around.

As I drove up the strip, heavy drops started to pound my car. The street was deserted, and the lights in all the shops remained off. It was still early, though, so maybe I wouldn't be the only one here today. If I was, that would give me time to rummage through my mom's journal more. I pulled into my usual spot and braced myself for the quick run through the rain to the shelter of the overhang. I tucked the journal and faery book under my jacket and grasped the keys in my hand. I was just about to throw open the door when I caught a reflection of a figure in my rearview mirror.

I looked closer and saw it was Ashe standing in the same spot as yesterday. Only this time he was wearing a jacket and was soaking wet. *What was he doing here?* I had two choices. I could ignore him for walking away so abruptly last night and go open the store or I could confront him. Who was I kidding? There was only one choice. I pulled the book and journal out of my jacket and set them back down on the seat. I looked in the rearview mirror to make sure he was still there. When I saw him, my body began to boil with intensity.

I had to see where this feeling was taking me. I took a brave breath and shot open the door. I took a moment to look at him. It was dark, but my vision was strangely clear even though he was across the street. He was even more gorgeous and endearing with rain rolling off his hair and down his cheeks and over his lips. Each raindrop on my skin aroused a part of my body. I was scared to take a step toward him, knowing that if I took this path, I might be tearing apart the road that River and I spent eighteen years building, but I couldn't deny what my body needed, and right now it was Ashe.

I took a step, and a wave of emotion pulsed up the balls of my feet. Light enveloped me and blinded my senses. Everything around me disappeared: the shops, the street, the rain, my car, and Ashe. I was alone with the light. I should have felt scared, but I didn't. I felt warm and happy. I closed my eyes and let the surrealism of the moment take hold of me. I felt at home within the light. A hand touched my cheek lightly and forced me to open my eyes. Ashe had joined me in the light and brought all his beauty with him. His eyes spoke words that his lips could never express. His hand warmed my cheek. I placed my hand on top of his and closed my eyes to feel his energy enter me.

Here within the light, I realized he was familiar and not a stranger. If River was home, Ashe was my heart. Two parts of me that I needed and could never live without. Ashe was the missing piece and now the hole in my heart could mend and start anew. As I opened my eyes, I knew this was the defining moment I would never be able to take back. Ashe leaned into me, but then the light went dark and he disappeared. I was back on the street, standing in the rain in front of the store with my car door ajar. I looked around desperately.

"Arie, what are you doing standing in the rain? You're soaking wet." Starling came running over. "Oh my God, girl. The inside of your car is soaked, too." She slammed the door.

I was still in a state of shock. She put her arms around me, and the chill that was seeping through my wet clothes started to dissipate in the warmth of her embrace. She shoved me under the canopy.

"Do you have your keys?"

I dropped them into her hand while my mind was still racing through the moments that had just taken place. I couldn't speak. I wanted that moment so badly. I *needed* that moment so badly even if it wasn't real. But it was real, right? I could kill Starling! I managed to glare at her.

"What? You're mad at me for getting you out of the rain? Really?" She shoved the key into the lock and pushed open the door and heaved me through it. "What is up with you, girl? I think it's time we talked." She rushed to the back.

I heard the heater kick on and the rush of heat flowed through the vent and filled the room. I looked like a wet rat. I hope I didn't smell like one, too. I really didn't want to sit in the store all day soaking wet. Starling sprinted passed me to the front door.

"I'll be right back. You need dry clothes."

She read my mind. I needed to sort through what was real and what wasn't. Did that actually happen outside, or was I having a vision? If Starling hadn't shown up, I wondered what would have happened. The thought made me perk up. If that was my destiny in that light, then there was hope for me after all. Starling rushed back over with a handful of clothes. Convenient that she had a clothing boutique next door, I guess.

"Here. Go put these on."

She shoved the clothes to me and twirled me around and gave me a push toward the bathroom. I sloshed across the floor.

"Don't worry. I have socks and shoes for you, too."

Damn, that girl knew everything I was thinking. I closed the bathroom door and started to strip away the wet clothes. I was truly soaked. I caught sight of my ring, which was changing colors again. I wondered what made it glow. I thought about it as I got dressed. Starling had picked out a beautiful oversized turquoise sweater and a pair of leggings. Not my usual attire, but comfy and simple, which was definitely my style. The ring glowed when I came in contact with the book and when I thought about my mom. I had visions, too. All of this started on my birthday. There was an obvious significance, but what it was and what was happening, was still as much of a mystery as ever.

I needed to get in touch with Sierra. And where the hell was River? I went back out into the store to find Starling sitting at the desk looking through my mom's journal.

"Star!" I raced up to her and grabbed it out of her hands. "Why did you get this out of my car?"

"Whoa, back off. I didn't realize it was a journal until a second ago, and I didn't get it out of your car. It was just sitting here. Had I known what it was I would never have opened it."

I hugged the journal close to me. "Ahhh, I'm sorry. I didn't mean to yell at you. I was just surprised to see it. I thought I left it in the car, but I must have brought it in." I knew that wasn't the truth, but what was I going to tell her? That it has a mind of its own apparently. That would go over well. Starling stood up.

"Look, you need to tell me what's going on. River came by yesterday, and he was pretty upset. He wouldn't tell me why, but he said you needed someone to talk to because you weren't talking to him. So, spill it. What the hell is going on? Don't try to lie to me because I can see right through it."

And she could. She always knew when I was lying, but lately I was getting good at it. Too good. "Okay, but sit. You're making me nervous." She towered over me by a good eight inches. She sat down in my chair, and I scooted up onto the desk. "Weird things have been happening lately."

"Weirder than your strange attraction to animals?"

"Correction. Their strange attraction to me."

"Whatever. You know what I mean."

"Well, the way you said it makes it sound creepy and dirty."

She started laughing. "I guess you're right. Ewww."

I joined her in the silly moment until she broke it up.

"What else has been going on?"

I told her about the heightened sensations I was feeling, but only around River and Ashe. Ashe took a little more explaining. I also told her about the ring, the visions, and the journal. I ended with the vision she just crashed.

"Wow!" That was all she could muster.

"I told you. Weird."

"Yeah, but you failed to warn me of the hotness, too."

I could feel myself blush. "Sorry. Rewind disclaimer. There is hotness happening, too."

"Dually noted! I don't know what to say, Arie. For once I am speechless."

"I'm torn, Star. I don't know what's real and what's a vision. Is Ashe just a figment of my imagination? He feels so real. And what about River? And then there's my mom's death or murder. I feel like it's all too much at once. So, yes, River is right to worry because I feel like I am going crazy."

"That is a lot. I don't know, but whatever you need, just ask me, okay? I can deal with weird. What I can't deal with is you going through all of this by yourself."

"What if River's mom is right, and the visions did kill my mom? They have been getting pretty intense, and I have been blacking out a lot. I'm not ready to die, Star. I feel like I've just learned how to live again, how to be happy. " She stood up and wrapped me in her embrace.

"I promise we'll figure this all out. I can't lose you and neither can River. We'll make sure of that."

Her words were comforting, but didn't change the fact that something big was coming, and my idea of reality was about to change even more than it already had. "Thanks, Star. You're a good friend."

"You bet your ass I am, and you better not forget it. Now, tell me more about Ashe." She giggled and sat back down.

I knew she was trying to lighten the mood, but I just couldn't ride the wave with her. I was starting to get worried about River.

"Was yesterday the last time you saw River?"

"Yeah, why?"

"I just haven't heard from him after our encounter the other night, and it's not really like him to disappear."

"He mentioned something about his parents coming back and needing to pick them up at the airport. Maybe he's just preoccupied with that."

"You're probably right. I've been trying to get a hold of his mom, but it keeps going to voicemail."

"Why don't you just try calling River?"

I gave her a knowing glance.

"Right, awkward. Okay, well, I'll try calling him then."

She grabbed my phone and looked up his number and called him. "Voicemail."

She handed me the phone. I slid off the counter. "See. MIA."

"I'm sure everything is fine. Why don't we close up and go over there now? It's not like anyone is going to come out in this storm."

She was right. No one but us was stupid enough to be out. "It's okay. I think I am just going to clean up around the store and do some inventory today. Take advantage of the quiet."

"All right, I guess I should do the same. I'll be next door. Let's get dinner after, okay?" She stood up and walked to the door.

"It's a date."

"I'll come get you later."

She closed the door and rushed next door as the rain pounded the pavement. I went over to my mom's journal. *What was with these books?* I needed to try Sierra again. I grabbed my phone and pressed her number. This time it rang. *Finally!* After several rings, it connected, but it was quiet. Dead air. "Hello? Sierra?" Then the phone disconnected. *Okay, that was weird.* I dialed again, but this time it went straight to voicemail again. *Ugh!* I wondered if the storm was messing up cell service. I decided to try River's phone again, but it went straight to voicemail. I didn't have his dad's number, so I gave up frustrated and even more worried. This was just so unlike him. I fell into my chair and stared at my mom's journal for a moment before picking it up. My ring started glowing brighter than it had before. So much so it was blinding. I closed my eyes instinctively. The warmth the glow summoned had me yearning for my mom's touch.

When I opened them, I was surrounded by forest trees and beautiful wildflowers. Butterflies flew around freely, and squirrels scurried across the dirt foraging for food. A light shone through the spaces in the branches and created an iridescent glow. I thought I was alone until I heard a girl screech in terror. The adrenaline kicked up several notches. I started running in the direction of the scream, throwing tree branches out of my way and crunching leaves beneath my feet. I could see an opening ahead. I was about to break through the forest wall to come to the girl's aid, but someone had beaten me there.

A beautiful man, or at least what I thought was a man, was standing over an angelic frame. She looked to be about my age. The man and the girl were surrounded by the same iridescent glow of the forest, making it hard to see them clearly. A boy about the same age as the girl with the same glow came running from behind the man, which was opposite of where I was standing. Hiding in the forest wall, I spotted another glow, but couldn't make out the figure. I could tell by the man's body language he was in despair as was the boy. The man placed his hand on the girl's cheek, and a bright light filled it.

Oh my God! Was I in the faery book? That would be nuts! Even with all the weird things happening, this would have to make the crazy list. This was the scene from the last page of my book, only the kids were older. This was the page I always avoided as a child because of the dark nature of the ending. *Why was I seeing this? How was I seeing this?* The light filled the man's hand, and the glow around the girl faded and disappeared. He cupped the light protectively with both hands and looked at the sky and let out a terrifying cry.

Until now, there had been no sounds besides the forest and the ones that I made running here. I scrunched in fear and sorrow. The pain this man felt filled the forest with decay. The boy stood tall, but defeated, as the man walked over to him. I wish I could hear what they were saying. Then, as fast as the blink of an eye, the man touched the boy's face and he collapsed, holding the boy's light in his other hand. *Did he just kill him?*

I started to panic as I realized this could be the man who killed my mom. There was nothing I could do for the girl or boy, so I spun around and started running frantically back through the forest the way I came. Tears came in waves as I switched between breathing and crying as I ran. From what, I had no idea. I was alone in an unfamiliar world.

I was running so fast that I failed to notice the trail of butterflies following me. They passed by my side and fluttered manically in front of me, making it impossible to see and forcing me to slow down. As soon as I stopped, they circled around me trapping me in the middle.

At first, I was scared that the man would catch up to me, but then a quiet calm overtook my senses and dried my eyes and soothed my beating heart. If I was going to die, I hope it was as peaceful as this. A bright light filled the center of the butterfly whirlwind, and then I was back in the store, sitting in my chair holding the faery book instead of my mom's journal. Everything else was the same. The door opened, and Starling popped her head in.

"Ready for dinner?"

Everything else was the same except for the time. I had been trapped in the vision for eight hours.

"Arie, you ready to go?"

"Yeah, I'm ready." I grabbed the book and journal and tucked my phone into my back pocket and followed Starling out the door, turning off the lights and locking the door.

Chapter Fourteen

Starling was great at putting me at ease. Just being around her made me feel better. We had stopped at a small Chinese place to eat. She filled me in on things going on with the family and her nonexistent love life with Donut Dan. She hated that I nicknamed him that, but it fit. The first time I "met" Dan he said two words, *hi* and *bye*. It was a very deep conversation. Star said even less. It was funny how she got so tongue-tied around him. The girl never shuts up otherwise. She was such an amazing spirit. I envied her for it. I also loved her for it. It reminded me of my mom.

I refrained from telling her about the book vision. To be honest, it was creeping me out, and I didn't really want to relive it right now. Two full days had gone by since I had heard from River, and I was getting anxious. I decided to drop by on my way home. It was almost eight p.m., so he should be home unless he really was picking up his parents today. It was kind of an ordeal because the closest airport was a few hours away, maybe more in this rain. But really they should be home by now. As I drove up the driveway, I noticed a light on inside. I saw River's truck around the side. They were finally home.

Okay, now that I knew he was safe, did I really have the courage to face him? Even if I didn't, I needed to talk to Sierra. It just couldn't wait any longer. Not after that last vision.

I parked in the same spot as earlier and went up to the door. With every knock my heart jumped. My stomach started twisting in knots thinking about the almost kiss I had with Ashe, or didn't have, because who knew if it was real? I sounded crazy! I could hear footsteps approach the door. River opened it. He looked sullen.

"What's wrong?" I could tell something wasn't right.

"Come in."

He moved aside to let me inside the house. He was wearing a plain white t-shirt and a pair of jeans. White socks covered his feet. I turned to face him. "What's going on? Are your parents home?" The look on his face broke my heart.

"My mom is."

He didn't move. "Where's your dad?" I was almost scared to ask.

"He stayed. My mom was going to stay too, but she wasn't feeling good, so she came home."

"Okay, so why do you look like someone just died? You had me really freaked out for a second." I punched him in the arm.

"Ouch. I'm just exhausted, Arie. It's been a long few days." He sighed and looked at the floor.

Oh crap! Did he know about Ashe? How could he? *I* barely knew anything about him. Something was off.

"Ummm, okay, well, can I talk to your mom?"

"She's asleep. She has a really bad flu or something."

"Starling's mom had the flu, too. It must really be going around right now."

"Must be," he said quietly, almost under his breath like it was meant just for him.

He walked into the kitchen, so I followed him. "I hope she's okay. Is there anything I can do?" He grabbed two glasses and filled them with water. He handed me one.

"She just needs to rest." He took a big gulp.

The silence was awkward, which wasn't normal for us. I wasn't sure what to say, though. I fidgeted with the glass for a few seconds. "I was getting worried because I hadn't heard from you since…" I couldn't finish the sentence. He knew what I was referencing.

"Yeah, sorry. I had some stuff to do yesterday, and today I was picking up my mom."

He seemed so distant. His mind was somewhere else. He couldn't possibly know, and what happened to waiting for as long as it took? Why was I getting so mad? He didn't do anything wrong. *I did.* Yet, I was scared. I was scared I was going to lose him. I didn't think I could survive without him. I was on the verge of tears. He noticed, so he walked around the counter and took me into his arms.

"Hey, it's going to be okay. I'm fine. I just had stuff to take care of. I didn't mean to scare you, bug."

I loved that he called me that. He hadn't used my nickname since my mom's funeral. His words warmed my soul with a much-needed reassurance that he wasn't going anywhere. I loved him so much. I sank into him and let him comfort me. He brushed my hair with his fingers and kissed my head.

"I love you, Arie. I'm not going anywhere."

That did it for me. The tears came quietly and disobediently. My hardened heart cracked like a dried up lake, knowing that I was not only going to break this man's heart, but I was going to crush it, and I was one day going to lose him. I wanted to savor every moment I had with him no matter how selfish it was. Right now he was mine, and no one could take that from me.

I wouldn't let this moment go unrecognized. I might not be able to say I love you back, but I could let him in again, something I never thought possible. That was the least I could do. He deserved all of me, not just the broken parts. I looked up into his crystal blue eyes and gave all my heart to him. I stood on my tippy toes and kissed him with every morsel of love and appreciation I had in me. His lips were soft and tender.

He reciprocated momentarily, but then pulled away.

A tear trickled from my eye. He looked me in the eyes and brushed it from my face. Without saying a word, he gently kissed my cheek where the tear had fallen, lingering in the moment for a few seconds. I tightened my hold on his hair in anguish because in this moment we both knew things were going to change. *I could feel it.* He looked at me carefully again and gently stroked my cheekbone with his thumb.

"I love you, Arie. No matter what."

He kissed my lips with determined gentleness. He went and sat down on the couch. I followed and sat in the smaller couch across from him. Nothing else needed to be said. We quietly knew where things stood between us. He bent over his knees and rubbed his face. He looked tired.

"You look like you could use a week's worth of sleep. I should go." I started to get up.

"I'm not letting you go home in this storm. Just stay. We can just sleep together like we used to."

I missed that. The days after my mom died I would fall asleep in the safety of his arms. It was the only way I could sleep. Ever since I distanced myself and that ceased, I never slept more than three hours at a time. It would be nice to sleep a full night again without nightmares.

"Okay." I managed a small smile. He put his hand on mine and helped me up. He led me to his room never letting go.

I woke up in the security of River's arms as I had for so many nights in the past. He gave me one of his shirts to sleep in. We didn't say much when we came to his room. There wasn't anything to say that we didn't already feel. Saying it aloud would have made it all too real for both of us, something neither of us was ready to submit to. I took in his naturally invigorating scent and imprinted it to memory.

It was still early, and I knew he needed his sleep, so I slowly and carefully unwrapped myself from him and inched out of bed. I slipped on my socks and pulled on my leggings. I walked out into the hallway and listened for any sounds of life besides mine. The house was silent. I quietly walked to the kitchen and started a pot of coffee. The sun was just starting to peek over the horizon, so I grabbed a quilt off the couch and scurried outside. The morning dew kissed my exposed skin and the fog surrounded me as I made my way to the porch swing and sat down. The fog was thick this morning. It always was in the late fall and early spring. I loved it. Sometimes it felt suffocating, but it also felt cleansing. I tucked my feet into the blanket and sat still with my eyes closed, letting my other senses take over. Dawn and dusk would always be my absolutely favorite times of the day, especially dawn because I was truly alone with peaceful thoughts.

I heard the door creak open. Sierra was standing there holding two cups of coffee.

"Good morning, Arie." She handed me a cup.

"Hi, I'm sorry. Did I wake you? How are you feeling?"

"No, sweetie. I was awake, and I'm feeling a little better. River told me that you needed to talk to me?" She inquired.

I didn't know how to start this conversation or how much to tell her because of the whole Ashe and River thing. "Ummm... yeah. I was wondering where you got my mom's ring."

"Do you mind if I sit with you?"

"No, of course not." She was even beautiful rolling out of bed. She sat next to me careful not to spill our coffees.

"Your mom gave me that ring on the morning just before she..."

"Died. You can say it. It's been two years. I should be able to handle hearing it now."

"I prefer saying passed."

We sat there in silence remembering my mom in our own private memories. "Why would she give it to you, especially that day? I never saw her without that ring." She took a slow sip of coffee, probably contemplating how to tell me the horrible truth and the lies surrounding my mother's death.

"Your mom knew her time was up, and she wanted to make sure that her ring made it into your hands. She trusted me."

"But why did you keep it from me for so long?" Tears were filling my eyes. I felt betrayed because she knew how hard it was on me not being able to have that one piece of my mom all these years. "You saw what it did to me thinking it was gone."

"Your mom made it very clear that you were not to get the ring until you turned eighteen. And before you ask why, she never told me. The thing that worked so well with our friendship was we didn't need to ask a lot of questions to know that we loved each other. We just needed to be there for each other and listen. That's what I did for your mom. It killed me when she came to me that day. I was about to lose my best friend, and there was nothing I could do about it. I had to just listen and be the best person I could be for her in that moment."

She was choking back her own grief as she spoke. I couldn't hold back the tears anymore. I put down the coffee, knowing it probably wasn't the smartest thing to be holding.

"I just don't understand how she knew she was going to die. Did someone tell her they were going to kill her? Everyone loved my mom."

"Everyone and everything, sweetie. She was a remarkable woman, and her spirit will always be here for us."

"River said you told him she had visions and that you thought that was what killed her?"

"I did tell him that, but I really don't know what happened. I want to believe she died peacefully. When she said goodbye to me, she seemed like she had accepted it."

I started crying harder. "But why didn't she say goodbye to me?" I was crying so hard I was shaking and could barely get the sentence out of my mouth. She put down her coffee and wrapped her arms tight around me and whispered into my ear.

"That's why she was outside, sweetie. She was going to say goodbye."

All the pain I had been holding onto the past two years came rushing out and filled my world with darkness, sorrow, and loneliness. All I had ever wanted was the chance to tell her how much I loved her and to be able to say goodbye. Knowing she was on her way to give me that chance before she died ripped through me like a grenade tearing me to pieces in an explosion of memories. I missed my chance by only a few moments. The thought made me crazy.

Sierra held me firmly until my convulsions passed. She rubbed my back and rested her cheek on my head like my mom would when I was upset. I didn't know what I would do if I didn't have River and his parents.

"Is everything okay?"

River had popped his head out. It had been awhile since he had witnessed an "Arie meltdown," but I wondered at what point it would get old for him. When he would have enough of the broken bits of me and move on.

"I think she is going to be just fine," Sierra said for both of us. "I should go rest."

She got up, and River took her place. She grabbed both of our coffee cups and went inside.

"You okay?"

He put his arm around me. I was still clenching my knees closely to my chest in an attempt to control the convulsions. I let my body lean into him. "You're too good to me, River. What did I ever do to deserve such unconditional affection from you?"

"We were meant for each other, Arie. We were born only a few months apart, we are neighbors, and our moms were best friends. It was written before we even existed. There will never be anyone else for me. You are the reason I am here."

My heart bled with sadness. I knew what I had to do. "I love you too, River." I sunk my face into his chest and held onto the moment for as long as he would let me.

"Did you find out what you needed to from my mom?"

"Not entirely, but it was something at least."

"Good. Just don't shut me out, okay? I can help you figure out what's happening. I want to help you."

"I know, River. That's the only thing keeping me going." And it really was. What was I thinking letting myself get sucked in by Ashe? My heart was so conflicted, but River had been with me my whole life, and I knew that he always would be. You couldn't buy that kind of loyalty. He was mine. *Forever.*

Chapter Fifteen

Friday came quickly. The storm had passed leaving the town soaked but clean. The smell of freshly washed asphalt filled the street outside the store. I felt like I had come to a standstill with everything.

The store had been busy since the storm let up, and in between rushes, I was taking inventory and placing orders. I had to stay late last night just to get the inventory completed. Nothing extraordinary had happened. Ashe all but disappeared from existence, and River was giving me space but checking in regularly. Starling had finally given in and asked Donut Dan to dinner, so once again, I was on my own for the night. I thought about going home, but decided to stay at the store and cozy up in a couch chair in the reading nook to read through my mom's journal more.

Here it felt intimate and less intimidating than the house I grew up in and was now way too big for just me. While there were memories here, there were more there that haunted me day and night.

I hung the closed sign in the window and locked the front door. I grabbed the journal off the desk and checked my phone for messages. Nothing. I left my phone behind and took the journal to the chair. I curled up and flipped through to the last page I had left off on where my dad had summoned my mom to the forest. I admired my mom's writing for a moment and then flipped through to pick the next story to read. I stopped on the story dated one day before my seventh birthday, September 22nd.

I woke up in the meadow where the butterflies frequented. I didn't know how I got here, but I was hoping I would see Teve again. It had been six years since I had been visited by him. I missed him terribly, and my heart longed for his touch. The thought of seeing him again excited me. I sat up and looked around for him. I was alone with a half moon and the twinkling stars. The breeze was warm and gentle as it caressed my skin. Where was he? I heard a noise come from the forest wall and jumped up in anticipation. I wanted to run to him. I needed a dose of him. It had been too long, and I didn't know how much longer my heart could survive without him. If it wasn't for Arie, I would have been lost long ago. A deer poked through the brush and walked straight toward me without hesitation. I was amazed, but disappointed. It stopped in front of me and raised its nose to my hand as I reached out for it. Then before I could touch it, a noise from the forest startled it and it ran in the opposite direction. Teve! I started to run toward the forest, but slid to a stop when a shadow moved into my path. Its presence felt dark and cold, and fear pumped through my veins. I had fallen from my slide and was hysterically pushing back away from it. When I got my footing again, I stood up and started to run back to the meadow, but the shadow had blocked my path. I froze. The breeze picked up and raised goose bumps on my neck as it carried a whisper to me.

"When nature calls, she will listen, cry in despair, and fight with her heart."

I was paralyzed with fear keeping a watchful eye on the shadow in between glancing up to the house where Arie was sleeping. Then, the shadow was gone. I let out a fearful cry and fell to the ground as I shed a flood of tears. I was alone and confused. What was that? Where was Teve? Was it talking about Arie? Nature has only ever interacted with me outside the realm of normalcy. It has ignored her existence since she was born. It had to be talking about me, right? A terrified thought crossed through my mind, causing me to jump up and sprint to the house to Arie. I tore through the back door and raced up the stairs. I, quietly but forcefully, opened her bedroom door and peeked in. She was sleeping peacefully as I had left her just hours before. Her milky skin glowing from the moon's reflection against her auburn coffee locks. She was even more beautiful in her sleep. I let out a sigh of relief and walked over to her window and closed the curtains, but only after I scoured the meadow, looking for any signs of the shadow or Teve. All was quiet and normal again. I closed the curtains and walked over to Arie. I pushed back a piece of hair that was covering her face and kissed her on the head. I couldn't help but look at her in a different light now. Something had changed because of the revelation in the meadow and I could never take it back, only hope that it wasn't talking about her. I couldn't bear to think of her having to endure any kind of pain. She was still so young and innocent, and I would protect her until the day I died and then after.

I looked up from the journal and remembered the morning of my seventh birthday. I had woken up feeling different, something that nature had immediately noticed. I remembered thinking my mom was crying now realizing it was because of her vision. *She knew I was like her, too.* She was afraid for me. Her vision had been a warning, and her nightmare came true the moment I woke up that morning. Oh God, what she must have felt! The despair must have been her death, but what did it mean fight with my heart? Was it talking about River and Ashe? But why would I fight? I had made up my mind. Or was it talking about something else? I closed the journal in frustration. Every answer I thought I was getting closer to only made more questions surface. What the hell was I? Did others exist, or were my mom and me just freaks of nature?

My ring started glowing again, and I felt compelled to go to the front door. I got up and walked over to it and peered outside. The shadow figure was back.

It's weird, because sometimes I felt fear in its presence and sometimes I felt comfort. Right now I felt neither. I wasn't afraid, and at this point, it seemed like my only option to finding out what happened to my mom and discovering more about myself. I inhaled all the strength and confidence I could and hesitantly reached for the doorknob and turned it, knowing I was crossing the threshold of safety. I stepped outside, never taking my eyes off the shadow. It remained still until I stepped off the curb. It then descended into the thick-forested park.

I picked up speed as I followed it into the thicket. It was moving quickly, and I thought I had lost sight of it until I reached a clearing. It was the same clearing I saw in my vision of the faery book, only this time I was alone. The shadow had dissolved, and the only glow was from the light of the moon. Then, from the opposite side of the clearing, the shadow emerged and approached me slowly as if floating on a billowing cloud. My throat tightened, as it got closer to me, which caused my adrenaline to spike.

I wanted to stay strong, but as I struggled for breath I was beginning to weaken. I felt my knees buckling, and it took everything in me to stay erect. I felt dizzy, and my eyes were filling with water. The shadow stopped a few inches in front of me, and a hand quickly broke through the darkness and gently touched my cheek. Breath filled my lungs easily, and the strength returned to my legs. The hand was frail and soft and reminded me of my mom's. It felt warm on my skin, and I felt the need to place my hand over it. As I did, I felt a surge of power fill me with love.

A blinding glow enveloped the figure as it emerged from the shadow. I squinted in a desperate need to see who was hidden within the light. As the glow faded, my eyes widened in shock and gut-wrenching disbelief. It was my mom, but this time it wasn't a vision, right? I was awake when I followed the shadow here. I never blacked out.

I gripped her hand on my cheek as she smiled at me softly. She was here or at least a part of her was. I didn't care how or why I just wanted to stay in this moment forever. "Mom, how...?"

"Shhhhh, my sweet Arie. My essence will always be with you if you believe."

"I will always believe. I promise."

"I don't have much time. There's a fight coming, my sweet dear Arie. One that started when you turned seven and the essence within you activated. You will have to make a choice that will affect everyone. Be cautious and mindful. I stayed as long as I could to protect you, but all I can do now is watch and do what I can from where I am now."

"But I don't understand. Where are you? Are you still alive? Why can't I come with you?"

"I'm sorry, Arie, but I have to go now. You will never be wrong if you follow your heart."

She started to fade. I gripped on tightly to her hand trying to keep her with me, but it too faded. Tears fell hard and fast.

"Don't cry, my sweet Arie. You will see me again."

As she was fading, she leaned in and kissed my forehead, transferring something deep within me. She was gone, and I was alone again, surrounded by towering trees above and low lying grass below. I was drained of emotions and exhausted. I just wanted to lie down and give up. What was I hanging on to?

I had nothing left anymore. So I did. I lay down on the grass and gave into the night, closing my eyes and breathing in the peace of the surrounding silence. The chirping crickets and the fluttering wings of some flying night creatures began to lull me to sleep. I wanted peace like this to last forever.

"Wow, I don't know if I should join you or call you crazy."

I opened my eyes to see Starling standing above me.

"So should I lie down with you or bring you home?"

I couldn't help it. I started crying again. The kind of cry that breaks your heart to watch. I wanted to say something, but I couldn't. She knew that all I needed was someone to be here with me, so she just quietly lay down next to me and squeezed my hand. At some point, my water well had to dry up, because I honestly didn't know how much more I could take. A lot of time had passed along with many tears.

"Can I ask you something, Arie?"

"Of course," I managed to sniffle out.

"It's obvious to everyone around you that you're meant for greatness, so why haven't you seen that yet?"

That was an abrupt and fair question. "Honestly, Star, it's hard to imagine everything that I am is meant for anything good when all that has happened since my birth has brought suffering to me and those closest to me. My father left my mom leaving her heart eternally broken, then my mom died, and now River is stuck loving someone who doesn't know how to reciprocate the same love. All bad, Star, so tell me again how I am supposed to see the good in all of this?"

"Arie, you have this intoxicating light that you carry all around you, and while things that have happened seem unbearable right now, I just know that you are going to rise above them and be the salvation of so many. People are innately drawn to you, and that will be your saving grace."

"You have always been so good at seeing the positive in everything. I wish I was more like that."

"You're more than that, and it's just a matter of time until you see it."

She sat up and looked down at me. "Was that your way of telling me it's time to go?"

"Well, it is almost midnight, and it's not always the smartest thing for two girls to be hanging out in the middle of nowhere."

"Yeah, I guess."

"Can I ask you another question?"

"Sure." I sat up and looked at her.

"Why are you out here?" she asked plainly.

Another great question. I just didn't know how to answer it. I wasn't sure if what happened was real or not, and at this point, I was either going to sound like a person meant for great things or a complete nut case, so I lied.

"I just needed to breathe, you know?"

"I do know."

"Now, can I ask you a question?" I asked.

She stood up, so I followed her lead.

"Of course, if you don't mind walking and talking." She started to lead us out of the clearing and back into the forest the way I had come.

"What happened with your date, and how did you find me?"

"That, my dear, is two questions. The date with Dan was awesome. I had him drop me off at my car, which I left at the boutique. I noticed your car was still there, and when I didn't find you in the shop, I came out here looking for you. It's not like this is the first time you have retreated out here."

She picked up the pace a little.

"True, but I don't remember ever seeing that clearing before. Do you?"

"Honestly, I don't wander around like you do, so I would have no idea. Listen, we should really get back."

Her voice was sounding more and more anxious with every step we took. That's when I felt something. Were we being followed? "Star, why are you going so fast?" She didn't respond, but instead started a jogging pace. I struggled to keep up with her because of how drained I was from the night's events. "Star, you're kind of freaking me out."

"We need to get back. Now!"

She grabbed my hand and started pulling me with her. We were running now, and my heart was pumping hard to keep the breaths coming. We pushed through thick bushes, jumped over protruding tree branches, and plowed through tall grass. I didn't remember any of this, but I wasn't really paying attention when I was following the shadow. The only sounds that filled the night were Starling's and my heavy panting and shoes crunching through the park. She never slowed down and never let me fall back.

What was happening? Who or what were we running from? I dared to glance behind us and could have sworn I saw more than one shadow trailing closely behind us, but it also could have been the natural shadows of the forest. The fact that I wasn't sure was enough to kick me into high gear. We jumped through the break in the thick brush and ran out of the park and across the street. Starling threw open my shop door and shoved me inside and locked the door forcibly. She pulled down the blinds and turned around to face me as she caught her breath.

"What the hell, Star?" I was bending over trying to catch my breath.

"I'm sorry. I just had this sudden urge to run like we were being chased."

"What if I told you we were being chased? Why do I get the feeling that you wouldn't be surprised?" I stood up and looked at her accusingly, but she remained quiet. "Is there something you aren't telling me, Star?"

"Dammit, Arie. I want to make up some elaborate lie to protect you like I am supposed to, but I can't seem to lie to you. But I'm bound to secrecy, so all I can tell you is that I'm on your side and I'm here to protect you, but first and foremost, I'm your friend."

She took a few steps toward me, and instinctively, I took a few steps back. Her words stung. How long has she been betraying me? How could I be such a fool? I loved her like a sister and now another piece of my heart was chipped away with her sudden revelation of lies.

"I don't even know what to ask about first? Do I start by asking about the years of lies, or do I ask what you mean by you are on my side? What other side would you be on?" I backed up to a bookcase, creating a larger distance between us. I was fighting back tears. I would not let this destroy me. I was stronger than that.

"You have to just trust me for now. There's nothing I can say to change how things have transpired. All I can do is be by your side and prove to you that my friendship has always been real and always will be. I meant it earlier when I said you were destined for greater things, and I am here to make sure that happens."

What the hell was she trying to tell me? I had never been into the cryptic crap, and that's all I had been getting lately, pieces of information that I somehow had to put together on my own. "I don't know how to deal with this right now."

"Tell me what I can do," she pleaded.

"You can leave, Star. I need you to leave." I didn't know what else to say. My head was spinning, trying to piece together all the events that had been leading up to this moment since my birthday and even before.

"I can't just leave you here alone after what we just ran away from."

"How would you being here be of any protection from that?" I pointed outside. Again, she remained silent. "Forget it. You can't tell me that either, I suppose." She shook her head.

"Let me just call River. I'll stay out of your way until he gets here." She pulled her phone out of her back pocket and walked to the back of the store.

I let the tension release from my muscles. I could feel she was nothing for me to fear, but that didn't change the fact that she lied to me, and she knew more about me than I did and yet wouldn't... correction... couldn't tell me.

I walked over to the door and lifted the blinds to peek out. The streetlights provided ample light to confirm that there was nothing outside anymore, but I didn't feel any less safe not knowing what was after us. I jumped at the sound of Starling's sudden return to the front of the store.

"Sorry, I didn't mean to scare you. River is down the street getting a bite, so he'll be here in a minute."

I didn't turn around. I couldn't face her.

"Look, Arie, I love you and I know you feel like I wronged you, but that was never my choice to make. I made a promise to watch over you, and I won't break that promise, not even if you hate me and never forgive me."

There was a knock on the window-framed door. I lifted a blind to verify it was River and opened the door for him. He came in, and his presence added to the awkward tension in the air.

"Okay, well, I guess I'll go now."

As she passed by me, she squeezed my shoulder lightly and walked out the front door only giving River a passing glance. My heart sank a little as she closed the door behind her. "Just let me get my things." I walked to the reading nook and grabbed the journal and walked back to the front where River was.

"Do you want to talk about it?"

"No, not really." I collected my keys and my phone and turned off the lights as we left the store.

Chapter Sixteen

I knew I owed River some sort of explanation. He insisted on bringing me home, so I compromised and let him only if we drove home in my car. I didn't want to be stuck at home all weekend without a car. Honestly, who knew when I would need a quick getaway, but really who knew if there was any escape from what was coming my way. As I drove down the dark country road, I watched the forest on both sides cautiously. I was still on high alert, thinking something could jump out onto the road at any moment. I drove faster than usual. River broke the silence first.

"Arie, we need to talk."

He didn't look at me as he spoke. The anxiety the weight his words carried tightened my stomach. "Okay."

"Not here," he responded.

Even worse. I refrained from pressing him further. I was afraid to hear what he had to say after losing my best friend only minutes ago. I continued to drive us home. I was about to pull into his driveway when he stopped me.

"Can we go to your house?"

"Sure." I continued down the road to a break in the trees where my driveway was. I pulled in and parked. I was about to get out when River gripped my hand to stop me. Tingles spread like wildfire over my skin. It was fascinating that he could still do that to me. I looked at him and admired his beauty and purity in the moonlight. How long until the image I held of him was shattered?

"Would you mind if we went to our spot?"

It was a mildly warm night with a nice breeze, but after sharing the spot with Ashe it felt wrong, but how could I tell him that? "Okay."

We got out of the car and walked through the meadow to our spot. River held my hand tightly. I was nervous for so many reasons: the talk River was about to have with me, the shadows that chased me earlier that could show up here, and my apparent pending fate waiting around the corner. When we reached our spot, we sat down and enjoyed the terminally innocent silence for a moment. River released an uncomfortable sigh.

"I saw you here the other night."

He knew he didn't have to say anything more. Shame filled me from the inside out. That's why he was so upset the other night. I didn't know how to explain. There weren't really any words to explain what I was feeling.

"I..."

"You don't need to say anything. I don't want you to say anything. I just thought you should know."

His voice was soft and forgiving, which made all of this so much harder, and amidst all of this, someone or something was after me for some unknown reason. "I'm sorry," was all I could say.

He wrapped his arm around me and held me close as we sat listening to the night full of life and hope.

River wouldn't let me drive him home. We left with things unsettled, but at this point, there wasn't anything I could do to resolve the issues suffocating us. Before he left, he made sure the house was safe, and I was locked tight inside it. He wanted to stay, but the air was so thick between us, we both thought it better that he didn't, but instead checked in by phone every few hours. I made sure to plug in my phone to charge and sat on the reading bench overlooking the meadow lost in my thoughts. I couldn't imagine what it must have felt like for River to see me with someone else. It had always been just the two of us.

This was unfamiliar territory for both of us. Painful unfamiliarity. He was the last person I would ever want to hurt. I loved him so much.

As I was dazing, the fog was slithering through the yard and covering the meadow. Fall was such an incredible season. As my thought faded, a figure emerged from the fog. It was Ashe. He seemed to float right up to the window, activating flutters in my heart. Even locked up inside the house, I could feel him. I placed my hand on the window. He returned the gesture and placed his on mine through the glass. The energy between us was so intense I thought the window would crack. His eyes were mesmerizing and made me weak with the intensity they studied me.

I wanted him. I needed him. I craved him.

I got up and went to the back door. He met me on the other side. I could feel the world changing around me as I pondered opening the door, but I couldn't resist. I unlocked it and joined him in the fog. We locked ourselves in the moment before speaking. He was every girl's fantasy guy. He always had on a fitted t-shirt and jeans, but wore it like a tuxedo. How did I get so lucky to have the most handsome guys on the planet want me? I never thought I was more than ordinary.

"Hi." *So stupid!* Was that really all I could say? Yes, yes, it was. I found myself somewhat dumbstruck around him.

"Hi."

"Your entrances are sort of creepy." I nervously twisted a lock of my hair around my finger.

"Creepy. That's a new one." He smiled smoothly.

"I didn't mean you were creepy. I meant the way you just show up, good or bad weather, is creepy."

"Mysterious." He winked.

"Fine, mysterious, not creepy." Were we really having an argument over my choice of words?

"Thank you!" His smile took on a mischievous nature.

"You're welcome." I stood awkwardly in the same spot. My heart was pounding, my knees were weak, and my skin was on fire. God, how he made my body ache for him!

"I wanted to see you, so I hope it's okay that I popped in like this."

He wanted to see me! I was not going to lie, that made me a little giddy. "Ummm, yeah."

"Would you mind if we walked a little?"

His voice was like calm currents on a crystal blue lake. How could I say no to that? "Sure." He had me speechless.

The fog was still thin enough that the moonlight could cast a beautiful glow around us. We walked side-by-side close enough to touch, but didn't. We walked past the meadow onto a trail that led to Deer Creek.

"I like being around you."

He was honest about his feelings. It was refreshing.

"I like being around you, too."

With that, he smiled at me. When we made it to the creek, we spotted a family of deer drinking. "If you're really still they won't be scared away." This was the same family that introduced themselves to me the other night. We sat down on some large riverbed rocks and watched them drink and forage. I wanted him to touch me, even if it was just for a second. I loved the way he made me feel, but he seemed so reluctant to make any physical contact with me. "Can I ask you a question?"

"Of course." His full attention was on me.

"Is there something wrong with me?" I asked him shyly.

"Now, why would you think that?"

"Well, because when I see you, it's only for a short time, and you don't seem to want to touch me." I was a little embarrassed telling him so.

He smiled coyly as he caught a piece of my hair flying in front of my face. I braced for his skin to touch mine. He tucked the hair behind my ear, gently grazing the top of it, sending chills down my spine. My body tensed in anticipation. He clutched his hand behind my head and pulled me into him slowly. As his lips were about to touch mine, he paused and stared deeply into my eyes, arousing that primal need for him.

The green specks hidden within his hazel eyes looked as if they were glowing in mutual anticipation. After a tortuous amount of time passed, his lips pressed against mine. I wasn't prepared for what happened in the next blissful moment. A beautiful wind of light swirled around our bodies and carried us to another plane of existence. His lips were hot and soft against mine. It took my breath away. I felt myself losing consciousness. So did he, so he held me tighter and pulled away and made me focus on him.

"You need to stay with me, Arie. I need to show you something."

The light was still entrapping us inside our own little hideaway. He again pressed his lips to mine and kissed me passionately with desperation and need. I could feel his love for me reach parts of me I didn't know could be aroused. I could feel the very essence of my existence rising to the surface with every brush of his lips. As if he was mine. Not only right now, but he had always been. The primal need for him was real and embedded deep inside me. I pressed my lips hard on his as my body temperature rose. I wrapped my arms around his neck and held him in the embrace.

His arms ventured down my shoulder blades, meeting at the center and sliding down to the dimple on my lower back, sending shockwaves with every move. I could feel his heart beat against his chest as if it was trying to force its way out to join with mine. My fingers combed through his dark short strands and clung onto locks as my breathing grew heavier.

The light emitted a warm, but tingly sensation around us, further escalating our desire. Our lips were forever connected in a kiss that would put the gods to shame. As our kiss deepened, a vision flashed through me. It was Ashe and me caught up in a similar embrace, but we were somewhere else and we looked different, but our essence felt the same. We were in love, but I could feel that our days were numbered by the desperation in the intimate moment.

Tears were falling from my eyes as he kissed me, which he gently rubbed away with his thumbs as they cupped both sides of my face. It was hard to decipher between reality and the vision, both moments equally as intense and intimate.

I pulled away from his lips and looked to the sky as I let out an excited breath. His lips explored the side of my neck, causing everything in my body to tense up in pleasure and then suddenly weaken. Another vision flashed. It was me in the clearing, lying on the ground in the damp low lying grass surrounded by a faint glow. My body was lifeless, but my mind was swirling with memories as my eyes focused on the full moon above. Butterflies were circling me, kicking up a light breeze that tickled my skin trying to arouse it awake.

One single tear fell from my eye as I realized in this moment that I would no longer kiss my soul mate again nor feel the warmth of my protector. I would no longer run barefoot across the grass that now cradled my unmoving body. This life was ending. I was afraid of the unknown. I was afraid to die. I could sense my breathing grow shallower and the blood flow to my heart start to slow down. My body was becoming cold. I didn't know how much longer I could hold on, but I wanted to. I wanted to say goodbye to them. I wanted to say I was sorry for not being stronger. I wanted to tell them how much I loved them. I wanted to live.

The moon's light began to blur as a person's shadow hung over my dying body. A deep burning prickled my cheek, making me want to scream in pain, but there was nothing left in me to do so. The shadow went out of focus, and the light around me faded until I was alone in the dark and then there was nothing. No sounds, no sensations, no light.

I screamed as the vision ended, causing the light to scatter and reveal its source as hundreds of fireflies. I started falling to the ground as my body went limp. Ashe caught me just before I hit the ground and pulled me into him. He held me tight and caressed my long hair as my body spasmed aggressively. I forced my eyes to stay closed and tried to block out the sounds around me. I was pretty sure I just witnessed my own death.

"What just happened?" My voice was broken and shaky.

"I'm sorry. I thought if we were in the light it would be okay." He put distance between us now that I had calmed down.

"Is that why you never touch me?" I pulled my knees into my chest and hugged them tight.

"Yes." He sounded defeated and sad.

"Did you see it, too?"

"Yes."

"So, then you know that I'm going to die." I looked at him apprehensively, scared to hear a confirmation of my assumption.

"I do," he said melancholically.

He couldn't look at me.

"Oh my God," I muttered under my breath. I knew we all had an expiration date, but I didn't look any older in my vision than I was now, so was I to assume I was going to die soon? I buried my face in my knees and tried to drown out the dark thoughts clouding my mind. I pictured River and his parents at my funeral, broken hearted having to bury the last of the Belle lineage. And then there was Starling. She would be losing a sister. What about me, my life, a future unrecognized? My stomach hurt, the pain coming from a place of anguish.

Ashe sat next to me still as a rock, staring at the creek. He seemed to know he couldn't offer me any words of comfort, so he remained silent. We sat there and watched the deer finish their evening routine and disappear in the forest. As soon as they left, the frogs croaked again and the crickets sang. The fog was getting thicker and the wetness was sticking to my skin and a chill was starting to spread over me.

"Were we... are we... in love?" I struggled to get the words out as I watched the grass glisten from the dew under the moonlight.

"Yes, to both," he said confidently.

He finally made eye contact again and smiled at me softly. I stared at him as I let that sink in. He was beautiful with the dewdrops layering his hair and leaving a sticky glow on his face, making him shine in the moonlight. He sat with his arms lazily perched on his bent knees as if he was in the middle of a modeling shoot. The specks in his eyes still gleamed, making the hazel glow like an amber gemstone. Funny that it was called a gemstone when it was actually sap fossilized over millions of years from prehistoric trees. I wondered if he was prehistoric, too. What an odd thought! It was also a symbol of courage and believed to be the soul of all living things. "Will you walk me back?"

"I would be honored." He stood up and absently held his hand out to me, but then quickly retracted it.

"It's okay. I'm okay now," I said softly. I pushed myself up and walked in front of him back down the path to my house. I looked back to catch another glance at him as the word *boyfriend* ran through my head. I blushed shyly and turned back to watch my footing as I walked the uneven ground. I now understood why he made me feel the way I did, but I didn't know what to do with it or how River fit into it. As I broke through the forest into the meadow, I looked back, but Ashe was gone. I wasn't surprised this time, but it didn't make it an easier. My heart ached as I made my way up to the house, alone.

Chapter Seventeen

As I lay in bed, I tried to pick apart my visions. My vision with Ashe felt so real, but we looked different. Our hair was lighter, and our eyes were glowing amber. We felt connected on a universal level, like the way you should with your soul mate, but we were held in a desperate final moment. What could have been happening that would tear two people apart so tragically? I could feel my soul losing its other half. I could feel myself dying inside as he kissed me his last goodbye. And then there was my death.

How could the fates be so cruel to show me my own demise? The figure standing above me was so blurry that I couldn't get a clear picture of whom it was. I assume the person who caused my death. The pain I felt in my final moments was immense. The burn on my cheek seemed to reach deep into my core and pull the life right out of me. Remembering sent goose bumps up my arms. Maybe I was shown the vision to try to prevent it, but then there was Ashe, who looked so defeated as if my fate was written in the stars.

And then there was the kiss and the light!

What was it about his touch that was capable of manifesting these visions? I should have asked him more questions, but I was still in shock by the time he vanished. *Next time.* I hoped there was a next time. I stared out my window as I contemplated all the different ways to ask him a laundry list of questions. My eyes grew heavy quickly from the exhausting night, so rather than fight it, I closed them and let sweet sleep embrace me.

A loud pounding echoed in my sleep. I tossed and turned in bed trying to shake off the noise until I realized the pounding wasn't coming from my dream. It was coming from downstairs. I shot open my eyes, squinting at the light shining through the window. The pounding got louder and then stopped. I heard the front door open and then slam. Footsteps charged up the stairs.

"Arie?" There was true panic in River's voice. I sat up quickly.

"Yeah, I'm here. I'm okay." I rubbed my eyes as he plowed into my room.

"Seriously, Arie, what happened to checking in every few hours?" He looked like he ran the whole way here with his hair disheveled and the sweat glistening on his bare chest. His perfectly sculpted chest and abs.

Ugh! I slammed my head back on the bed and threw the pillow over my head. "I'm sorry. I fell asleep. But in my defense, it's been way more than a few hours, so I am not the only one who forgot to check in." I heard him approach the bed and felt it sink as he sat next to me. He lifted the pillow off my head.

"Fair rebuttal," he smiled sweetly. "I'm glad you're all right. You had me a little worried."

"A little? You almost broke down my front door! Next time do yourself and my door a favor and just start by using the key."

"Okay, maybe more than a little." He softly caressed my arm.

His touch felt different. It was still comforting, but it didn't send chills through me. I wondered if last night had something to do with it. Maybe the sensory overload from the visions blew a fuse in me.

"I need to get back home. My mom is still pretty sick."

I sat up again. I was starting to get worried about her. "What's wrong with her?"

"I don't know. I thought it was the flu, but she's not getting any better. I have a doctor coming to visit later, so I'll let you know." He stood up.

"Okay, thanks." He left my room, and I heard the front door lock a minute later. I was going to make a point of visiting her later today, but right now, I wanted to dig through my mom's journal some more. I threw off the sheets and hopped out of bed. I went downstairs into the kitchen and poured myself a bowl of cereal. I watched life wander around the meadow as I ate breakfast. It was breathtaking. The fog had lifted, leaving a layer of dewdrops on everything that glistened in the rising sun's rays. So many things had happened over the last few weeks that I hadn't had time to stop and really breathe. This might be the last time I would get the chance. With that thought, I decided I wanted to visit my mom in the meadow.

After I finished the cereal, I put the bowl into the sink and grabbed the journal off the reading nook and headed outside. The sun was still making its way above the horizon, casting a magical glow across the meadow. Dragonflies and butterflies danced from dewdrop to dewdrop drinking water and chasing each other. The innocent nature of their existence made me jealous.

Beautiful butterfly flowers like the one left at the store mysteriously grew all around my mother's gravestone. I was awestruck at the beauty of so many in one place. They were magnificent and perfect in honor of my mom's memory. At this point, questioning how they got there would be pointless.

I sat down and leaned against the backside of her gravestone. My ring started to pulse beautiful colors of pink, purple, blue, and white. I could feel the essence of life comfort me as my heart still mourned my loss. I opened the journal and rifled through the pages. I was hoping one of my mom's visions would tell me when my last days were and how it happened. I spent the better half of the day reading through all the stories. They were mainly sweet visits by my dad. Some even included me when I was younger.

He sounded like an amazing man and would have a made a loving father. It made me sad that I never got to meet him, but at least now, I knew he wasn't just another deadbeat father. He loved my mom and me and wanted to be with us. I wondered how he died. I assumed he was dead since he was appearing to my mom in visions like she was now appearing to me. I wondered if when I died I would be reunited with both of them. Was that what my mom meant when she said we would be reunited soon? That the ring would help me find her when I too pass from this life?

The last entry was the day before my sixteenth birthday. I was dreading this entry, but I knew it was coming. I thought about skipping right to it when I first started to read, but I was afraid it would make me not want to read anymore, and then I would miss something important. It was dated September 22, 2011.

Today I felt life slowly seeping out of my body. I was tired and surrounded by a deep sadness. I spent the day in the meadow meditating. Several animals had approached me as if they were saying their goodbyes. There were so many. Deer, squirrels, birds, dragonflies, and butterflies. It was surreal having them all approach me at the same time. I knew and could feel something was wrong.

With Arie's sixteenth birthday just a few hours away, I was dreading the feelings rushing through me. I was hoping to see Teve today, but what I didn't expect was the impending doom weighing me down. I knew Arie was meant for greatness, but what that was, I didn't know. Teve had never told me what he did to me the day he disappeared. It wasn't until the first creature, a butterfly, landed on my hand, followed by hundreds more, that I knew he wasn't human. I had fallen in love with him the first time I saw him walking along the path to Deer Creek and never questioned that love. He never gave me a reason to question it. I was alone in this house at age eighteen, donated by an elderly couple who had visited me every day at the foster home in town. They died shortly after their donation. They would have adopted me, but they were in bad health and the state wouldn't allow them to. I met Teve the day I moved in. He said he lived down the road, but I never did go there. He was twenty-five and the most handsome man I had ever seen. He had sandy blonde hair that almost touched his shoulders and the most beautiful amber eyes. His chest was chiseled with amazing care and his abs were defined and perfect. I had become speechless that first day I saw him walking with his shirt off, glowing from the sweat of the mid-afternoon sun. Nature had made the most beautiful creature in this man and he had the inner beauty to match. We spent every sunset by the creek getting to know each other, my most favorite being our more intimate conversations. He was so gentle with me, and his touch made my blood boil and my heart skip beats. I thought I would get to spend the rest of my life with this man, but I was wrong. I got to spend the rest of his life with him, and I was grateful for every touch and whisper.

The day he disappeared we had snuggled in the meadow in the spot he nicknamed butterfly circle. It was our little secret, and our mere presence seemed to make the energy of the world come alive within it. We had made love for the first time that day. After, he had laid his head on my belly and rubbed it gently with his hand. A warmth had covered the area and made me squirm in delight. That light touch of his hand was the most intimate moment we had ever shared, and it was just a simple gesture. He had taken my hand after that and promised me he would love me until the end of days. I assumed that meant we would be married, but then he was gone and I was left pregnant and alone. I was so grateful that Sierra and Hudson had moved in down the road. She saved me.

Now I sat in the same spot we had made love for the first and only time and waited for him to return. Hoping he would come back. As the sun fell below the valley, I was feeling less and less confident. Arie was spending the evening with River, so I decided I would stay out here until she got home. I was desperate to see him. I could feel my body weakening, so I lay down on the grass and watched the stars twinkle in musical unison. It felt like hours had passed, but then my wish came true. Teve appeared above me, but this time he looked sad. I stood up to face him.

The look in his eyes could melt a woman's heart and break it at the same time. He placed his hand upon my cheek and showed me his pain. It was my death. The vision only lasted a second, but the damage had dug deep in both of us. My body had weakened so much he had to carry the weight of my limp body to the ground. He caressed my hair as I cried quietly into the comfort of his arms. It broke my heart to leave Arie all alone.

"She won't be alone," he said as if he had read my mind. "She will always have us looking after her. She has a destiny to fulfill that was written before she was born. Your death is just one of many that are necessary to lead up to the full moon that will propel her into a higher level of consciousness where all beings exist through their essence. She is the only one who can maintain that balance and therefore she is a great and dangerous asset. Make sure she gets the ring after her eighteenth birthday and not a day before and you will see her again."

My head started hurting, and the noises of the forest escalated. I covered my ears tightly and closed my eyes. I no longer felt Teve. I opened my eyes slowly, and I was again alone in the darkness. I saw a car's headlights pull into the driveway and heard car doors slam, so I somberly made my way back to the house. I wanted to spend every moment with Arie in the precious little time we had left.

And my mom did. We stayed up until the sun rose, talking about my father and the creatures and life and death and especially love. We only spent a few hours napping and then spent every moment of my sixteenth birthday together until River and I went to the meadow. Had I known what was going to happen I wouldn't have left her side. And now, more people were going to die because of me, including myself, although my dad didn't mention my death. The sun was setting, and the energy that had surrounded me was all but gone. My dad had mentioned a full moon. The next one was in less than two weeks. In my vision I died under a full moon.

Did I really only have two weeks left? How would I spend these last moments of my life? I needed to find someone to take care of the store. Maybe Starling or River? And then there was the house and all the memories locked up in the attic.

A full-blown panic attack consumed me. I sobbed between breaths as the reality of my death finally hit me. What would I tell River? I didn't know if I could, but I wanted to give him the chance to say goodbye. I wouldn't take that from him.

I wanted to visit his mom, so maybe she would be able to help me decide what to do. I collected myself and the journal and went back to the house.

By the time I drove to River's house, it was well past late. I probably should have waited until the morning, but time was trickling away quickly and I wanted more answers and I knew Sierra had to have more. I hoped she was still awake and not too sick.

I knocked on the door, but no one answered. River's truck was gone, which was strange, and all the lights were off, but if Sierra was that sick she should be home. I put my ear to the door, but it was silent on the other end. I hated barging in, but I did anyway.

"Hello? Sierra?" I called out as I opened the door. I turned on the hall light and walked quietly through the kitchen and down the hallway, turning on lights as I went. "Sierra?"

The door to her room was closed, so I knocked lightly. I heard a soft voice answer me, but I couldn't make out what she said. I turned the knob slowly and poked my head in. Sierra was lying on the bed only lit by the moonlight from the open window. She looked sick and frail underneath the comforter. Her face was paler than usual, and her eyes were sunken. I was frozen in disbelief.

"It's okay, honey. You can come in," she murmured.

I slowly walked to her bedside. She looked even worse than I thought. "What's wrong with you?" My voice was shaky.

"It's my time, Arie." She could barely talk.

"What, no. Why? Where's River?" I was starting to have a panic attack. She pulled her hand out from under the blanket and put it on mine, giving it a gentle squeeze.

"I'm meant to die in order to help take you to the next level in your life's fate."

I was shaking my head in disagreement. "No, not you, Sierra. Please, not you. I can't lose you, too."

"It's as it should be. Hudson has already gone. You would have felt his essence when he passed, and River knew that our lives here were numbered. We all knew."

"Everyone except me!" I had raised my voice unintentionally, but I was pissed. Why was I the only one who didn't know what I was? And when would I have felt Hudson's essence... *the light at the bookstore in the rain*. My happiness in that moment was now fractured and overshadowed by remorse.

"Our job was to protect you until this day came and then lend you our energy for the final phase of your ascension. We made a choice to do this for you, and we were all honored to do it. The only one who wasn't given a choice was your mom, but in the end, she understood what her life's purpose was and she accepted it. She did it for you."

Tears were free flowing again. I was having a hard time processing everything she was telling me. "I saw myself die, Sierra. What purpose is it for you giving up your life for me when I am just going to die at the next full moon? Because I don't see the point!" I stood up and walked to the window and glared out.

"I know you don't understand right now, but you will."

I was hysterically crying to myself. I was going to lose the ones closest to me, and it was my fault. A horrifying thought crossed my mind. River. Oh my God, was I going to lose River, too? I turned back to Sierra to ask her, but her eyes were closed. I walked to her bedside to tuck her arms back in. She was so still. *Too still!* I touched her cheek, and a light immediately burned in my hand. I tried to pull it back, but a force stronger than me held tight and entered my body. The light finally unlatched its hold on me, and I stumbled back, falling to the floor. Sierra's lifeless body immediately disappeared, and a million butterflies were left in her place, leaving nothing behind that was my Sierra.

They swirled around me, lifting me off the ground and then flew out the window. I didn't know what to think. I was in total shock. I stood staring at the empty bed. I was internally distraught having lost another mother. Despair chewed away at my heart, and the pain in my stomach was almost unbearable, but I held my ground. If this was my fate it was time to be strong.

If she truly believed we would all be together again, then I would hold onto that and let it carry me through the rest of my days however long or short that might be. I needed to be strong for what was to come. This was the defining moment of my true purpose. Would I let the grief overtake, or would I rise against it and be strong so I could fulfill my destiny whatever that might be?

I stood up and brushed myself off as if I could brush away the years of pain. I wouldn't let their deaths be in vain! Whatever it was I would stand up to it and fight with all my heart!

Chapter Eighteen

I sat on River's back patio enjoying the numbness of my mind and letting my body settle into the new surge of energy Sierra had gifted me. I wanted to wait here until River came home. I tried to call him to no avail. He needed to know his mom was gone. I wasn't sure how he would take it. It sounded like he knew it was coming, but I would still think it would be hard for him.

The fog was thick, making it hard to see anything. In fact, the air was hauntingly silent. A dark feeling rode in with the fog and kissed the tip of my nose. My vision was blurring, and I suddenly became tired and weak. I tried to stand up to go inside, but I couldn't move. The panic adrenalized me, but didn't do me any good other than snap me out of the daze.

The fog became darker. It started taking on the shape of shadowed figures. It reached down into my throat, cutting off my airway. I was paralyzed. The shadows surrounded me and lifted me off the swinging bench, carrying me into the forest. I still couldn't move as I floated across the fog and struggled for breaths. Was this how I was destined to spend the last few weeks of my life? A prisoner of the shadows? I wanted to scream for help, but couldn't. I was a prisoner in my own mind. As they passed the threshold into the forest, something pushed through the shadows and grabbed me. I was so weak and sleepy that I could barely keep my eyes open. I was still floating, but at a much quicker pace and the ride was rough. Nausea was building inside me. After what seemed like an eternity, I felt the damp grass beneath me and cold hands cupped my cheeks. I was starting to feel the energy build back up in me.

"Arie, wake up."

Was that Ashe? I opened my eyes and locked eyes with him. We were in the butterfly circle. "What happened? Did you carry me here?" He brushed his fingers through my damp hair and then unexpectedly pressed his lips on mine. It instantly felt like he was breathing new life into me. As I inhaled his kiss, my lungs burned for more.

He made my whole body feel alive with every touch. I found the bottom of his shirt and pulled it over his head. He pressed his lips on mine again. How was this moment even possible? No visions interrupting us this time. His kiss had me flying with the fireflies that lit up the circle.

"Arie."

I was once again paralyzed, but this time by my own guilt. River's voice had pierced through the moment and jabbed me in the gut. Ashe rose off me cautiously and put his shirt back on. I stood up quickly. The look in River's eyes could have killed me if I let it.

"River, I..." What could I possibly say to make this better?

He glared at Ashe. "You need to be going now."

"Wait, what? River, you don't understand. He saved me from the shadows. They were carrying me into..."

He cut me off sharply and addressed Ashe. "You shouldn't be here."

"What do you mean he 'shouldn't be here'? Did you not just hear what I said?"

Ashe put his hand on my shoulder. "It's okay, Arie. He's right. I shouldn't be here." He kissed my forehead and started to walk into the fog.

"River, what are you doing? He just saved me. You aren't going to just let him leave like that are you?" He didn't respond. I stepped out of the circle and ran after Ashe. When I caught up to him, I grabbed his hand, and an electric pulse shocked it away. River caught me before I hit the ground. I watched as Ashe disappeared again.

River picked me up and carried me back into the house. He laid me on the couch and put my blanket over me. Without saying a word, he went to the kitchen and got me a glass of water. As he handed it to me, I sat up and took a sip. He sat on the couch next to me with his back facing me.

Things could not be any more uncomfortable. First, I needed to tell him his mom turned into a million butterflies and then there's being caught in the act with Ashe. *Lovely!* I reached out and touched his back to which he immediately flinched, something he had never done before. This was going to be harder than I thought.

"Before we talk about what you just saw, there's something else I need to tell you." His back was still to me.

"If it's about my mom, I already know."

He seemed so distant and cold as he spoke. "Oh, how?"

"We knew it was coming and she asked me to leave, so I wouldn't see it. She thought it would make it less difficult for me." He was unmoving physically and emotionally.

"So, if you guys knew this was coming, why didn't you tell me? I was there when she disappeared into a sea of butterflies, River. Didn't you think of saving me from that?"

"You'll witness more deaths, Arie. You need their essence. That was their purpose in this life. To protect you and build up life's essence for you to take when it is your time to ascend. You just need to accept this as your reality now and appreciate what you are and what you are meant for."

"Which is what exactly? No one has given me a clear answer, River. I hate riddles with a passion and I suck at them, so if my whole purpose is wrapped up tight into one big riddle, then we are all screwed." He started laughing. "What is so funny?"

"You really do suck at riddles."

He continued to chuckle at my expense, so I punched him awkwardly in the shoulder. Not easy to do from my angle. His laughter faded out. "Are we going to talk about what you just saw?" He stood up and looked outside.

"What's there to say? You're free to choose who you love."

I stood up and joined him, putting my hand gently on his back. "Is it fair that I love you both in completely different ways?"

"You will need to make a choice soon."

I knew he was right, which made me sad, because I needed both of them in my life. "I know," I said somberly. "Do you want to talk about your parents?"

"No."

I was terrified to ask the next question. "Am I going to lose you, too?" My stomach was in knots, and I could feel a panic attack coming on.

"No, not like that. I will be by your side for as long as you want me to be and for as long as I can."

I let out a sigh of relief. He let me rest my head on his shoulder, but he offered no affection in return. "Do you know what's going to happen to me or what I am?"

"I was only told that I was to protect you. Other than that, it's all blind faith and the feeling deep inside me that I love you and I want to protect you. Some know more than others, but only what they need to know in order to fulfill their purpose. I imagine if you tracked everyone down and asked what they knew, you could piece it together, but some are already gone. We are in the final phase, and the next full moon will take all your energy."

I let that settle on me for a few minutes as we stood in silence. "What happened out there tonight with the shadows? I was completely paralyzed, and I could feel their darkness."

"Just like the belief that if there is a heaven, then there's a hell. With all good there's a reflection of the bad.

There are those who follow the darkness and those who follow the light we call essence. The darkness would do anything to keep you from ascending, which is why you need protecting, and you need to be extra cautious. You're powerless against them until your ascension."

"You keep talking to me like I know what this 'ascension' is." I was getting frustrated.

"To be honest, I don't know what it entails."

"I saw my death, River. Do I have to die in order to ascend, or do the dark shadows get to me before?" He shrugged at my question and finally put his arm around me.

"I don't know, but if you don't ascend it means I failed, which probably means I died, because I would never let that happen." The pure ferocity in his voice resonated in the stillness around us, securing his unconditional and undying devotion to me.

"Do you know if my mom was one of us?"

"She wasn't. She was human, but carried an essence similar to ours, which is why she was chosen to bring you into this world."

I let out an embarrassingly loud yawn.

"You're tired. You need to sleep. I won't be leaving your side anymore. Go get some rest."

"What about you?" I stretched my arms above my head.

"I'll sleep on the couch when I get tired."

I wanted to offer him my mom's bed since sleeping with me was obviously out of the question after tonight, but I still couldn't handle the idea of anyone else sleeping in there, and I was definitely not in an emotional state to be sleeping in it. "Ummm, okay. Good night then."

"Goodnight, Arie."

He never turned away from the window. It was like a switch flipped, and he was now a watch dog instead of my River. I wondered if things would ever be the same between us again.

I wanted to question him about Ashe. It seemed like he knew him, and there was definitely more to it than either one of them was telling me, but how did I ask him after the betrayal he just witnessed? *I couldn't.* That would definitely be like rubbing salt in an already raw wound. Time was running out, and while I had some answers, they were encrypted and I was left without the deciphering tools.

I missed Starling. I needed my best friend. I was still disappointed that she lied to me, but I was starting to understand that it wasn't entirely her fault or something she wanted to do. I grabbed my phone and sent her a text.

Hey, are you there?

Yeah. What's up?

Can you meet me at the lookout tomorrow?

Of course! What time?

Sunrise?

See you then.

Tomorrow was Sunday, and the lookout was my Sunday spot. I felt better knowing we were going to patch things up and maybe I would solve another piece of the puzzle. I turned off my phone and threw it onto the dresser on my way to my window. I sat on the ledge and looked out. I saw Ashe standing across the way. He acknowledged me with a sneaky smile and a wink. I had two protectors tonight, and I loved them both. I smiled back, grateful that he hadn't left after all. Every time he disappeared, I feared would be the last time I saw him.

I went to sleep knowing that I was safe, but that I would be the one to hurt one of those amazing hearts who were keeping me so. Was that what the vision meant when it said I would have to fight with my heart? I just hope my heart was strong enough, and more importantly, I hope their hearts were, too.

Chapter Nineteen

Getting out of the house to meet Starling wasn't an easy task. River was obsessed with not leaving my side, day or night. We finally agreed on him shadowing me from a distance, so Star and I could have our own private girlie talk. All I had to do was mention things like PMS, and he was convinced. Men were too easy to get rid of. I pulled into the parking lot at the lookout in the preserved park. Star's car wasn't here yet, so I decided to wait at my usual spot. River parked as far away as possible and stood outside his car, leaning on it like a model in all his hotness. I could have it worse. I could have an overweight pitted-faced protector. He was sexy and more than easy on the eyes. I just wished my heart belonged solely to him.

I disappeared up and over a little hill, which I knew would make River nervous, but it was my spot, so he knew where to find me. It was a gorgeous Sunday morning, and the sky was free of any impending storms. The sun was reaching out to me warming my skin as the morning chill burned off. I was anxious to talk to Star. I felt a strong need to apologize for doubting her friendship, and I wanted to know what her purpose was in all of this. Maybe she even knew what I was and if River and she were like me, too. It seemed like they must be since they were playing such a pivotal role in my ascension.

Thinking about the ascension filled me with anxiety. Who could blame me? The ascension was a big unknown and riding on blind faith was never my thing. I turned to the thicket, thinking I heard something. I was on heightened alert after what happened last night. A fox jumped out and ran toward me with its nose dragging along the ground. It paused right next to me, lifted its nose, and looked right at me. A set of familiar purple eyes stared at me. It was *my* fox. I reached out and petted its head. It sniffed my hand and then crawled onto my lap and made itself comfortable. Nature never ceased to amaze me. It reacted just like it had when I was a child, only now it was larger by at least fifty pounds. It was heavy on my small lap, but I absently caressed its fur as if it was my pet as I stared down into the valley.

After some time passed, I was starting to get worried about Star. I checked my phone, but there wasn't a message from her. The fox had fallen asleep on me, so I gently coaxed it awake and scooted it off into the forest. I went back over the hill to my car. River was still standing against his car.

"Did Star happen to call or text you?"

He pulled his phone out of his pocket to check. "No, what time was she supposed to be here?"

"A while ago. I am going to try to give her a call." I tried to call her on my phone, but there was no service. "Dammit Even if she tried to call, I have no service. Do you?"

"One bar. Let me try."

I was stamping my foot impatiently. He put down the phone.

"It wouldn't go through."

"I'm going to go to her house. Maybe she just overslept." I rushed to my car.

"I'll be right behind you."

River jumped into his car and drove up behind mine. No way was he going to let me out of his sight if something was up with Star. Who was I kidding? There was no way he was going to let me out of his sight, period! As I drove out of the canyon, I tried Star again. Her phone went straight to voicemail. That was seriously my pet peeve! I hated going straight to voicemail.

I threw my phone onto the passenger seat and drove through town to get to Star's condo. She lived at the edge of town in one of the beautifully renovated condos that once was a huge three-story warehouse building. I pulled into the lot and rushed through a greenbelt, passing several doors until I reached hers on the end. She had a gorgeous view of the forest on the end. Footsteps stomped up behind me.

"Dammit, Arie! How can I protect you if you're just going to take off like that?"

"I thought you were a runner." I shot him a sarcastic glare.

"It was a rhetorical question."

"I'm not as weak as you all think. I can kick ass with the best of them." I knocked on Star's door. There was no answer, so I rang the doorbell. From inside, I could hear movement and then feet shuffling toward us.

"Who is it?" Star's voice was muffled through the soundproof wood.

"It's Arie." I spit out a huge sigh of relief. She was okay.

"Oh my God," she spat out.

I heard her voice much clearer now. She unlatched the locks and opened the door. She looked like something worse than what the cat dragged in. When she spotted River behind me, a blush of embarrassment covered her face. She grabbed my arm, pulled me in, and closed the door.

"You'll have to wait outside, River. I'm not decent."

She shouted loud enough for him to hear through the door and loud enough to give me a headache. I could hear an irritated mumbling come from outside. It was actually kind of funny. "You better have a good reason for standing me up."

Right on cue, a half-naked Donut Dan passed by us into the kitchen. Not that my jaw should be dropping to the floor, but it was. "Really? Well, if your hair could only talk." I had to giggle.

"Oh no, is it that bad?" She grabbed my hand and pulled me into the bathroom, locking us in.

"Don't get me wrong. I am totally happy for you, but you scared the shit out of me. And just in case you forgot, I'm being hunted down by shadow-stalking demons of some sort. Not really the time to be hooking it up."

"I know. I'm sorry. I was just really upset, and he came by just to watch a movie and then things happened."

She washed her face quickly and ran a brush through her hair while simultaneously brushing her teeth. Of course, she looked gorgeous just like that with no makeup. "We need to talk."

"We do. Let me get rid of Dan." She left me alone in the bathroom.

After a quick look in the mirror, I huffed at my image and went into the living room and sat down. Within minutes, she was shoving Dan out the door. The look on River's face was priceless. *Ha-ha*. She fell into the seat next to me.

"Look, I'm sorry for not telling you the full truth," she said somberly.

"I just feel like you could have told me sooner. Like maybe before we were chased down," I pointed out.

"I was getting ready to, since you're so close to ascending, but there was never a good time. You kept having episodes. That ring you're wearing is supposed to unlock everything for you. How and when I don't know, but it's been pretty active lately, so it probably has something to do with the full moon."

"Are you like me?" I wanted her to say yes, so I didn't feel so alone in this.

"Yes and no. It's hard to explain. Did River tell you about your mom?"

"He said that she was human, but had an essence similar to him and me."

"That's right. I was chosen for the same reason. My essence is close to yours, but I'm fully human. After your mother died, River came to me and placed his hand upon my cheek. I passed out, so I'm not sure what happened, but he explained to me that I was chosen to protect you until your ascension after your eighteenth birthday. So, when I say you saved me, I meant it. This gave me purpose. You gave me purpose."

Her voice was starting to tremble as she held back her emotions. Her high school years seemed so perfect, so to hear that things were less than perfect was a bit of a shock.

"All of this is crazy, Star. To hear I'm not human has got to be the weirdest most unbelievable thing that someone could be told, yet here I am, not human. My whole perception of reality shifted in the blink of an eye."

"It was hard to believe for me, as well, but I could feel it, so I had faith in it because I believe that only the truest of things come from deep within you. You feel it, right?"

"Do I ever! I feel everything, Star. I feel like a walking bolt of lightning charged by my emotions."

"You have to be careful. What you're feeling is because your essence is preparing you, but with them out of control and heightened, you can't trust in them fully. Your body is in an amplified state of awareness, but your mind isn't yet, so just be careful."

"Are you referring to Ashe?" I cringed at the possible answer.

"I don't know anything about Ashe, but I do know everything about River, and he's one of a kind. He would die for you. Just remember that, okay?"

She put her hand upon my leg to make sure her point got across. I looked to the door where River was probably standing guard, and it made me feel awful all over again. He would do anything for me. I would do anything for him too, except possibly give him the one thing he wanted most, my heart. "I'm glad we're okay."

"Me too." She grabbed me in her signature hug. "Nothing has changed, Arie. Friends 'til the end."

"Friends 'til the end." I squeezed her back. A pounding on the front door interrupted our love fest, causing us to giggle. "Maybe we should let him in now." She stood up and opened the door for River.

"It's about time, and what was the donut guy doing here?" He snapped.

Star and I shared secretive glances.

"Never mind. I don't want to know. Now that the cat's out of the bag, we need to have a plan. Last night the shadows got too close. I didn't realize they were already aware of your existence, so we need to make sure she's never out of our sight." River was now pacing like a caged animal ready to pounce.

"You guys, I am not totally useless. Now that I know what is going on, I can look out for myself, too. There is one thing I need to ask, though." River froze mid-step as if he knew what I was going to ask.

"What is it?" Star jumped in before River could divert the discussion.

I looked directly at River, forcing him to make eye contact. "It seemed like you knew Ashe. You told him he wasn't supposed to be here, but you didn't act like he was a threat to me, so please tell me, who is he? Why do I feel connected to him somehow?" His face immediately revealed all the pain that I had inflicted on him since Ashe entered my life. It killed me to see that I was the source of such pain for him.

"Because you *are* connected. You're connected to everything, Arie. If he stays away from you, he is not a *lethal* threat to you."

The way he said lethal made chills rush over me. I knew that was all I was going to get from him, and the conversation was not exactly comfortable for either one of us, so I let it go.

I needed my routine to keep my sanity intact, so I spent the next week accompanied by a bodyguard to and from the bookstore. If it wasn't River, it was Starling. I loved them, but no one should spend that much time together. It just wasn't healthy for the relationship. I read through my mom's journal again to see if I had missed something, but I didn't find anything new. My ring hadn't glowed all week, and I didn't have any visions. At night, I was plagued with nightmares of visions in replay mode and the death of my mom. It took so much time for those nightmares to stop and now they had returned with a vengeance, featuring the shadow that I had seen in my vision flashing across the yard from her lifeless body.

Ashe was staying hidden for the most part, but I could feel when he was around. My body would heat up, and tingles would captivate my attention. I missed seeing him. I wondered if this was how it felt for my mom after Teve disappeared. I was still undecided about my feelings for River, so I chose to ignore them for now.

The full moon was looming in the very near future, and I needed to focus on what that meant for me. River said the shadows were lying low, but to not underestimate their capabilities and their thirst for power. It scared the hell out of me. Just their presence paralyzed me. I didn't want to know what else they would do to me if they got to me again, so while having bodyguards was somewhat annoying, I welcomed it. I just wished we knew what the ascension was. All of us were clueless. Again, the unknown was terrifying.

I sat in the reading nook at the store. A storm had moved in, and the streets were deserted. It was only three in the afternoon, but it could have easily passed for midnight. It was pitch black outside. I liked watching the raindrops hit the glass and race down the windowpane. It was pure and serene. My childhood faery book was nestled on my lap. My connection with my mom was fizzling out as the full moon neared, and my loneliness was increasing. Nothing in my body was telling me that the ascension was a good thing. I felt emptier than I had ever felt before.

As I continued to watch the raindrops fall, I imagined all the tears I had shed over the last two years. They were all for my mom. She was the only one I was naturally connected to. Now that the connection was nearly severed, I had no idea what would become of me. I was secretly hoping River or Ashe would be my release from the deep reaches of depression that my mind was falling into, but their existence and my heart's conflict for both of them, only made things worse. I would ruin somebody, and that was enough to drive me crazy.

A reflection in the window startled me out of my daze. I turned to face the little girl who had bought the faery book a few weeks ago. Her face lit up when she saw my book resting on my lap. "Well, hello. Did you come back for another book?" I leaned forward and reached for her. My ring started to glow brightly.

"Oooooh, that's pretty," she said in awe.

I pulled back my hand quickly, and it ceased to glow. *What was that?*

"Thank you. It was my mom's." I wrapped my other hand over it, afraid it would start again.

"I wish I had one," she gleamed from ear to ear.

She was such a beautiful girl, and I could feel the purity of her essence, something I didn't feel in people very often. She was definitely special. "Where's your..." Her mom burst into the store, dripping wet with a panicked look on her face.

"Amary, don't ever leave me like that again," she bellowed. She bent down to her daughter and took her face gently in her hands. "You scared me." She pulled her into a deep embrace.

Watching them warmed my heart. I got up. "Let me go get you a towel to dry off a bit." I went into the bathroom and quickly grabbed a towel from underneath the sink and rushed back to them. The mom was still holding the little girl. "Here's the towel." The mom stood up and took it.

"Thank you so much. Sorry about bursting in here." She started to dry off her daughter first.

"Please don't be sorry. Is Amary short for something?"

"Yes, for Amaryllis." She started to work on herself with the towel.

"That's beautiful. Amaryllis is a flower, right?"

"Yes." She looked surprised. "Not many people know that."

I bent down to Amary. "Can you do your mom a favor and not scare her like that again?"

She nodded her head. Her eyes were a golden amber color and offset her chestnut hair and fair skin. She smiled shyly at me with a little hint of shame. I patted her head as I stood up.

"She must really like you. I was next door looking at a dress, and then all of a sudden she was gone."

Starling came through the door with a look of relief as she spotted us. "Thank goodness you found her." She walked over and joined us. "You gave your mom quite the scare, little one," she said sweetly.

"I'm sorry," Amary announced quietly to all of us.

"It's okay, sweetie. Just please don't do that again." She bent down and picked her up. "You're getting so big, Amary. I can barely carry you anymore." A sadness washed over her expression that only another mother would understand. "We should be going now." She looked at Star. "Would you mind wrapping the dress for me, so it doesn't get wet?"

"Absolutely." She led the way to the door and held it open for them. As the darkness enveloped them, Star turned back to me quickly. "I'll be back in a little bit. We can get dinner." She closed the door.

The only reason they let me be alone in the store was because they believed that I was safe inside, since I had only been threatened outside. I know if they didn't truly believe it they wouldn't hesitate for a second to guard the doors. I scooped up the book from the chair and then sat back down. I studied my ring carefully.

That was the brightest I had seen it glow since my last vision here, and it was reacting to the little girl, but she was just a girl. *Or was she?* My mom and Star were more than just human, so maybe there was a chance she was, too. I did feel something special in her. If my suspicion was correct, then there had to be more like them. What that meant I had no idea. At least not yet, but I hoped that little girl was safe if she was one of them. I found myself worried about her, but until I knew what I was, I didn't know how I could help anyone else.

Chapter Twenty

The storm had gotten progressively worse, so Star and I decided to grab takeout and eat it at my house. She was on watch duty tonight, which meant a much-needed girl's sleepover. She really was a lot of fun, and I didn't think I could take another awkward night with River.

He barely spoke to me unless it had to do with the ascension. It hurt how distant he was from me now. I was losing my connection with him and my mom at the same time. It was almost too much to handle. I was so thankful for my friendship with Star. If I didn't have her, I would be a mess.

We ran into the house with takeout bags over our heads to shield us from the torrential downpour. We charged through the door and locked it behind us. Lightning lit up the sky and the dark house. "Wow, we've seen some crazy storms, but this is nuts!" We put our bags on the kitchen island.

"Yeah, this one seems a little out of control," she said worriedly.

"You sound concerned." I grabbed the kitchen towel and tried to dry myself off and then handed it to her.

"It's just weird timing, you know? The full moon is only a few days away. Maybe I'm just being paranoid." She took the towel and dried off. "Let's eat. I'm starving."

We pulled the hot soup out of the bags and ate straight from the containers at the island.

"So, how are things with you and River?" She took a bite of soup.

"Weird. I hate it. I mean, I understand, but I never told him I didn't want to be with him. I just need time to figure out things."

"He knows you care for him, Arie, but he needs to know that you love him. And I mean more than anyone else, including Ashe. He's just hurting right now, but never doubt his loyalty to you. No matter what you decide, he will always be by your side."

"I know." I thought talking to Star about this would make me feel better, but it only made me feel worse. I think she picked up on it because she changed the subject.

"That little girl was cute."

"She was, but you know, she felt different." I stirred my soup as I blew on it to cool it down.

"What do you mean?" She inquired.

"It's hard to explain. I can feel the difference between yours and River's essence compared to other people, but I never attributed much to it until recently. Now I know why you feel different, and she feels like you guys, so I'm kind of worried about her. How many more of you are there?"

"I don't know. I don't feel it like you do. Hell, I thought I was normal until River came to me."

"That was the first thing I have really felt all week, and my ring reacted to her presence." Star stopped eating and looked at me completely frozen. "What, Star?"

"That doesn't strike you as odd?"

"Well, yeah, which is why I mentioned it."

She whipped out her phone.

"Who are you texting?"

"River. Has your ring ever done that to anyone else?"

"Nothing alive."

She was still texting. She tapped her fingernails impatiently on the granite while she waited for a response from River.

"Can you at least tell me what is going on in that little mind of yours? Either tell me that or stop tapping because something is about to drive me over the edge."

She stopped.

"Sorry, I'm just anxious. We can't take anything out of the ordinary for granted."

"I agree. Did he text you back yet?"

"No, and your service sucks here."

"Geez, tell me how you really feel. The service is better upstairs." She jumped up and ran up the stairs. I got up and carried my soup to the nook to finish eating. The storm was damn scary, but it was beautiful. The lightning lit up the sky like a Christmas tree in the middle of the town square. The thunder that followed wasn't so awesome. It was so loud it shook the ground and windows. It was one angry storm. If it was looking for its presence to be felt, it succeeded. I jumped every time it roared.

Another bolt of lightning lit up the forest and flashed an image of Amary barefoot in a pretty pink knee-length nightgown. "What the..." Did I just see that? Another bolt flew from the clouds, and there she was again against the forest line, only this time a shadow was holding her and she looked terrified. I jumped up, spilling my soup everywhere. "Oh my God." I ran to the door and stormed outside without even thinking. The rain pelted me as I ran toward the spot where I saw her standing, but she was gone, and a large figure stood in her place. I stopped quickly, slipping on the wet grass. The figure raised its finger to its lips and blew out a *shhhhh*. Before I could scream, it lunged at me, and everything went black.

My head hurt like hell, and I felt groggy and nauseous. *What happened?* I couldn't think. I could feel my sopping wet clothes sticking to my skin. Think, Arie. I was with Star in the kitchen and then... *Oh no!* I remembered. *Amary!* I tried to sit up faster than my body was willing to let me, which resulted in a painful head rush that left my head spinning with the room. Room? Where was I? It was pitch black, but my eyes were starting to adjust. I relied on my other senses. The floor was rough. It almost felt like concrete, and it smelled musty. I could taste the rot on my tongue. The spinning stopped, so I started to crawl around the room. The floor was definitely concrete or rock of some sort. I kept moving along, trying to find a wall I could follow. Hopefully to an exit. My knee ran into a clump on the ground. I felt in front of me and squinted to get a better look.

It was Amary. I scooped her up and put her on my lap. My eyes were starting to adjust to the darkness. I could hear her breathing deeply. Her hair was covering her face, so I swept it out of the way and tucked it behind her ears. Who could do this to a little girl? I rocked her as my body vibrated with fear. Where were we, and how did we get here?

A horrifying vision took the place of my temporary blindness. Amary was sleeping in her bed as a shadow lurked over her. Amary's mom came into the room and tucked her in. The shadow reached out for her mom's neck and held tight.

I screamed, "Nooooo!" which broke me free of the vision. I didn't know what happened to her mom, but I hoped she was all right. My heart was racing as the fear that filled her mom's heart consumed me.

Amary's breathing changed, and she started to stir.

I whispered into her ear, "It's okay, Amary. It's Arie from the bookstore. I have you, sweetie. I won't let anything happen to you." Unfortunately, something already had and would haunt her forever. Her eyes sprang open, and the fear that filled them would haunt me forever. She started shaking uncontrollably and whimpering softly. All I could do was hold her tight and shush her softly while I rocked her. I swore two things to myself: that I would protect her as if she were my own, and I would get revenge on whomever did this to her.

After a while, she fell back to sleep. I needed to get us out of here. A dim light started to shine through a crack in the wall, illuminating the room. We were surrounded by rocks and concrete molded into a room, but almost like a cave. It was definitely fabricated from someone's hands rather than a natural occurrence, though. In the corner, I spotted a blanket lying on a rock. I shifted her in my arms and carried her with me to retrieve it. I grabbed it, trying to be careful not to stir her, and spread it out the best I could onto the ground. I slowly and gently laid her on it and wrapped the blanket over her, bunching up the end into a pillow for her head. As a mother would do, I petted her hair softly as a reassurance more for me that she would be fine.

I got up and walked to the crack filtering light in. I looked out and saw only forest. I could hear a waterfall close by. That was probably where the musty smell was originating. I pushed on the wall, but it was solid. I followed it around, trying to find a door of some sort, but there was nothing. If there was a way in, there had to be a way out. I crawled along the ground and even climbed the walls to see if there was an opening near the ceiling, but was unsuccessful. I had no idea how much time had passed, but Amary began stirring again.

I ran over to her side. I didn't want her to wake up alone. I sat down next to her and rubbed her back, hoping to lull her back to sleep to avoid this nightmare. A butterfly flew through the crack and landed on the rock next to us. It opened and closed its wings slowly. It was brilliant with red and orange colors painted on its wings and a firefly like glow surrounding it. A flash of light overtook it, and it flew back out of the crack. Ashe stood where the light exploded. Shock took control of me. I wanted to say something, but there were no words. He rushed to my side and placed one hand upon Amary's head and one hand upon my back that sparked me back to life.

"Are you guys okay?" he asked with a mixture of anger and concern.

"I really don't know how to answer that. Physically, yes. What did I just see, Ashe?" I was still stunned by his sudden manifestation.

"There isn't time to explain right now, but I promise I will."

He placed his hand upon my cheek, sending shivers through me and then gently kissed my lips. I could almost taste the relief that he had found us unharmed.

"Are you ready?" he asked softly.

"Ready for what?" A beautiful light surrounded us in a warmth of comfort. I wrapped my arms around Ashe and buried my face into his chest.

Chapter Twenty-One

I watched as the light around us changed between a beautiful spectrum of colors. We hadn't moved positions, but it felt like the ground had fallen away, and we were floating through a peaceful sound wave across the universe. I felt Ashe's energy consume my fear and fight its way into my heart. It wouldn't have to fight too hard. My heart belonged with him, but was also pulling for River. *Maybe it would have to fight a little.* The light began to fade and exposed us to the glow of the rising sun and the smells of an awakening forest. Only this was not *my* forest. It was more lush and green with beautiful tropical plants that boasted reds, oranges, and yellows. I even saw some blues and purples.

We were surrounded by beauty in its purest form. The buzzing of dragonfly wings mixed with the chirping of a lovebird's song. Everywhere butterflies were either hopping from flower to flower or resting. There were so many you couldn't tell where the flowers ended and the butterflies began. There were easily hundreds of them. As beautiful as it was, the feeling that took my body hostage was so much more.

The prickling of energy pulsed on my skin like a live wire. With every move and gentle touch of the breeze, I wanted to scream in ecstasy. With every intake of breath came a hurricane of foreign aromas. A group of purple flowers close by caught my attention. With every step toward them came the deep awareness of the ground beneath me as the grass flattened, and the dirt surfaced. As

I suspected, the flowers were the mysterious purple flowers shaped like butterflies that were left in the bookstore. I touched one, and the three petals immediately came alive and butterflies scattered gracefully. My eyes lit up as if I was an infant experiencing something for the first time.

The magic that captured us was something out of my childhood fairytales. I couldn't help but touch a few more petals to watch them transform in front of me. Smiling ear to ear, I touched them one by one and squealed quietly with giddiness. This caused a domino effect, and within moments, all the petals had come alive, and the butterflies spiraled around me trapping me in a tornado. As their speed increased, a light sparked into a rainbow of colors. I spun in the opposite direction like a child spinning in circles in the wind.

My body felt alive with all the essence of the forest. This would be a moment I would never forget. As the light dissipated, Amary's face was lit up in awe as she watched me. I ran to her side.

"Amary."

"I want my mommy." She melted in my arms.

Ashe shook his head and gave me a look that shot arrows at my heart and erased all the previous blissful moments in the fairy-tale forest. I squeezed my eyes shut tightly and held her in my arms. She was only four and all alone. I hoped she was more resilient than I had been. This would be the hardest thing she would ever go through, but I would be there for her and protect her as River had done for me.

"I know you have a million questions, but we really need to get going," he said softly.

"Go where, Ashe? You're right. I do have a million questions, and I understand right now is not the best time. All of this may be normal for you, but it's not for us. It looks like we were dropped in the middle of the Neverland forest after visiting the dark side. This is all levels of crazy." My voice was harsh and made Amary cringe under my grip. "I'm sorry. I didn't mean to scare you I'm just lost... I don't know what's real and what's not, and I don't know who I can trust or if I can even trust my own feelings anymore."

Amary quietly whimpered on my lap as I rubbed her back to soothe her. Ashe bent down to eye level. He grabbed my chin in his hand and gently forced me to look at him.

"You know you can trust me. That feeling you get when we're together can't be fabricated." He released my chin and put his hand over my heart. "What you feel here can always be trusted."

When he let go, I released a deep breath that I hadn't even known I was holding. It left me feeling dizzy and happily dazed until the reality of our situation set in.

He stood up. "We need to be going now. I can carry her."

I stood up with her cradled in my arms. She had a death grip around my neck. I whispered into her ear, "It's okay. I promise. You can trust him." She believed me without question. I handed her off to Ashe who held her as if she weighed next to nothing. She buried her head into his chest and held on tight.

"Can't you just do that nifty light trick again?" I waved my hands in the air as if I was composing an orchestra. He started laughing. "Are you seriously laughing at me right now?"

"I wish it worked that way all the time. I wasn't even sure I could do it that time. I have only ever been able to do that by myself. It takes a lot of light to do what I just did, so I won't be able to do that again for a while. Maybe never after what I just pulled off. I have a feeling you helped a little, though." He winked.

"Me? How could I have helped? I have never done that before."

"Oh, but you have. Remember the rainy day in the parking lot when I was waiting for you outside your store?"

Ummm, yes! I had every moment with him etched in my brain forever. "That wasn't me. A dear friend passed his light on to me."

"I'm sorry, Arie."

"Yeah, me too."

"Hopefully, it wasn't all bad, though." His sultry smile made my knees weak.

"Wow, okay. More on that later. Shall we?" I moved aside for him to lead the way. He walked so quietly and smoothly it could be mistaken for flying. How was so graceful. I, on the other hand, was not. Not from lack of trying either. I followed him on a barely beaten path that beckoned for me to trip on a protruding tree branch or to get tangled in a wild vine. I could only imagine what those vines could do to me if they came alive like the butterfly flowers with their spiky thorns and sticky fur. They were beautiful, but menacing-looking. We were in the middle of an enchanted forest with no end in sight. I was feeling drained. Surprisingly, I wasn't hungry, though, but I was worried that Amary might be. "Ashe, can you stop for a second?"

"Of course."

I caught up and rubbed Amary's head softly. "Sweetie, are you hungry?" She shook her head, but made no attempt to talk.

"You won't get hungry here."

I was about to open my mouth to ask a question, but decided to file it inside my many folders full of questions for now. I looked at Amary again and gave him a worried look.

"She'll be fine. She has you."

His words were honest and warm. I loved that every time he spoke I felt safe. He started to walk again, and I followed willingly.

I could see a break in the thicket ahead. I was anxious to start my round of questioning, but I was also worried that we were still in danger. Someone had taken us, and when they discovered we were missing, I imagined they would be pretty angry. Above all, I was terrified to tell Amary her mom was gone. Just thinking about it made me sick to my stomach.

Ashe passed the threshold into the clearing ahead first. He turned around and waited until I caught up. He carried Amary like it was nothing, and she stayed buried in his chest as if she were frozen, probably frozen with fear. His smile looked unfazed from the long journey we just took through the forest.

I actually didn't feel tired either. In fact, my energy level was higher than it had been all week, and I felt great aside from being kidnapped and the impending talk I would be having with Amary in the near future. Even in light of everything that had happened, Ashe's smile still made my toes tingle and my stomach swirl in knots. I blushed as the thought of kissing him again rushed through my mind.

I reached them at the edge and dropped my jaw in astonishment. What lay before us was the most unbelievable landscape I had ever seen. My mom would have loved to have been able to paint this. To the right of us, a raging waterfall fell from a cliff and emptied into a creek that flowed through the valley directly in front of us. The valley went on as far as the eye could see. A meadow lay to the left of us and was covered with exotic flowers of every color of the rainbow and then some. Where there weren't flowers there were deep green grass blades thick and glossy without a hint of brown to them.

All kinds of mysterious flying insects flew around, chasing each other and eating from the flowers. The only things missing were little fairies sitting on the flower blooms giggling. I must have let out a noise as I took in the world around us because Amary finally peeked her head up, and the light in her eyes made my heart melt. She was beautiful, innocent, and precious, and I was afraid this might be the last time I would see that smile light her soul up like this again.

I imprinted the image into my mind. I wanted to remember her in this moment, so I could remind her that there was a time when she was genuinely happy.

"This is an amazing place, but how do we get back home?" I asked.

"This is your home, or at least it was," he replied.

"I think it's time we had that talk, Ashe."

"Follow me."

With Amary in hand, he walked along the edge of the forest line and through a small break to reveal a clearing with a beautiful cabin made of natural wood and windows everywhere. The color of the wood blended perfectly with the trees around it. As I looked beyond it, several more houses, similar in style but not quite as grand, appeared. Were they there a moment ago? They were all scattered throughout the trees. Some even expanded into the trees like the kind of tree houses kids built in their own backyards.

Ashe looked down at Amary. "Would you like to meet some friends your age, Amary?" She nodded hesitantly. "Let's go then."

I followed them around the side of the house to the backyard. The view from the backyard was equally unbelievable. Several young kids played in the calm waters of the river that flowed by while others dug in the sand.

Ashe put Amary down. She stared toward the kids, but made no moves to join them. She looked at me for permission.

"I think it's okay if you want to go play." She still didn't move, but looked back and watched them play. A little girl that looked to be a couple of years older than her came running toward us with a flower in her hand.

"Hi, I'm Iris." She handed Amary a bright pink flower bloom. Amary took it shyly. The older girl towered over Amary by at least a half a foot, so she bent down. "Would you like to come play with us, Amary?"

How did she know her name? I looked at Ashe with a questioning glance. He winked in response. Iris took Amary's hand, and when Amary took a couple of steps with her, she led her down to the riverbed. All the other kids immediately flocked around her. Amary stayed behind Iris, but then a smile lit up her face, and her stiff stance relaxed as she eased right in with the kids.

"Should I even bother asking how Iris knew Amary's name?"

Ashe smiled coyly. "Let's go inside. There's someone you should meet."

I looked down at Amary playing with her new friends. She seemed content, but it made me uneasy to lose sight of her.

"She's safe here," Ashe said confidently.

I *felt* that we were all safe here, but I couldn't help but feel a strong bond with her. Tingles shot up my arm when Ashe took my hand in his. The energy of this place was starting to surge through me again. He led me to the back patio of the grand house. The walls slid away to open up to the outside world, inviting the inside out and the outside in.

The inside of the house was as equally amazing as the outside. Everything was simple and meant for a purpose whether it was for lounging or eating. There was nothing out of place and nothing flashy or unnecessary. As I stepped over the threshold, I felt like I walked through a wall of electricity. It buzzed in my ears and raised the hairs on my body. As soon I was all the way inside the house, the feeling disappeared, leaving a light after buzz on my skin. "What was that?"

"What was what?" He looked at me quizzically.

"You didn't feel that?"

"No, I'm sorry. I'm afraid I didn't."

He let go of my hand suddenly and stiffened. If we were safe, why was he afraid? Before I saw him, I *felt* him. A strong tall man with blond shoulder-length hair entered the room. I didn't even know where he came from. One minute Ashe and I were alone, and then the next, I felt his energy wisp around me and he was standing there. He was handsome and looked to be in his late twenties maybe early thirties, although his energy felt ancient. I felt an instant draw to him that was as strong as my draw to Ashe, only different. Ashe immediately bowed his head and looked at the floor, while I couldn't keep my eyes off him.

"Thank you for finding her. Can you please leave us a moment?" The man asked.

It was more of a command than a question, although one that would come from a friend or father rather than from someone in power. Ashe left the room quietly without looking at either of us. The uncomfortable silence was making me anxious, or it could be that I was left alone with a complete stranger that elicited that type of response from Ashe.

"There's no reason to fear me, my child." He kept his distance, but relaxed his posture.

"Who are you?"

"I believe in your world I would be referred to as your dad."

What could I say to that? Nothing. Because the life drained out of me.

Chapter Twenty-Two

I came running from the meadow to find my mom lying on the ground. River just behind me. A shadow fled from my mother's lifeless body. Just as the shadow reached the forest line, it revealed its true form, my father.

I sat up quickly, choking and panicking. River sat next to me on the couch in the grand house that now seemed to suffocate me rather than welcome me. He took my face in his hand and caressed my cheek with his thumb.

"Arie, focus. It's okay. I'm here."

His blue eyes locked on mine intensely, trying to break me from my nightmare, but little did he know, I was now living my nightmare. My chest sunk and rose quickly as the panic attack forced itself deeper inside me, and tears rolled freely down my cheeks. When I jumped up to run, River seized me around the waist and pulled me onto his lap and squeezed me tightly. I wanted to scream, but I couldn't catch my breath.

"Shhhhh. You need to calm down, Arie. I promise you're safe. Shhhhh."

All I could do was shake my head and squeeze my eyes shut, trying to force myself to wake up. River continued to shush me and hold me. My breathing started to flow more evenly, and my body started to relax into him. I kept my eyes closed and burrowed my head into his chest. He was the only person I felt truly safe with.

After a few minutes passed and my mind cleared, I remembered that I was now responsible for a little four-year-old girl. A new kind of panic washed over me. I popped my eyes open. "Amary!"

"She's okay. She's still outside playing, and Starling is with her. Amaryllis fits right in here."

I sat up and looked at him. "Where's here, River, and how did you find me?"

He brushed my cheek with his soft, but strong hand and brought his lips to mine. As they pressed up against mine, a vision swirled in my head. It was River kissing me, but we were here in this world. In this house. In another time. I looked as I had in my vision with Ashe, my eyes amber instead of blue and a soft glow around me. My hair was a lighter shade of brown and my skin milky white. I pulled away from him and looked into his crystal blue eyes confused. "I don't understand, River."

My father came back into the room. River stood up, bowed his head discreetly and left through the back without saying a word.

"May I?" He waved his hand out referencing the couch.

I nodded and lowered my eyes to my feet. He came over and sat on the other side of the couch, being careful not to get too close to me.

"Are you okay? Did they hurt you?" He sounded genuinely concerned.

I shook my head. He was a stranger, but I knew he was my father. I could feel it, but I was at a loss for words.

"Amaryllis is adjusting well."

I looked at him and saw he was looking outside. "For now, until I tell her that her mom's gone." He looked back at me. He was magnificent. His essence hugged me with warmth.

"Yes, that will be hard. I know you have questions, but I think it would be best if you rested a bit. You and Amaryllis will be safe here until your ascension."

I thought carefully about what I was going to say next. I needed to ask him about him being there when my mom died, but wasn't sure how to ask.

"What is it, my child?"

"I had a vision. I saw you leaving my mom's body the day she..." It was still so hard to talk about even now.

"Yes, what is your question?"

"Did you... I mean... do you know what happened to my mom?" I put my head down in shame for what I was implying.

"I do, but now is not the time. You've been through a lot, and I'm concerned that you're still in shock. How about we revisit this conversation later?"

I nodded my head in understanding, but I scrunched my face in frustration. When I pouted, my mom said I looked like a squirrel because my face narrowed and my lips pursed. I didn't understand this world, and I didn't want to offend anyone. I was a little scared, so I stayed quiet and followed the rules, for now. I pulled my legs into my chest and rested my chin on my knees.

"Can I ask where we are?"

He let out a belly laugh that took me by surprise.

"Yes, my child. As with your reality, we don't really have a name for our reality. See, this is my reality, and the other one has been your reality. Although now I guess both realities are yours." He observed the blank expression on my face. "I guess that didn't help, did it?"

"So, there are two worlds?"

"Not exactly. There is one world, but several realities within it. The one you came from is one, and this is another, but there is another one. Most people don't know about it because it's only possible to live within one reality per lifetime."

"Then how am I here? And River, Star, and Amary?"

He stood studiously tall.

"You aren't going to tell me, are you?" I asked doubtfully.

He let out another laugh.

"Not right now, my child, but I promise you will know everything in due time. Would it be too forward for me to ask for a hug?" He stretched out his hands toward me.

I stood up and fell into his arms. He wrapped them tightly around me and rested his chin on my head. I saw a tear fall down to the floor. I looked up at him and saw his amber eyes filled with tears.

"I'm sorry, my child. I have waited a long time to hold you in my arms."

The purity of his heart covered me and brought tears to my own eyes, something I didn't expect, but welcomed. To know that I had finally found my father and to know that he wasn't dead and wanted me as much as I wanted him was the internal boost I needed to conquer whatever was waiting for me in the ascension. I melted into his arms and snuggled my face into his broad chest. We stayed like that for several minutes. "I've missed you, too."

He kissed my head and pulled away from me, taking my face in his hands gently.

"We have eternity to look forward to now." He smiled sweetly, released my cheeks, and walked into the backyard.

What did he mean we had eternity? I let the thought spin in my head. River came up behind me and kissed me gently on the neck. He blanketed me with warmth with every touch. I would never feel as safe as I did when I was with him. It was such a different feeling from Ashe. When Ashe touched me, I felt invincible.

Today was the first day since River saw me with Ashe that he had showed me any type of affection. His touch felt soft and inviting. He wrapped his hands around my waist and pulled my back into his hard abs. I loved how safe I felt when I was with him, and I was more than happy to have my River back.

The problem was that I felt that way about Ashe, too. For now, I would take what I could get. I had so much to think and worry about that for one day I just wanted to let it all go.

"Did you have a good talk with your dad?" He spoke softly into my ear that sent chills down my neck.

"Yes, cryptic and short, but good. How is Amary doing?"

"She's having a great time."

"Does she know that we aren't home?" I asked.

"I don't think so. I think she might be too young to understand."

I watched her outside splashing in the water with several other kids. She was laughing as if everything in the world was perfect. I wished I could keep it that way for her. "How did you and Star get here?"

"Tivon came to us when you disappeared. He asked us to come here with him to help find you. By the time we were ready to set out to look for you, Ashe had brought you back."

His name resonating from River's mouth made me twinge with guilt. "Where is Ashe?"

"He left." He pulled away and walked to the back patio. "He doesn't belong here." And with that, he made his way down to the river.

Why did he keep saying that? If Ashe didn't belong in my reality and he didn't belong here, where did he belong, and why did I feel the way I did about him? Not knowing was driving me crazy!

I needed to clear my head, so I went outside and sat on a chair on the back porch. Amary spotted me and ran up to me, smiling. She gave me a huge hug that filled me with happiness and sadness. I squeezed her back and kissed her on the head. She looked up at me.

"I love it here. Do you love it here?" she questioned me.

I stroked her hair as we spoke. "I do."

"When will my mom be here?"

Her question shot directly to my chest. I hugged her firmly to hide my discomfort. "I don't know, sweetie."

"I hope it's soon. She'll love it here." She ran back down to play in the river.

I forced the tears to retreat. I was going to be strong for her, for us! As I watched everyone, I knew this was not the place to clear my head. I needed to be alone with the essence of the naturally serene world. I got up and snuck around the side of the house and escaped deep into the forest. I felt the faint buzz of life teasing my skin as I inched my way past branches, vines, flowers, and bushes. I passed families of raccoons, chipmunks, birds, butterflies, and dragonflies among many others. The forest was full of life, prosperity, and hope. I could feel the brightness of its essence feed my much-needed starving soul. Just as I was soaking in the sun's rays, I felt the energy change and a soft breath on the back of my neck.

"I was hoping you would venture out."

The familiar voice sent my heart racing and caused my breaths to deepen. A hand slowly brushed aside my hair, and a sensual kiss touched my neck, propelling my body into a state of instability. I melted back into Ashe's body, letting myself mold to his chest. He wrapped one arm around my waist and one around my chest and gracefully spun me around. In one fell swoop, his lips were on mine, not giving my body a chance to recover from the encounter.

With his lips pressed against mine passionately, I raked my fingers through his hair as I reveled in the powerful exchange between us. The fire lit inside me, and he responded desperately, carrying me to the ground. He broke free from my grasp and smiled. He caressed my temple with his thumb.

"I love you," he said intensely.

I was flustered. I knew how I felt, but there was still River. "I...uh..." His lips stopped me from saying more.

He pulled away slowly, "You don't need to say anything. I know your heart is conflicted. I just wanted you to know that I'm yours and only yours in this reality and any other."

A noise from close by caused us both to sit up in a high alert position.

"Arie!" My father's voice yelled in the forest just in front of us.

Ashe bent down and whispered into my ear, "I have to go." He kissed my ear and quickly rose and disappeared.

"I'm here." I stood up. His worried expression pained me.

"It's not safe for you out here, Arie. You must stay close to the village until the full moon."

"I'm sorry. I wasn't thinking. I just needed to be alone." I looked down at my feet in shame. In a flash, he was in front of me, pulling up my chin.

"You don't ever need to hide your face from me, my child."

His words comforted me. He took me in a gentle hug and then led me back to the village. I looked over my shoulder in the direction Ashe traveled. I already missed him and hoped the time for our next reunion wasn't too far away.

"There's a special place I go to clear my head that is safe if you would like to see it?"

"I would like that very much." I was still uncomfortable with my newfound relationship with my father, but I was beginning to warm up to it.

He walked me back through the forest and past the village that seemed to go on for miles and to the side of the waterfall that had introduced me to their world. I followed him behind the cascading water over a riverbed of rocks to the other side. When I emerged from behind the waterfall, I was confronted with a drastically dropping cliff and an absolutely splendid view of the valley and a receding ocean. The sun was beginning to set, and an almost full moon had already begun to rise high above it. This place just kept getting more magical by the minute.

"This is where I come when I need to be alone. No one knows about it except me. I happened upon it shortly after I had to leave you and your mother. It was the only place that kept me sane. Leaving my family behind was the single hardest thing I have ever had to do, and I hope the last. I don't know if I could handle something like that again. Your mom was always so much stronger than me."

He looked off into the great expanse that lay before us, dazing as if he was remembering my mom. A sadness was reflected in his eyes.

"Thank you for sharing this with me… and about my mom. She loved you very much." He turned to me and smiled through the tear that betrayed his masculine exterior.

"Thank you for telling me that. It broke my heart every day I was away from you two and saw what she went through. A love like ours is very rare, and I will cherish it 'til the day my life is truly over here."

"What are you… I mean, what are we?" I fought the urge to look down.

"Some people in your reality call us fairies, angels, or guardians, but that wouldn't be completely accurate."

"What would be?" I was trying unsuccessfully to not sound completely stunned. The idea that I was part fairy or angel or whatever was unbelievable.

"We're the essence that lives in nature. Some here call us nature spirits."

While I was in complete shock, it totally made sense. My mom and I had always had a special connection with nature. "Am I…a nature spirit?" I asked carefully not sure if I wanted to know.

"That, my child, is a hard question to answer. In a way, yes. Right now, you are."

What did he mean by 'right now'? Before I could ask, he was heading back the way we came. "Take as much time as you need."

He seemed to vanish within the mist of the waterfall. It broke my heart when I thought about what my mom and he went through being separated, and it made me think how broken I would be if I was ever separated from River or Ashe. Would I survive as they had done for so long without each other? I didn't know if I was strong enough, but now that I had Amaryllis to protect I might be, but I wasn't willing to find out. One way or another I would keep both of them in my life, even if that meant I couldn't have either one of them the way I wanted.

Chapter Twenty-Three

I could have sat in my dad's private sanctuary forever. It was so serene. The sun seemed to set slower here, so I was able to admire the bright pinks and oranges that expanded for miles across the smog-less sky. The moon had already taken position high in the sky, and with only a sliver away from a full moon, I was reminded of my impending ascension or death, whatever it might be.

I sucked in a cleansing breath and washed away everything that had happened since my birthday. I focused on the beauty of the world that surrounded me and the tingling sensation that had resided on my skin since I came here, in this other reality. I wondered how many others existed. Was Ashe from this one or another one? The fact that he could be here and in my home reality brought me to the conclusion that he could manifest anywhere. Of course, I could be wrong.

My dad had done the same. He had traveled between both realities freely, but why hadn't he gone before now? He saw how much pain my mom was experiencing. Why didn't he do as Ashe had been doing? I watched as birds dive bombed from the sky into the water in hopes of getting dinner or maybe just to sip water. Ducks, dispersed sporadically on the water, bobbled up and down with the waves of the currents as they napped. I could hear the buzzing of insect wings all around me. Even some grasshoppers chirped a song of serenity. The light mildly-tempered breeze freshened the air for all the creatures to breathe.

A sudden chill crawled over the surface of my body that caught my breath in my chest. I could sense something behind me, but was paralyzed with too much fear to turn around. *I thought I was safe here?*

"It's just me," Ashe said smoothly.

My shoulders relaxed, and my lungs remembered how to inhale.

"I didn't mean to scare you." He sat next to me.

"What was that?" I rubbed the spooky feeling off my arms.

"This place is shielded from anyone but you and your dad, so the organic elements react to intruders to alarm you."

"That's handy and weird." My body settled and soaked up the warmth of having Ashe by my side. "How did you know where to find me?"

"I followed you."

"Oh." I pause for a moment and then asked, "So, can I start my questioning now?" I fidgeted with my pant leg.

"Yes." He chuckled.

How can he make a chuckle sound so damn sexy? Now, all I wanted to do was kiss him again. To feel his energy fill me all over. "I'm not sure where to start. I have so many."

"How about I start?"

He reached out and stroked my fidgeting hand and took it in his. The feeling that consumed me made my head dizzy. He brought my hand to his lips and lightly kissed it, leaving behind prickles of static. His eyes watched mine as he relished in my reaction to his touch.

"Do you enjoy watching me suffer?"

"Are you suffering?" He looked somewhat concerned.

I giggled shyly. "No, 'suffering' would definitely not be the word for it." I secretly noted that I might die, though, if he didn't kiss me soon. "I have my first question."

"Oh, okay, I thought you needed me to help start off the interrogation." He smiled.

His smile was like water on flames. The sizzle reverberated through my head. "How do you do it? How do you make me feel like this?"

"That is a fully loaded question whether you realize it or not." He winked.

"Does that mean you aren't going to answer it?" I raised an eyebrow at him.

"I'll do even better. I'll show you," he said as he leaned in and kissed me.

The immediate response he summoned from deep within me was a desperation for more. I swung my leg over and straddled him as I pulled on the roots of his hair. His kiss maddeningly deepened as he grabbed me around the waist and pushed on the small of my back to get me closer. I could feel our hearts pounding against our chests. I was drawn to him like a butterfly to a flower full of nectar. I craved every inch of him. My senses were heightening with the approaching full moon, and I could feel his kiss forcing me into a hidden place in our deep-rooted connection. My mind erased words and thoughts, and memories exploded in a moment of near death-like visions.

A little boy hid in a shadow cast by a towering tree. I was a little girl, and he watched as I chased butterflies in a field. The same field I later die in. He walked over with a butterfly on his finger and showed me proudly. Mesmerized by the unfamiliarity of him, I reached out my hand and giggled as the butterfly adorned with shades of orange, red, and yellow hopped onto my finger. A moment later, we watched as it joined the other butterflies in a game of chase. He took my hand, and a foreign sensation made my body shiver all over. He smiled in recognition. My father emerged from the forest and shooed away the little boy like a child shooing away a fly. He stepped aside and revealed another little boy that was hidden behind him. He encouragingly pushed him toward me. I recognized him from the village. We both smiled at each other awkwardly.

I was older now, sitting against a tree trunk hidden deep within the forest, writing in a journal. I was surprised to see Ashe appear from behind a large, green tropical foliage that had kept my spot a secret for so long. His smile melted my heart and tickled my bare toes. He was the little boy carrying the beautiful butterfly. He sat across from me, crossed his legs, and absorbed my presence. He was gorgeous, enchanting, and forbidden, but the way he made me feel lit my heart on fire. Something I couldn't deny my core. He was meant for me and me for him. Our essence screamed to be united as one. He leaned over slowly and grazed my cheek with his lips. A sound came from beyond my hideaway, forcing Ashe to leave quickly. I touched my cheek that still burned with his lips. I wanted it to stay forever like a tattoo that permanently marked the beauty of its meaning into its owner. River plowed through the plants and almost stumbled over me. Guilt consumed me as I watched the purity of concern fade into innocent adoration. He was there to protect me, love me, and be my everything. Something I couldn't reciprocate now, knowing that nature had chosen Ashe for me.

The last vision was my father standing over me. I looked to be mid-teens. We were surrounded by the same iridescent glow of the forest. River came running from behind my father, and Ashe was hidden behind the forest wall. Both my father and River were crying. My father placed his hand upon my cheek, and a bright light illuminated in it. The light filled his hand until the glow around me faded and disappeared. My dad cupped the light protectively with both hands and looked at the sky and let out a terrifying cry. His skin drank the light. River kneeled in front of him with pleading eyes. My father reached out and touched his cheek and stole the essence from him. River's body went limp and fell to the ground. His essence was now a part of my father as well.

My mind went blank, and a spark of anguish separated me from Ashe's embrace. I jumped off his lap and cupped my hand over my mouth as tears broke through the tough exterior I was trying so hard to build. The guilt and pain of what I had just seen forced me to the ground. "I killed him. It was my fault. Oh my God! He died for me. He left here to be with me there. This can't be. How can this be?" My tears turned into increasingly loud whimpers, and my chest hardened as if it had forgotten the rhythm of inhaling and exhaling. The sounds of the world became too loud to bear, and the brightness of the retreating sun blinded my retinas. I curled into a ball and started babbling incoherently the thoughts that poisoned me.

I kept my eyes closed tightly and tried to drown out the deafening sounds around me. Not even the touch of Ashe could bring me out of this. I had died in this reality, and River loved me so much he followed me. He gave up everything to be with me. The depression deepened as I mentally listed all my betrayals. First, by kicking him out of my life after my mom died, then out of my heart when Ashe arrived, and finally, the ultimate betrayal of murder. He deserved better than me, but how do you convince someone of that who died for you?

All of a sudden, I didn't know how to live anymore. I couldn't remember how to breathe. I could *feel* everything and nothing at the same time. I managed to scratch out, "You need to go." I could feel how bad that hurt Ashe, but he was the reason why I had betrayed River in both realities. He needed to leave. When I still felt him near, I yelled through gritted teeth, "You don't belong here!" I don't know whom those words hurt more. I was angry, but sending him away felt like I was killing a part of me that lived so vibrantly inside me, in my essence.

"I'm sorry, Arie. I didn't know you would see that. If I could have stopped it, I would have. I..."

I covered my ears again to block out his penetrating voice that was seducing my mind to forget the truth that I bared witness to only moments ago. "I can't, Ashe. You need to go." I don't know what it was about our connection, but I could feel his heart break, or it could just be that I was feeling mine break. Either way I didn't need to see his face to feel his despair. It added to my own pain.

After a few quiet painful minutes passed, and my body ached from the tension it bore, I looked up to confirm that Ashe had gone. Not that I needed to. I felt empty the moment he left. He gave up so easily. Would River have given up so easily? The sting of rejection hurt like hell.

I stood up, wiped the tears from my face and stretched out my aching muscles. They all felt the gravity of what had transpired. I needed to get away. I needed to find that spot behind the tropical foliage hidden deep within the forest that was my own private place of solitude where Ashe first kissed me, burning a tattoo of emotions into my cheek.

I ran over the wet river rock, catching myself every time I slipped, and I burst out from behind the waterfall not sure which direction to run. I closed my eyes and tried to summon the memories of my other life. I let out a frustrated sigh and opened my eyes.

A butterfly shaded with many colors of purple fluttered over and landed on my shoulder like a parrot on a pirate. It flew off and into the forest. A soft glow surrounded it. I knew I was meant to follow it, so I did unquestioningly. Once I entered the forest, I could only see the soft glow the butterfly emitted in front of me. Still shaken, I trudged on my bare feet through mossy mud that squeezed its way through my toes, hacked past thick foliage, and climbed over wild tree branches penetrating the ground. In my reality, I would be scraped and bruised, but here nothing seemed to hurt me. It was as if my body was invincible. The visions had explained so much about River and Ashe's love for me and about my death, however, I still didn't know how I died.

Did this mean I wasn't going to die tomorrow? Was that vision the same as the other ones, or was I destined to repeat this life as I had the other? Torn between two loves only to die too young to figure it all out. I stopped to swallow down the panic attack. I might not have been physically harmed, but I was bruised and broken inside.

The glow was fading in the distance, so I picked up speed to try to catch up, but I wasn't fast enough. When it disappeared, I surveyed my surroundings to get a grip on where I was. The sun had finally set, and the light of the moon was bright enough that rays shot through the canopy above. I had no idea where I was, how far I had gone, or how to get back. What the hell was I thinking? I felt alone and scared and in danger.

My eye caught sight of the soft glow of the butterfly tucked beneath some large green leaves next to a tree trunk. I walked over and pushed the leaves aside and saw the butterfly resting on a small rock next to my childhood hiding spot. Relief washed over me as I nestled underneath the leaves and perched up against the trunk. This was where my first betrayal of River took place. Right here when Ashe marked my cheek forever. I touched my cheek and closed my eyes, trying to remember the feeling, but also wanting to take it back and forget. I pulled my knees in close to my chest and wrapped my arms around them tightly. It was too dangerous for me to go back tonight, and since the temperature seemed to be pleasantly constant here, I knew I would be okay. I was hidden from sight, and I could feel I was safe here. The butterfly stopped pumping its wings, and the glow faded as it fell still for the night. What a strange companion to have, but beautiful and unconditionally forgiving. I followed its lead and rested my head on my knees and closed my eyes, hoping sleep would take me before my thoughts ran wild again.

I had calmed down considerably, and I wanted to keep it that way. What I really wanted was to find a way to love

River as I loved Ashe. To feel like I was floating on stars when he touched me. To know deep down that he was my other half. The perfect match to my essence. The missing piece that made me complete and safe and not alone.

My ascension was tomorrow night, and I still had no idea what that meant. Would I still be me, or would I become one of them again? There was no mention of River and Star ascending, so did that mean they would go back, and I would stay here? The thought terrified me. They were my strength beneath all my weaknesses. I needed them.

If ascending meant I would have to say goodbye to them like my dad had to do to my mom, I would refuse. I couldn't bear to do to them what he did to my mom, whether he had a choice or not. I could tell there was always something missing from her. She was never quite whole. I needed more answers before I agreed to this. I wasn't even sure if I had a choice, but I needed to know. I couldn't go into this relying on blind faith. Not if ruining the lives of the two people closest to me was part of the deal. My heart ached just thinking about them.

They would be worried that I was missing. Should I go back now or wait until sunrise when it was safer? Only I wasn't sure it was safer. I had grown up in a reality where dark meant danger and light meant safety. Everything I relied on were the things that my mom taught me in the other reality.

If I became one of them again, would it be like my mom never existed? Like she didn't hold me when I was scared, or read her stories to me, or teach me how to treat the natural beauty of the world around me? Would she cease to exist if all my memories faded? The panic started to rise in my chest again, and my breathing came fast and hard as tears threatened to prove my strength wrong. I couldn't stay here all night. I needed to know everything *now*! I took deep breaths to slow down my breathing and to call back the attack clawing its way up my throat. The butterfly stayed still as I stood up and crawled back out of my hidden safe house.

I stood up and looked in every direction, hoping the forest would tell me which way to go. I cursed myself for not paying better attention to how I got here. I was also regretting not wearing shoes. The inhabitants of this reality might like the feel of gritty mud between their toes, but I didn't. I was a mess. My hair was all knotted up, my clothes were filthy, and my eyes were swollen. I didn't know what I was going to do, so I just stood there watching the wind play with the flower petals and leaves around me.

My ring was glowing faintly as the world danced quietly around me. It was calming, so much so that I was starting to feel drowsy. I knew I was tired, but to feel this heavy seemed a little odd. There was no way I would make it ten feet feeling like this. Maybe I should just sleep it off. I caught myself from falling just as the forest starting spiraling around me. I fell to my knees and crawled back into the safety of my hideaway before passing out next to my sleeping butterfly.

Chapter Twenty-Four

I didn't know if I was dreaming or stuck in that heavy fog-like state of awakening when you try to wake up, but no matter how hard you fight, your eyes betray you and close. I was only mildly aware of myself. I couldn't remember where I fell asleep or why. I wanted so bad to wake up, fearing the worst if I didn't. How long had I been sleeping? I attempted again to open my eyelids. As I did, I saw a sliver of my surroundings. I couldn't be sure, but it didn't feel like I was in my secret hideaway. Where was I then? I could still feel the soft grass beneath my cheek and the now dried mud between my toes.

I struggled with movement in my fingers first. It was tougher than I thought. Once they started to wiggle, I tried to open my eyes wider. I could see that my ring was glowing brightly now. I felt nauseous from the sleep coma, and the light stung my eyes. I closed them again trying to adjust to the world slowly this time. I started to move my toes and fingers again. Satisfied that I could probably manage propping myself up on my hands and knees, I opened my eyes again still feeling very groggy.

I weakly pushed myself up on my knees and rested my weight back on my legs as my eyes worked at focusing on something, anything. I could feel beads of sweat start to cover my face as the nausea intensified. I hated throwing up. I needed to get this under control quickly.

I took slow, even breaths while I registered my waking place. I was still in the forest alone, but I was no longer in my hideaway. Wherever I was, it was even more beautiful than everything else I had seen here so far, which already seemed unimaginable. The exotic flowers towered high above me and more stunning flowers drooped from the tree branches even higher above them. A light morning haze hung in the air and what looked like stars illuminated the area and buzzed in my ears. Large dewdrops fell from the plants every few seconds, hitting the ground with a soft vibration that tickled my toes.

Once my head started to clear and the nausea receded, I could fully appreciate the gifts that nature was bestowing upon me. I felt like I was becoming one with it. As the light breeze swayed the blades of grass together, they seemed to whisper to me. I looked down and finally registered that I was wearing something entirely different than what I fell asleep in. It was a lovely purplish blue full-length princess cut dress made of buttery soft satin. It was fitted from the waist up with beautiful flutter sleeves and a low bust line and flared out softly from the waist. I had never worn anything like this, let alone owned it.

Star had dresses like this in her boutique and even tried to give me one to wear for prom, but I couldn't take it. Not even borrow it. Besides, I didn't go to prom, anyway. River wanted me to, but I was way out of that way of thinking at that point. Happy was not my place, and proms were happy.

I was somewhat mortified that someone had put me in this dress while I slept. Even more mortified not knowing who. I was also suddenly worried about ruining the dress. It was too exquisite for me to be rolling around the grass in.

I anchored my hands on the ground feeling the tickle of the blades and pushed myself up. I felt a little dizzy at first, but quickly refocused. My ring was emitting a beautiful purple color that matched my dress. Where was I? A tingle started to flow through me that sent a wave of elation down to my core. I sucked in a deep breath trying to hold the feeling inside.

The brightly lit stars swirled around me causing a whirlwind of flames to erupt around me. Closer up, I saw they were beautiful insects that were a cross between a butterfly and a dragonfly all decorated in purples and blues with iridescent wings. They had to be nature's most incredible creation, and they were dancing around me like I was. They grazed my skin as they whisked by. They created their own weather around me like the eye of an out of control forest fire, but it came in the form of sensations heating me up from the inside out.

Goosebumps frolicked at the base of my hairline on my neck and behind my ears. My butterfly friend penetrated the tornado and perched itself on my ring and watched quietly as it pulsed its wings slowly. The whirlwind flew apart without warning, and the hybrids hid beneath the haze of the morning air, back to business as usual as if their world had gone uninterrupted. My butterfly hopped off my ring and flew to a nearby flower just sprouting from the ground.

Behind the haze, I could make out a dark cloud floating in my direction. I froze with fear. Had the dark ones found me and taken me here? But it was so beautiful here. Nothing like the dark place Amary and I had been trapped in.

As the cloud moved closer, I could make out a celestial light in the center. I watched it in amazement as it took my mother's form. I didn't move, fearing any slight shift would make her disappear. Her essence immediately joined with mine and made me feel whole once again. Her face lit up as she finished her approach and stopped only a few feet in front of me.

I wanted to touch her, but I waited patiently for her to explain why she had come. In life, she seemed otherworldly. Now, here in this reality, it just magnified her inner beauty even more.

"The ring helped you find me," she said kindly.

I rubbed the ring. "I guess," I said unsure. "How did I get here in this dress?"

"This place and that dress are for your ascension tonight."

She didn't really answer my question, but I accepted it just the same, because she was my mother and I trusted her more than anyone else in existence. "How much time do we have?"

"Not a lot and I'm afraid the reason I'm here may hurt you, but it's time for you to know the truth about my death."

A layer of ice coated my chest, making it impossible to breathe. The last two years had been unimaginably impossible for me because I was always weighted down with guilt of not knowing what happened to her. Hope of one day vindicating her death was the only thing that kept me going through the motions of everyday life. "I know that Dad was there that day."

"Yes, my dear. He was saying goodbye. Something I wish you were able to do. Maybe it would have saved you from so much pain."

"When did you find out you were going to die?"

"I could feel it in my essence. It was fading. I didn't know how much time I had, so I was trying to be with you as much as I could and give you the chance to say goodbye. I was going to tell you."

"Wait, I don't understand. Your essence was fading? But you aren't like Sierra and Hudson. Why would your life just fade? Does that mean you weren't killed?" I was blurting out so quickly that my tongue could barely keep up with my lips to form the words clearly.

My heart was starting to ache, feeling that somehow her death was my fault.

"Shhhhh, my dear."

She reached out her arms, inviting me into her embrace. I obeyed and fell into her. Her familiar fragrance and the safety of her arms filled my senses with happy memories. I couldn't hold back the tears. As much as I wanted to be strong, I just couldn't with her.

"I miss you so much."

She tightened her grip around me and rested her cheek against mine. I could feel her warm breath on my ear as she whispered me into another realm of existence.

"I'll show you now," she said while petting my thick newly groomed hair.

My body felt light as air. I couldn't physically feel my mom holding me anymore, but I knew she was. I was standing within a bright light that I shielded from my eyes. The illusion of my mom's death became visible as the light burnt out. *Oh no, not again.* My heart started racing. I knew what I was about to relive, and it was any wonder how my heart survived these constant revivals. Something was different, though. My mom was lying on the ground, alone. I wasn't standing over her with River as I had seen so many times in the past. Instead, a glow emitted from her body. It swirled around, and I tracked it as it raced to the butterfly circle where River and I were. The light joined with the butterflies as they trapped us inside the eye of the tornado. As the light faded from the butterflies, my body started to glow and then dispel as my skin absorbed it. I was in a state of disbelief as I watched.

I had finally learned the truth of my mom's death. I killed her! This was it. All my hope had been falsified, and I no longer wanted to live. There was nothing worth living for if it meant I had to live with the guilt of my mom's murder. I was still paralyzed in shock. The only sign of physical life came from the tears that escaped down like a rushing a river. I was physically still here, but all signs of life inside me had died in this one earth shattering moment. I wanted to scream, run, do something other than stand here frozen in time facing what was, up until now, the worst moment of my life. I guess they were one in the same now. Why was I still here? I slammed my eyes shut, and my body finally went limp and fell to the ground.

When I opened my eyes again, it was as it was when I woke up just moments ago. My cheek rested on the soft beds of grass with the dried mud still between my toes. Where was my mom? I jumped up quickly and spun in circles, surveying everything for any signs of her. She was gone, and everything was unchanged.

Was it just a dream, or had she really been here? Maybe there was still a shred of hope that I didn't kill her. The thought went straight to my heart and chiseled away at the essence that gave me life. A sudden gust of wind picked up and carried a message in the disguise of my mom's voice. "I'm so sorry, my dear."

I collapsed to my knees, not caring if I ruined the beautiful gown that was bestowed upon me by God knows who. *It was real. I had killed her!* My chest burned as I choked back uncontrollable tears. The only reason I existed was because of her. She had carried me in her womb, taught me the ways of the world, protected me from danger, and loved me unconditionally, all for me to take her life, so I could what? Live? Ascend?

Or was I going to die tonight? Maybe that was the ascension. Or maybe the shadow stalkers killed me. I could feel the darkness eating me from the inside out. While the outside of me still pulsed with inconceivable energy, inside was rotting. I was rotting, and I was numb. The unknown no longer scared me. Fear would mean I could still feel, and I didn't. No fear, no hate, no love, no hope.

My mom had died because of me, a choice she never made, and now I would never be the same Arie again. My innocence stripped, my sorrow wiped away, and my walls impenetrable. I buried my head into my knees and pounded the anger out of me until my fists felt raw. I was still invincible, so the only scars I made were unseen and only for my own private misery.

River seemed to be alluding to some sort of battle brewing, and I could only assume I was in the middle of it with all the fuss that was being made over me. How Amary fit into all of this was still a complete mystery to me, but I needed something to focus on.

My mother's death was to save me, so I would not let the importance of her death go unnoticed or unappreciated. I would fulfill my destiny, and then I would release myself to the essence of the world and be free of all my pain, guilt, and emptiness. What the world chose to do with it was of no concern to me. There would be nothing left of me but a glowing ball of light much like an exploding planet, free of everything and shooting pieces back into the universe to consume.

The tears had stopped, and my chest loosened, allowing oxygen to breathe life into my lungs. I felt defeated and hardened. My mission was on autopilot, controlled by an emotionless vessel. I stood up and mechanically brushed the dirt from my dress, tied my hair up into a knot, and headed back to the village that now I knew instinctively how to find.

Chapter Twenty-Five

Stomping through the forest felt much different now than it had only hours ago. So much had been lost because of me. My protective shell of numbness shielded my physical and emotional state of awareness, which also numbed the effects of my rapidly approaching ascension. I didn't feel the prickles of electricity on my skin nor the natural energy of the forest.

As my legs scratched past thorny bushes, I looked down to see they were leaving their mark on me whereas before they hadn't. Somehow my emotions were closely linked to the effect this reality had on me and since I had given up, so had it, offering no protection and leaving me vulnerable. The sun was high above the sky, so there were less than twelve hours before the full moon was at its peak and when I would meet a fate that had been planned out for me long before I was alive.

For the first time in my life, I felt completely lost. I let my body lead the way as I blankly followed.

A sound charging toward me had me battling between running for my life or confronting whatever it was. Before I could decide, Ashe ran through the trees, grabbed my hand, and dragged me behind him as he continued running. "Ashe, stop!" I tugged my arm free and felt the fresh bruises forming. "What are you doing?" He stopped and tried to pick me up.

"We have to go," he said calmly but insistent.

I struggled against his efforts. "Stop it! Leave me alone!" I pushed him hard against the chest. He caught my wrists and spun me around so my back was pressed up against his chest with his arms holding me tightly. "Let me go, Ashe!" I tried to struggle again, but he was too strong, and I was too tired to fight anymore. I was exhausted and ready for this to be over.

"Stop fighting me," he whispered into my ear.

A shadow emerged onto us, quickly followed by several others. The shadow of the first one disappeared and revealed a young, tall, strong, dark haired man with a menacing look in his eyes. The other shadows hid their contents as they hung in the background.

"Good job, Ashe. That wasn't so hard. Perhaps we should have shown her the monster she is sooner."

His evil smirk made me want to spit in his face, but Ashe held me with an immobilizing death grip. "What is he talking about, Ashe?" He didn't dare to turn me around and face my emerging rage.

"Aw, somebody looks hurt. But wait, I thought you had given up?"

He moved closer to me, so this time I took the opportunity to spit at him. It was just short of his face and landed on his black shirt.

"Tell her, Ashe. Tell her how you were planted in both realities to watch her for us by gaining her trust and eventually her love."

As if my heart couldn't take anymore, the blood seemed to stop flowing to it, and the beats slowed down. I was struggling to find the words that could capture what I was feeling.

"I'm sorry, Arie. I wanted to tell you, but…"

I cut him off. "Let me guess. You couldn't," I said harshly and with every ounce of hate any one person could muster.

My anger was cut short by an evil laugh.

"So it is as the fates want it to be. Ashe and Arie together. It's sad really. Two hearts meant to be together yet can't be."

"What's he talking about, Ashe?" I asked sharply.

"You're asking the wrong person, Arie. Don't you remember me? Your good old friend, Pyrrhus? And here I thought you were gone for good and then I found you. A little girl in a new life playing with her little friends at school."

The memory of the shadow in the forest approaching me when I was hiding at school on my seventh birthday flashed in my head. "That was you?"

"It was. What a wonderful little life you had until you killed your mother."

He bit at my weakness. "And the other times? Were those all you?"

"Yes, you were your weakest in that reality. It was the best time to take you. Too bad your friends caught on before I could," he hissed as he stood only inches from my face, sending horrific terror through my soul.

Ashe was still holding my arms tightly. "Run," he whispered into my ear. He let me go, and I flew past him, away from what I could only assume were the dark ones. The pain of betrayal seeped in and lifted the emotional veil while fear pumped through my veins. My feet took flight and allowed me to run faster than I ever thought imaginable. I could hear a wind blowing behind me and trees falling over. They were destroying the forest as they gave chase. Would I be fast enough?

My ring began glowing fiercely, and my dress sparkled as if it stole all the stars from the night sky. I didn't know what was happening, but I felt light as air and stronger than a mother's bond. I was being protected. A breeze whipped past me, and Pyrrhus stood in front of me, bringing me to an abrupt halt.

"That wasn't very nice. I wasn't finished reminiscing about the good old days." I backed up, but caught a glimpse of the other shadows enclosing around me.

"All dressed up with nowhere to go. And I am fancying that ring."

His focus on my ring made me very uncomfortable. I hid it with my other hand. "You can't have it or me."

Laughing louder, he said, "Oh, really? Looks like you don't have a choice about either."

He was right, but I wasn't going to just hold up my arms and surrender, so as he got closer, I kicked him in the groin. He stood undaunted. Was he invincible here, too? He laughed louder.

"You amuse me, child. It's too bad we only have a short time together."

His touch on my arm burned like a blue flame. I screamed out in agony, followed by tears of pain as I fell to my knees. My scream echoed through the forest, and within a second, his hand was ripped off mine, and he hit a tree hard at least a hundred feet away. Men and women broke out of the other shadows and poised to fight, and here I was in the middle of it all. Did I even really know how to throw a punch correctly so I didn't break a finger? And would it even matter? My kick did nothing to Pyrrhus but entertain him.

When I spun around to locate him, he popped up next to me and reached out to grab me again. I flinched, remembering the crippling pain he inflicted just seconds ago. River suddenly appeared behind him and kicked him away from me.

"River!" He found me. Oh God, what if he was hurt because of me. Or worse. He wasn't like everyone else here. Hell, I didn't know what he was. The other shadow stalkers started to ascend on him. I had to do something. Just as one of them was about to lunge for me, I was flying across the ground away from the fighting. Arms wrapped around me, held me tightly as we watched the fight from afar. I knew it was Ashe. "Let me go, you coward. I have to help River."

"Calm down. He has help," he whispered.

I looked up and saw my dad and many other people from the village throwing punches and invisible lightning bolts that threw their opponents aside without touching them. It was chaotic and terrifying. I frantically searched the jumble of bodies for River. I saw him battling it out with Pyrrhus. Trees had been demolished in the fight and left a clearing. River was on the furthest side from me. I couldn't tell who was winning, but River looked pretty beat up, and Pyrrhus appeared untouched. "You have to help him, Ashe. Please." I was pleading with him now, but I knew if he was from here, he would fare much better against him than River.

"Do you promise you will stay here?"

"I promise. Please, just help him." He released me and was gone in a flash and joined River in the fight. My dad was fighting two people closer to me, and the rest were a blur. It was almost like watching a formal celebration as everyone waltzed across the dance floor.

I locked eyes on River and watched as he spit up blood, but stood up and continued fight. I had to cover my mouth to keep from letting out an anguished cry at the sight of him. He was losing, badly, but he said he would die protecting me if that's what it took. I hoped I was not witness to that now.

Ashe grabbed Pyrrhus before he could deliver what could have been a final blow to River. He tossed him into a bush and jumped on top of him. I couldn't see what was happening, but suddenly, they both retreated along with all the other shadow stalkers. I didn't waste any time rushing over to River. He was on the ground, bruised and bloody, but he was sitting up, which was a good sign, I think. I kneeled down in front of him and put his face in my hands as I surveyed his injuries. His eyes burned with pain other than physical.

"I thought I was going to lose you," he said.

I fought back the tears. "I thought I was going to lose *you*." I gently kissed his cheekbone where a knot was growing. He put his arm around my neck and pulled me in close. I inhaled his pain, love, and anger all in one universal breath.

"Thank you," Tivon said as he joined us. "Thank you for fighting with us, River. You could have died, and it proves to me how much you are willing to sacrifice for my daughter."

I peeled myself off him and confronted my father, enraged. "How could you let him come? How could you let him fight against... I don't even know what to call them! He's not like you! Here his injuries are just as real as where we come from. He can die!" I couldn't contain my anger. All the betrayal and fury and hate I was feeling spilled out all over my father.

"Arie, he tried to keep me from coming. I refused." He stood up.

"River, what were you thinking?" My tone came down a few octaves.

"I told you that I would never fail you no matter what."

I didn't know what to do with all my engorged emotions and conflicting feelings. There were too many eating at me and consuming my sanity. I wanted my wall back, but I knew better now. It had made me vulnerable and allowed *them* to find me. So, I raised my face to the sky, and I screamed. I screamed louder than any normal person could. I screamed to the unrisen moon, to the protective forest, and to my mother's memory. I screamed for River's pain and for Ashe's betrayal. I screamed for me. When I was done, I could feel every pair of eyes in the vicinity staring at me as if I commanded them to. I unapologetically faced my father, waiting for judgment.

"Do you feel better now?" River asked from behind me.

"It wasn't to make me feel better. It was to stop the noise in my head."

"I know so much of this has been hard on you and hard for your human mind to handle, but things will feel different after tonight." Tivon was trying, but all I wanted to know was the truth about everything.

"Is it true about my mom?"

River chimed in, "What about your mom?"

"I killed her," I said as strongly as I could.

"What? That's ridiculous!"

"No, she's right River, but you didn't kill her Arie."

River took my hand in his to comfort me for what I was about to hear and what he was about to learn about me. Would he still die to protect me after he found out what a monster I really was? That's what Pyrrhus called me. *A monster.*

"You didn't have a choice in the matter of your mom's life or death. When I chose her, I didn't know she would die when you came of age, just like I didn't know she was the other half of my essence. The day she died I went to say goodbye, but also to apologize to her. Will you let me show you?"

I nodded as he reached out his hand for me. I released my hand from River's and took my father's.

Again, I was catapulted into my worst nightmare, but this time voluntarily. Tivon stood over my mother's barely breathing body holding her hand and caressing her hair from her forehead. A tear fell from his eye and landed on the ground next to her ear. I could feel his pain as if I was him. His despair matched the despair I felt that day. He was broken. He spoke softly to her.

"I'm so sorry, my love. I didn't know this was your fate," he said.

"Shhhhh, Teve. I wouldn't change a thing. Arie is the most precious gift you could have given me and has completed my journey here. I didn't know what love was until I met you and had our child. She saved me, and one day she will save you from this pain, too. It is as it should be."

"I don't want to say goodbye, my love. Knowing you were here living was just enough to get me through the misery of being apart from you, but this…"

"Teve, nothing is forever. You taught me that, remember? Our story isn't finished. You must live for Arie now. Protect her, love her, and be there for her. And somehow I know that one day we will all be together again." She struggled to breathe.

"I love you, Ariana." He kissed her forehead and then was gone.

When I opened my eyes, I could see the pain my father had just relived with me. "Why didn't you just tell me instead of putting yourself through that again?"

"I could never *tell* you how much your mother means to me."

I knew he was right. I needed to feel his love for her to truly believe.

He dropped my hand gently. "We need to get prepared for tonight. This will not be the last time they try to stop the ascension."

He glided away to regroup with the others. I turned back to River. "Are you okay?"

"I should be asking you that."

"Do you see any bruises on me?" I retorted.

"Maybe not on the surface."

He was right. I was black and blue on the inside, and I wasn't sure when or if that would ever heal.

"His vision didn't release me from the responsibility of my mom's death. I'm still the reason she's gone. Whether intentional or not, it's still a burden I will always carry."

"Are you ready to go?" Tivon asked.

"Yes." I followed them silently through the forest back to the village with River protectively at my heels.

Chapter Twenty-Six

Before we had completely covered the distance from the end of the village to my father's house, Amary was running toward us. Her beautiful hair flew behind her, and her angelic face was lit up, not by the moon, but instead, by a pure innocent joy that only lived in the souls of a child. The purple in her dress sparkled with sequins reflecting the light from the night sky. It was stunning against her light skin.

She jumped up and threw her hands around my neck. "You're back! I missed you!"

I squeezed her back. It felt good to be loved so innocently. This was what I was missing being an only child. I didn't have the adoration or trust of a sibling although I had dreamed what it would be like on many occasions. Starling was a close second, but that certain unconditional love you could only get from family was absent. The kind of love that transcended friendship, hate, love, tragedy, and time. No matter what, you would be connected for better or for worst. "I missed you too, little buggie."

"Your dress is beautiful."

"Thank you, so is yours." She was wearing one similar to mine. I set her down, and she smiled unconcerned and held my hand all the way back to the house. The people that accompanied us back from my retrieval had dispersed among the village until it was just Amary, Tivon, River, and me when we arrived at the house. The familiar buzz crept across my skin as we passed over the threshold into the house.

Amary let out a giggle. "That tickles."

"You felt that?" I asked her.

"Yes, and it tickles every time."

I guess I can see where it could tickle. "What are we feeling when we walk in here? It feels similar to the feeling I got..." I stopped abruptly when I realized I was admitting to Ashe being at my dad's sanctuary. Tivon shot me an ashamed glare. I cowered guiltily.

"Feel what?" River asked.

Tivon addressed him. "I have naturally occurring organic alarms that recognize my essence line. It makes us aware of when someone outside of that enters."

Essence line? But Amary felt it, too. I went to open my mouth, but Tivon lifted his finger and shot me a look that spoke loud and clear. I stood quietly.

"Let's join the others out back," Tivon commanded.

When he spoke, you listened.

We all trailed behind him and filed out onto the porch. The sun was halfway down the sky now. It wouldn't be long before it set, and the full moon made its ascent. This might be the last time I would see its beauty light up the sky and its energy fill me with peace. Outside, kids still played in the river as if nothing had happened while the adults were on high alert. I could feel their uneasiness weighing down the air. There were several dozen, if not more, watching every move I made. It was unsettling.

Tivon bent down to Amary and lovingly told her, "Sweetie, can you please go play with your friends?"

"Okay." She ran down to the riverbed.

He nodded to the adults gathered around, and they knowingly nodded back and dispersed. "Shall we?" He motioned back into the house.

River and I sat down on the couch together, and Tivon sat in a chair across from us.

"Are you hurt, Arie?" I read the apprehension all over his face.

"No, but River is. We should get him some help." I looked over at him. His bruises were ripening, and the knot on his cheek doubled in size.

"I'll be fine." He brushed it off.

"That's not what I meant," Tivon added.

Oh. He was talking about my mother. "If I'm being honest, no. I'm not okay, but I needed to know what happened." I just never imagined it would be my fault, but I kept that to myself. I would carry that pain secretly with me until the end of my days. No one will ever let me believe it was my fault, but I knew the truth.

"River, would you mind leaving us, please?" Tivon asked.

He got up and joined Amary. I wondered where Star was.

"She went back," Tivon answered.

I was startled. I could have sworn I just thought that, but I must have said it out loud.

"No, you thought it. When you're here, I can hear your thoughts."

"And you're just now telling me this?" I felt uneasy now.

"That's why I didn't tell you before. It's *unsettling* having someone else in your head." He winked.

It didn't go unnoticed that he plucked that word from my thoughts, too. "I guess that's fair, but is there a way you could not, please?" I asked softly.

"Sure."

"So, you said Star went back. You mean back home?"

"Yes, she doesn't belong here. She's not like you or River."

"Right, she's like my mom."

"Yes." He looked at me oddly.

"If she's like them, is she... am I going to..." I could feel the panic fill my chest and the knots tighten in my stomach.

"You only take what you need, and that's for the universe to decide. You have no control over the fate of the others. I'm sorry."

"Things just keep getting worse. Why was I created if all I do is destroy?" He stayed quiet. "That wasn't a rhetorical question."

"I know, but there's no easy way to explain what your purpose is. You'll know everything you need to know tonight. I promise."

"You said Amary is in our blood line."

"Is that a question?"

"Yes."

"Do you know how you were created?"

"Ummm, is this that awkward father-daughter talk because I am way past that."

He started laughing loudly. "No, my child. I'm well aware of your knowledge of the creation of life. My question was do you know how you were created?"

"No."

"But you do know how you died here?"

"I know that I died, but I don't know how. Do you?"

"Unfortunately, no, I don't. I found you as you saw, lying in the grass under the full moon. That was before your mom. Losing you was the worst pain I had ever felt. I died with you that day. In my irrational moment of despair, I took your essence before the universe could, and I hid it within me. Then, I went to your mother's reality and scoured the earth until I met her. I knew she was the one. I placed my hand on her belly and trusted her with your essence, never telling her the truth. I had broken many natural laws by stealing your essence and doing what I did. I had a small span of time to recreate you in another reality before my body would consume it for itself as is our natural way."

I was speechless. Not only was he my father in the only reality I remembered, but he was also my true creator here.

"I know that's a lot to take in at once, and I know there is still so much more you want to know, but I think you need to rest some and I need to attend to some things for tonight," he said as he stood up and leaned over me and kissed me on the head. "I'm glad you're safe in my home once again, Arie. How I have missed you."

He walked out of the room to some other part of the house and left me to process. So many things had become clearer, but I still wasn't sure what role Amary played in all of this. I assumed what I saw in my vision was my dad taking River's essence, which he implanted in Sierra. I needed to talk to River before tonight.

Thinking about him brought Star to the forefront of my thoughts. I would one day carry the weight of her death as well. The closest thing to a sister I would ever have and I would be responsible for her demise. Would I even get to say goodbye, or would she die somewhere and her essence would just find me wherever I was? Sierra and Hudson were different, and their time was done when I turned eighteen to give me strength for the ascension, but when would I *need* Star? I cringed at the thought.

A beautiful young woman with the same golden eyes as all the other inhabitants here introduced herself.

"Hello, I'm Sage. It's so lovely to meet you."

"Hi, I'm Arie." I stood up and held out my hand.

Giggling, she said, "Yes, I know." She hugged me. "If you will follow me, I can show you to your room where you can rest."

She didn't wait for an answer. We walked down a long hallway.

"This is Amary's room," she said as we passed a door on the right.

We stopped at the last door in the hallway. She cracked the door open for me and stepped aside.

"It was nice meeting you, Arie," she said as she headed back down the hall.

I turned back to the door and pushed it open. *What!* It was my bedroom from home. Everything was exactly the same from the furniture, curtains, paint color, sheets, and the attached bathroom. The only difference was the view. Instead of the meadow, it was the riverbed. I spotted something on the bed and ran over to it. It was the blanket my mother had given me. I brushed the embroidery with my hand and then picked it up and hugged it. It even smelled like home. This made everything here seem so permanent already. The thought of not seeing Star again made me sad, and I still didn't know River's fate. Amary interrupted before my thoughts took a turn for the worse. She came running in and jumped onto the bed.

"Is this like your room at home, too?"

I loved her innocent happiness. "It is. What about your room?"

"Do you want to see?" she asked pleadingly with a huge smile.

"I would be honored." She jumped off the bed and grabbed my hand, pulling me impatiently with her. Her eagerness and strength made me laugh. We were in the hallway at her door in no time. Before she opened the door, she gave me a huge smile. She was so happy here, but I knew at some point she was going to ask about her mom again, and I would need to tell her the truth.

She pushed open her door and ran inside and jumped onto her bed, scooping up a giant-sized giraffe and snuggling into it.

"This is Giraffy."

I sat next to her. "Well, hello there. It's nice to meet you." I patted its head. Her room was enchanting. Her mom wasn't kidding when she said she loved fairies. The walls and ceiling were painted as an enchanted forest with fairies hidden among it. What was strange was the forest looked strikingly similar to the forest here with the oversized tropical flowers and giant trees. "Did your mom paint this?"

"Uh huh."

"It's beautiful."

"Looks like here, huh? All fairytales must have the same forest," she said innocently.

"They must. Your mom is an incredible artist. My mom was, too."

"Where is she?"

I sighed deeply. I didn't know if I was ready for this talk right now. "She got very sick and is no longer with us." *Please don't ask me how. Please, please, please.*

"Oh, my grandma got really sick too, and my mom said she went to heaven to be with my grandpa, and we would all be together again one day."

"One day," was all I could say. She scooted over to me and gave me a big hug. I wrapped my arms around her as my mom had done so many times in the past, and I squeezed her close to me. I looked up to see River standing in the doorway.

"Sweetie, I'm going to go talk to River in my room. Did you want me to tuck you in for a nap?"

"Okay," she said excitedly.

She crawled to the top of the bed and scurried under the sheets. I put Giraffy next to her since there was plenty of room on her full-sized bed and gave her a kiss on the forehead. "I'll come get you in a little bit."

"Okay."

She wrapped her arms around her stuffed friend and closed her eyes. I envied her for being able to sleep so peacefully. River moved out of the way as I closed her door, and he followed me down the hall to my room. I moved aside to let him go inside first.

"Wow, this looks exactly like your room at home." He leaned up against the door frame.

I filtered in behind him. "I know. I haven't decided if it's weird or thoughtful. On one hand, I know he wants me to feel at home here, but on the other hand, it solidifies the permanence of my new residence," I said sadly. I sat on the edge of my bed and buried my head in my knees.

"Do you know about Star?"

He stayed close to the doorway. To be fair, I hadn't invited him inside. I peeked up, "You can come in, you know." He inched in and sat on a chair close by. Once he got comfortable, I answered him. "Tivon told me she needed to go home."

"She wouldn't survive here. Her essence is too different. It can't sustain the basic necessities her body needs to live. She didn't leave without a fight. When word got out that you were missing, we all feared the worst. She wasn't strong enough to stay any longer, though. She would have died."

"So, she left not knowing if I was okay?" The guilt kept piling on. Had I never run away I would never have been in danger. Now, she was at home worrying about me. "I have to talk to her. I have to show her that I'm okay." I was begging.

"Even if you could, there's not enough time before the full moon is directly above us. In her heart, she will feel that you're alive."

"Alive, but not necessarily if I'm okay. It's just not good enough, River. I can't do that to her. I've already put her through so much." I stood up and headed for the door. River bolted in front of me.

"Where are you going?" he demanded.

"Ewwww. Don't talk to me like that." I tried to push him out of my way. "Are you kidding me, River? Get out of my way. I need to talk to my father." He did not budge.

He put his arms on my shoulder. "Arie, you need to listen to me very carefully. You need to rest for tonight. I promise I will make sure that she knows you're really okay."

I knew he would. He had never given me a reason to not believe in him. I was still pouting, though. He shook my shoulders just enough to get my attention.

"I promise."

For the first time since we started our little chat, I got to inspect his injuries from the fight up close. He looked much better. His knot had drastically reduced in size, and the bruises had already turned to yellow. I touched his cheek where the knot was. "How are you healing so quickly?"

He shied away from my hand. "It's this place. I might not be invincible, but my cells turnover at an accelerated rate, allowing the healing process to be faster."

"Yeah, I would say." I thought about that for a minute. If his cells were accelerated, did that mean he was aging quicker, too? "How long can you stay here?" I asked apprehensively.

"Long enough to make sure you get through tonight and are safe."

My heart sank. I would be saying goodbye to him in less than twenty-four hours. This was the little boy next door who ran around the meadow, sat in the butterfly circle with me staring at the stars, the young man who gave me my first kiss and was my first love and the man who I would leave alone in another reality with no mother or father. The only comfort I had was in knowing he would have Star. At least until the day my essence called upon hers to forfeit her life.

This whole thing was so screwed up. Either way I would be hurting the people I loved, so why not just go back to how things were before all this chaos started? "I'm not going to do it. I can't, River. Any way you look at this scenario people get hurt because of me, so I just want to go home and pretend none of this happened. I want to go back to Star and my house and the bookstore and you, River. I want to go back and be with you. Forever. I love you." Tears filled his eyes, but refused to fall.

"You have no idea how long I have been waiting for you to say that. To make a choice."

"I do know. I saw us, here, when we were a part of this world. You sacrificed your life here in this enchanted paradise free from pain to be with me. Now, I want to sacrifice something for you. I want to go back."

"You can't, Arie. Much like your father and Ashe, all you can do is visit and that's so limited over my life span in that reality. You aren't like me, and you aren't like them. You're special, and tonight, we'll all understand how much you're needed here."

He pulled me in and gave me what felt like a goodbye hug. "You're going to be there tonight, right?"

"I wouldn't miss it for the world."

We stood there for a long time soaking in the finality of the moment. I didn't know if I had made a choice for my heart, out of Ashe's betrayal, or because this was my last chance to, but my vessel was starting to hollow again. It was almost easier to live numbly, but here it was lethal.

I couldn't allow myself to check out. I needed to be strong for my mom, Tivon, River, Star, Amary, and myself. They all had sacrificed so much for this moment to happen, and I couldn't disgrace that kind of honor. He pulled away, breaking the unseen thread holding us together.

"I need to go, and you need to rest. I'll see you soon."

He kissed my head and turned to leave. My heart was racing, and my body was fidgeting with desperation and desire. "River, wait." As he turned back around to face me, I planted a sensual kiss on his lips. A kiss of love, lust, agony, heartache, and goodbye. He reciprocated the intensity, pushing his hands into the small of my back and lifting my feet off the ground. We were both still pure of heart, body, and soul, and I wanted to give that to him now if this was truly our last moment alone together. I knew he felt what I wanted, but he pushed away. He stroked my face as he hungrily took me in.

"I love you, Arie."

He kissed me softly and then left. My body slouched in response to the unintentional rejection. He was saving me in every way possible, keeping me innocent for as long as he could. I imagined tonight would change everything. It would change me.

As if my body knew it needed to refuel for tonight, it became heavy. I fell back onto the bed that mirrored my own, pulled my mother's blanket over me, and closed my eyes. My thoughts traveled to the battle over me, to the moment Ashe jumped on Pyrrhus who seemed to be leading the shadows. What did Ashe do or say to make them give up so easily, and why did he do it? It was hard to believe he loved me underneath all the lies and deceit unless he had a good reason. Maybe he was doing it all to protect me, or maybe he was just trying to move up in ranks on the other side. Whatever it was, it didn't change the fact that I couldn't trust him after what he did, and without trust, there couldn't be love.

My thoughts got fuzzy and muddled and eventually went silent.

Chapter Twenty-Seven

The quiet when I woke up was haunting. When I had fallen asleep, it was still light out, and I could hear the children's laughter outside. It was dark now and not a sound came from outside. I rubbed the sleepiness from my eyes and urged myself upright.

I wondered if Amary was still sleeping. I crawled out of bed, still a little unsteady on my feet and tiptoed to the door. It was silly, but I felt like I was a kid again, sneaking passed my mom's door to get a midnight treat. On many occasions she had caught me, and instead of punishing me, she would laugh and join me. The memory made me smile. I hoped I held onto those moments forever.

I opened the door quietly and was immediately confronted by Sage. I was a little startled by her presence.

"Did you have a nice nap?" she asked sweetly.

"Yes, thank you. I was just going to check on Amary."

"Oh, okay, let me take you to her."

Well, at least she didn't say no. That's usually what happened in the books I read in these kinds of bizarre scenarios. I was actually kind of expecting that, but relieved when I didn't get that response. In the books or movies, it was usually the moment the character realized they had actually been kidnapped rather than brought there out of their own free will. Sage led me to Amary's door and cracked it open.

"I'll be out here when you're ready."

Amary was on the floor playing with her fairy dolls with her back toward me.

"Hey, buggie."

"Arie," she squealed gleefully.

She jumped up and hugged me.

"Come play with me," she said as she dragged me over to the fairies.

"Sure, buggie." She was still wearing the dress from earlier as was I. Her hair was a mess from napping, so I snagged a brush off her little vanity before I sat down. "Would you mind if I brushed your hair?"

"Please. My mom usually does it. Do you know when she will be here?"

Daggers in the heart again. This was the first time she asked about her mom since we came here. She needed to know, but I didn't know what words to use for little four-year-old ears. How could I make her understand without her losing the light that brightens a room? I brushed her hair as I tried to form the right words. I didn't realize how thick her hair was. It was perfect like a little princess. "Buggie, has anybody told you why you are here or how you got here?"

"No, I'm just glad you're here with me."

She melted my heart with her innocent words. "I'm glad you're here, too." She continued to play with her fairies as I brushed her hair mindlessly just to give my hands something to do at this point. "Did they tell you I was... different?"

"Tivon told me you were special."

"Okay, special. Did he also mention that you are special, too?"

"He said I belonged here with them. That there was something special inside me that told him this was my home."

"That's right," I replied.

"Is my mom special like us, too?"

I put down the brush and picked her up onto my lap. "Your mom will always be special to you, but no, she's not like us."

"Does that mean she can't come live here with us?"

"Unfortunately, no, she can't, but she will always be your mom."

"But I miss her," she sniffled.

"When you miss her, just remember she's alive within you, through your memories and in your heart, okay, buggie?"

"Is that what you do when you miss your mommy?"

She was rubbing away the tears as they fell. I hugged her. "That's exactly what I do." I was trying hard to not join her in crying. I needed to be strong for her.

There was a knock on the door as it cracked open.

"It's time to get ready," Sage said.

I gave Amaryllis another hug, lifted her off my lap, and joined Sage at the door. "I'll see you soon, buggie."

"Okay." She smiled through swollen eyes.

I closed the door behind me as I watched her sit back down and play solemnly with her dolls again.

"What do I need to do to get ready for the ascension?"

"I'll take it from here, Sage. Thank you." Tivon appeared in the hallway, and Sage retreated.

"She mentioned getting ready for tonight?"

"Only you know if you're ready or not," he said.

"Since I have no idea what to be ready for, I guess I'm ready."

He chuckled. "There is much truth in that, my child. To be honest, your ascension is special, so no one knows what to expect. There are some things you do need to know, though. Follow me."

We went to the back patio where it was quiet for the first time. "Did everyone go home?"

"Yes, we have a curfew at sunset. We're safer during the day. The other ones that you call shadow stalkers move more freely at night, so we take the extra precaution."

"It must be hard living like this." I could only imagine living in a world where I never felt safe walking around at night. The beauty of the stars and moon would be a great loss.

"It didn't always used to be like this."

"Oh, really?"

"We all used to follow the light of our essence. It only took one event to reveal that deep within our essence there hides a darkness that feeds on the weak. The weak being those who have given into their emotions and given up on themselves. It consumes you. I don't really fault them for who they have become. Things took place out of their control and broke them. They lost their way and haven't been able to make it back."

"What was this event that changed the way of your world?"

"Your death, my child."

It *always* came back to me. What could I have possibly done to bring that much darkness out of a person to make them kill me? Tivon broke the silence.

"I'm sorry, but you need to know why you are here and why tonight is so important."

"Why would someone kill me?"

"Jealousy, hatred, greed, love."

"Did you just say 'love'?" *What was he saying?*

"Love is a powerful emotion. It drives people to do crazy things when it's not reciprocated. And you my child, were always well loved by all, and even more so by several boys. They all vied for your attention in different ways, but when one of them realized you had found your match and it wasn't him, the darkness was released."

"All of this is because of love or lack thereof?"

"You make it sound so much simpler than it is. Our reality is one of purity, peace, and tranquility. There is another reality full of darkness as is nature's way of keeping balance. Your reality is a combination of both. To have darkness here upsets that balance and can shatter the veils of all the realities and wreak havoc everywhere. It's my job to restore balance since you're my daughter. Only the one who darkness was brought upon can restore it. We are nature spirits, and this is our purpose."

When I said I wanted to know, I didn't realize I would be told all of this was my fault, and I was the only one who could fix it. I wasn't a damn superhero! I was an eighteen-year-old girl without a mother, a confused heart, and a little girl who needed me. It was a bit overwhelming. "Why is Amary here?"

"I split your light into two vessels just in case."

"Sure, okay, I get it. Insurance. But she's fourteen years younger than me."

"Yes. When I met her mom, she was only sixteen and newly pregnant. I felt her essence and knew she was another one like your mom. While she was sleeping, I gave her the rest of your essence by touching her belly as I had done with your mother. Unfortunately, the baby died. I thought your essence had, as well, but I knew when the dark ones brought her here it had waited for her mom to have another baby. Unfortunately, they found out before I did, because they were actively watching you. They must have felt Amary's essence when you met at the bookstore."

"Is she in danger?"

"Only until balance is restored. Then, she will be safe and so will you. You both need to be at the ascension since your essence is one. And then when she is eighteen, she will ascend, too."

"That explains why they took her. To separate us."

"Yes. When they realized they couldn't get to you, they took her."

That weighed heavy on me. If I had just let them take me that first time, her mom would still be alive. If she knew that, would she still look at me with adoration? We would do this together, and I would take care of her. I guess I was something of a big sister to her. We shared the same essence, which I believed made us who we were, so in my eyes we were family. I just hoped she could forgive me one day.

Sage interrupted us. "It's time to go," she said hastily and disappeared back into the house.

She returned with Amary. She was still holding onto one of her fairies. She bolted from Sage and ran to me, grabbing my hand anxiously.

"Where are we going?" she whispered.

I bent down to her. "For a little walk. Is that all right?"

She nodded. I kissed her on the head as River had done just a few hours ago. "We're ready. Is River walking with us?"

"Yes, but he will stay out of sight."

The gesture he made with his eyes was understood. Out of sight to protect us. I took a deep breath and nodded that we were ready. We stayed outside and went around until we hit the path through the village. A curfew might have been set in place, but I could feel hundreds of eyes watching us as we trotted by.

Their future rested on two pairs of shoulders. No pressure. At least Amary didn't have to carry that with her. I would carry all the burdens in the world if it meant I could shield her from any kind of darkness any of the realities offered.

The full moon lit our path as it plucked at the energy brewing around Amary and me. I could feel that something had already begun happening.

"What is that?" Amary asked as she rubbed her arm.

"Well, you know how we are special?"

"Yes."

"We are special because the sun and moon give us energy, so it tingles a little bit as it feeds our essence."

"What's 'essence'?"

"You know when something feels right or wrong, like throwing a toy or writing on the wall with a marker?"

"Yeah," she said guiltily.

I giggled at her response. "Our essence is what tells us when to feel that. Does that make sense? Some people call it a soul or their conscience, depending on what they believe in."

"Oh, okay. The little voice that says good or bad."

"Exactly and the sun and moon makes that feeling stronger, so we know better when something is good or bad." She must have understood or at least accepted my explanation because she got quiet for the rest of the walk.

We completed the journey in less than fifteen minutes. It seemed a lot longer earlier. Tivon's sudden stop in front of us startled me, so I pulled Amary close. He turned and stepped aside.

"This spot is sacred, and only you two can enter. What you see in there is for your eyes only. You will be safe. There are many of us surrounding the circle."

I nodded and kept Amary close to me as we shuffled passed Tivon. He pulled aside the humungous green tropical leaves that served as a doorway into the circle. I touched his cheek tenderly before we entered. "Thank you for giving me a second chance to live. For everything." I released him and pulled Amary through with me. I was not ready for what confronted us.

"Mommy," Amary broke from my hold and ran to her mom who was standing in the center of the circle next to mine.

Both looked as real as the moon high up above. All the moon's rays had focused its attention on this one magical circle not sharing any rays with any other corner of this reality. It was our moon. Our destiny. Our moms. My mom glided to me and embraced me. I couldn't help kneading at her back to see if she was real.

"I'm really here, Arie."

"How is this possible?" I looked her in the eyes in stark befuddlement to confirm she was here.

"I told you that the ring would lead you back to me, and it has," she said through tearful happiness.

"I can't believe you're here." She grabbed my face in her hands as if she was looking me over to make sure nothing had changed.

"You're more beautiful than the day I left you. Stronger, too. Your eyes tell the story of your pain. They also show the purity of your essence. This is what you were meant for. To save everyone. I am so proud of you, Arie, and I love you so very much."

Why did it sound like she was saying goodbye? I looked over at Amary and her mom, giggling and embracing. Was this all a fictitious vision giving us our innermost desire?

"You're not staying, are you?" I searched her eyes for the answer. She didn't need to answer. I already knew. "Is this a cruel joke?" My cheeks burned with anger as tears welled up.

"No, my love, it's not a joke. You need to make a choice." She grabbed my hand in hers.

"A choice? What choice?" Amary and her mother froze as they watched me blazing. I tried to bring it down to a whisper. "What choice, Mom?"

"We can't both stay. You have to choose."

I was speechless, paralyzed, and numb. How could I choose between my mom and Amary's mom? That wasn't a choice! That was a curse! My legs wobbled, and I fell to my mother's feet crying to the earth. "Why?! Why would you do this to me?! You're making me kill her all over again!" I yelled to the world.

My mom knelt next to me and shushed me like she used to when I was a child. "Shhhhh, my love. Everything will be okay. I know you will make the right choice. Just look deep inside and let your essence guide you."

We both knew what I would do, but I couldn't say it. Amary and her mother joined us. Her mother spoke in a reassuring voice.

"It's okay, Arie. She knows that she's special, and I'm not meant to be here. She understands."

I looked at Amary, and the agony and fear in her eyes told a different story. I studied the ground again. "I can't do it." I shook my head as I repeated those words until I found the strength to say it.

I stood up and took my mom's hands in mine. "I love you, Mom. No one will ever compare to your eternal beauty. No one will ever take your place in my heart, and I will remember every moment we spent together, good and bad. I know you will always be with me because you live here in the forest, in the trees, flowers, and butterflies. You live within me." I had managed to keep the tears at bay. "I choose Amary's mom." I heard the surprised sighs from Amary and her mom.

"I'm so proud of you, Arie. I knew you would do the right thing."

As she leaned in to kiss me, she began to fade. I felt her lips touch my forehead as her essence formed a beautiful funnel and swirled into my ring. My body exploded with light and all I felt was peace. I couldn't see anything, and my thoughts were wiped clean. Was this what dying felt like? Peaceful, quiet, and pain free? I felt myself lift off the ground and float toward the moon. I must be dead or dreaming, or was I ascending? A powerful surge of energy traveled from my fingers and toes and met at my core. I couldn't breathe as the force passed through me, and only one thought crossed my mind. This was the end.

Chapter Twenty-Eight

"Is she dead, Mommy?"

I could hear Amary's angelic voice in my head. I still felt as light as a falling snowflake. I managed a grunt as I tried to sit up. The dewy grass felt nice against my hot skin.

"Are you okay?" Amary's mom asked.

Did I even know her name? I picked her over my mom, and I didn't even have a name to put with her face. Reality nibbled on my limbs.

"Mommy, she's moving."

The ground vibrated as feet stomped over to me.

"What happened?"

I recognized the worry in River's voice immediately. "I'm fine." I made eye contact with River to calm him down. "Look, I'm fine."

"Is that..."

I cut him off, "Yes, it's Amary's mom." I turned to them. "I'm sorry, but I don't think I ever got your name."

"Misty," she said as she came closer with Amary.

River looked perplexed. "It's a long story," I told him.

"What you did for me, for us..." She stopped.

Not even she could believe what just happened, that I had chosen her over my own mother. "Please, don't."

She understood.

River helped me get up, but I felt good. Better than good. Physically, I felt like I was the strongest thing in existence.

"Did it work?" I asked River.

"I don't know."

Tivon charged in. "We have to go."

He didn't react to Misty's presence. Did he know I would be faced with this ultimatum? I felt my body heat up with silent fury.

"They're coming. We don't have much time," he said sternly.

"Who's coming? I thought this was supposed to restore balance? Aren't they supposed to, I don't know, disappear or something?"

"They have until sunrise."

"To do what?" I knew the answer before I finished asking it. "To kill us."

"It just takes one," he said gravely as his eyes moved to Amary.

"They wouldn't! Oh my God. They would!"

"Let's go then. Back to the safety of the village," River said as he grabbed me in one hand and Amary in the other.

Misty held onto Amary's other hand, and Tivon protected from behind. "Where are the others who were guarding the circle?"

"They're trying to head them off to give us more time," Tivon said as he urged us forward.

I was worried about Amary and Misty keeping up with us, but they were doing a good job. It didn't take us long to get here, and we were walking then, so we should be back to the village in a matter of minutes. We exited the circle and quickly started down the path.

With every rushed step we took, I could hear the fighting gain on us. Misty was starting to fall back since our speed was faster than a normal human. River kept dragging us, but she let go.

"I can't keep up with you. Please, just go and protect my baby. They don't want me. I'll hide until they are gone."

She was bending over, panting hard. I let go of River's hand and ran to her. "We're not leaving you! Who knows what they will do to you to get to us if they catch you. We'll carry you if we have to." She nodded in agreement, hearing in my voice that I wasn't going to take no for an answer.

I let my mom go so Amary wouldn't have to feel the same pain as I had, so I would guard both of them with my life if I had to. I reached out my hand, and she grabbed it.

"Thank you," she said sympathetically.

"Ready?" She nodded, so I ran alongside her, encouraging her speed by staying a few steps ahead of her, but only enough so she could keep up. A minute seemed like an hour when you were running for your life. I heard shouts in the distance from the side of us and then in front of us.

Oh no, they were cutting us off.

River and Amary were just ahead of us while Tivon stayed behind Misty and me. We were so close to the entrance of the village that I could make out the lights on in the windows of one of the houses, but we were too late. Shadows descended on Misty and me, but River and Amary had made it to safety. I let out a sigh of relief. I stopped quickly, hiding Misty behind me. Tivon jumped in front of me, but we were being surrounded and trapped like prey for a pack of wolves. Would we be picked off one by one, or would they attack at the same time? "Tell me what to do, Tivon."

"Don't get killed."

"I wasn't planning on it."

"Good."

We stood together tightly. Misty was trembling. "Just stay close to one of us, Misty." She didn't respond. I could hear Amary's cries for her mom getting further away as, I imagined, River was finding her a safe place, so he could come back to help us. At least I hoped that was what he was doing. "What happened to everyone else?"

"I don't know," Tivon said solemnly.

My stomach churned as I thought about all the people who just died to save me. "How are they so strong?" People started to break from their shadows. I heard Misty squeal in shock. If we didn't get back up soon, this wasn't going to be much of a fight.

"They get their power from the moon. Full moons, they are the strongest."

"Awesome, of course. Where do we get our power from then?"

"Both, but mainly the sun. That is why we are the safest in the daytime."

Pyrrhus emerged on us arrogantly. "Seems you're outnumbered, Tivon. Hello again, Arie."

The way my name rolled off his tongue like he was seducing each letter made me cringe. Misty pushed against our shoulders as she tried to get as far away from him as possible.

"Is it really true that you don't remember me, Arie?"

"Should I? You aren't much to look at." Although he wasn't hard on the eyes, the evil that reflected in his eyes made him look like a savage beast.

"Quite a tongue you have when the odds are against you."

"If you were going to kill me, I would be dead already." I glared at him.

"Then you should be more frightened. Imagine what I may want to do to you before the sun rises."

I spat at him. I couldn't help it. He brought that out in me.

Tivon interjected, "We'll see who plays with whom."

"I have been waiting a long time for this, Tivon. Maybe I'll keep you alive just long enough for you to see me kill your daughter, again."

The shock hit me like a fist in the face. He was the one I rejected and the one that was the root of all my pain. He was why I was transformed, why my mother died not once, but twice. He was the reason River gave up this charmed life to be with me in the other reality, and now he was stuck there to live out a mortal life alone. The rage built like a storm brewing underwater.

Tivon leveled me down. "Calm down, Arie. Your power is new and unknown."

"Yes, Arie, be careful. You wouldn't want to kill anybody else."

He was trying to rile me up. I took deep breaths and meditated like my mom taught me. I could feel my body stop pulsing with rage.

"Kill the mortal. Leave the other two alive," Pyrrhus commanded his minions.

Tivon and I shoved Misty between us. They couldn't kill her if they couldn't get to her. The shadow stalkers obediently closed in on us. Tivon and I prepared for battle. I kicked the closest one in the throat, launching him out of sight. *Holy crap! Did I just do that?* The confidence built in me as more crowded my space. As one grabbed my arm, I punched another one in the gut pounding him into the ground hard enough to split the earth. I wrenched free from the hold on my arm and elbowed him in the chest as I spun free. Misty was still between Tivon and me.

Tivon was holding his own, but didn't have the strength I had. I wondered how I could be stronger than him. River burst through the trees armed with fighters behind him. They dispersed and took out the shadow stalkers one at a time. It took two of us to fight one of them because their strength was so much more. I made sure Misty stayed glued to my back as I fought them off. There were so many, and they just kept coming. How did so many fall into darkness unnoticed?

River was making progress with the help of fighters on either side of him. My only concern was keeping Misty safe, so I stayed in one place and just fought them as they came at us. Pyrrhus managed to lure Tivon away from us with his taunting, leaving me alone to battle from all sides. I couldn't keep up with how many there were, and they were able to overpower me. It took four of them to hold me back. I was horrified when one of them locked Misty in a tight arm restraint. She whimpered for breath. I screamed out, "Nooooo! Please, let her go, and I'll come with you. I won't fight. Just let her go." The fighting ceased as my plea echoed through the forest like pollen being carried by a breeze. Everyone stood poised for battle, waiting for the next move to present itself. Pyrrhus bellowed with excitement.

"Did you hear that, everyone? She'll come with us if we let this worthless mortal live. That's so noble of you, Arie, but if you look around, you were going to be coming with us either way."

I surveyed the battlefield. We were down many fighters, River was covered in such a bloody mess I could barely recognize him, and Tivon was restrained by two shadow stalkers. *This wasn't happening.* "Please, don't hurt her. I'm begging you."

"Now you beg. It's a little late for that, Arie. You should have accepted me in your first life, and then none of this would have happened. You have the blood of all those fighters on your hands, along with your mother's, River's parents, and this one here. Who knows how many more when our numbers grow to epic proportions. And don't think lover boy here will be immune to my revenge."

My head was spinning. How could I get us out of this? It was hopeless.

"We are wasting time." He walked over to Misty and raised her head by her chin. She remained brave, looking at evil in the face.

"Please, don't do this." I couldn't help the tears from falling. Amary needed her, and my mom gave up a second chance at life for her to live. Misty locked eyes with me.

"Make sure she knows how much I love her."

A moment later, she was limp on the ground, and a dark cloud filled *Pyrrhus'* hand. It surrounded him in a fog of smoke and then seeped into every pore of his body. His face read ecstasy all over it.

"Noooooo!" I heard myself scream, but I felt disjointed from myself. A power from deep within me blew the four shadow stalkers off me. I charged Pyrrhus without even thinking. I could hear Tivon and River yelling for me to stop, but I couldn't. I had to avenge all the lives that he took, including mine. He turned to me, wielding something in his hand. I was moving too fast to make it out. Just I was about to launch on him, Ashe jumped in front of me, sandwiching himself in between us.

"What have you done?" Pyrrhus hissed through his teeth.

The life in Ashe's eyes dimmed as he reached for my cheek and stroked it gently.

"I love you," he said as he dropped to his knees.

I spotted the large dagger protruding from his back covered in blood. Pyrrhus was in as much shock as me. He looked up to the sky and let out a horrid shriek. In a matter of a second, he pulled out the dagger from Ashe's back and flew at me. He pinned me to the ground. His strength was unparalleled. Another kind of evil stared out from his eyes.

"You killed my brother, and for that I will finish you, and then for fun go after the little girl. Think about that as the light fades from your pathetic body."

The shock was just starting to register on my face from hearing that Ashe was this awful man's brother when his touch forced a vision on me.

I was standing in the clearing, admiring the butterflies when *Pyrrhus* approached me. He looked angry and bitter. He grabbed my arm, and I pushed him away. I walked away from him thinking that was the end of it, but then something punctured my lungs. I looked down and saw *the* dagger. The same one that had just killed Ashe.

I snapped out of it and looked straight into his eyes as he held the dagger above my heart ready to plunge it in. "I remember. I remember everything, *Pyrrhus*." I said his name with disdain. "I didn't love you then, and I could never love you now."

I could feel the sun rising before seeing it. The pull it had on me was magical as if we were one. He knew it too from the panic filling his retinas. He tried to ram the dagger into me, but I was stronger now. I wrapped my hand around the dagger and pulled it away from my chest, forcing him off me. Before I could use it on him, he retreated, followed by his followers.

Ashe. I jumped up and ran to his side. It was still dark out, but the sun would be peeking over the horizon any minute. Ashe remained bent over his knees. When I touched his shoulder, he flinched. "Ashe, what did you do?" I whimpered.

He used all his strength to pull up his head and looked at me. "I saved you."

All I could do was cry. Cry for the love we had in another life and for the love we could have had in this one. My heart bled with him. My essence was fueled by his, and it was decreasing by the second. "Fight, Ashe. Fight for us." He fell onto his side and laid his head on my lap.

I frantically searched all the eyes surrounding us until I found Tivon's. "There has to be something we can do, right? Please, tell me there's something."

He looked defeated. "He was wounded by the dagger of life and death. It's not for us to decide. I'm sorry, Arie. You've already lost so much."

I avoided River's stare. I knew this probably hurt him like hell, but in this moment, it was just Ashe and I as I cupped his head in my hand and caressed his temple. My other hand was covering the wound, trying to stop the bleeding. I rested my forehead on his, not caring that my tears were rolling down his face. "Oh, Ashe, we never had a chance, did we?"

"No, I guess not. Nature wasn't ready for our kind of union." I positioned myself carefully, so I could kiss him on the lips. They tasted salty from my tears, but sweet like his essence. The kiss transported me to the moment in River's backyard when a shadow approached me and a hand emerged, causing an explosion of fireworks between us. "That was you?"

"Yes, I had just found you again, and I couldn't resist. It was wrong, but I couldn't stay away from you, so I stopped fighting it. I love you, Arie, in life and death, forever."

My tears covered his face. "I love you, too."

Tivon stepped forward. "We need to go and leave it to nature's will."

He was still now and barely breathing. I didn't want to leave him here to die alone. "I'm not going to just leave him." The first ray of sunlight found his body and surrounded it, pushing me away with its natural energy. Tivon pulled me away as his body rose a few feet off the ground and then manifested into hundreds of butterflies. I screamed out, "Nooooo!" and fell into my father's arms. He was the only thing keeping me from collapsing. I hurt all over. My muscles burned, my heart ached, and my core felt ripped to shreds. Anything was better than this feeling, even death.

Chapter Twenty-Nine

I couldn't remember how I got back to my room in the village, but here I was lying in bed, still wearing my dress, but as clean as I was before the ascension. Another oddity. I was invincible from physical injury and always clean. I stared at my hands that were covered in Ashe's blood not so long ago. I didn't think my heart could hurt this much again, but it did. Only more proof that Ashe and I were meant for each other.

Could someone really live with a part of them dead? Would I be like a zombie walking around and going through the motions, but not really feeling? Tears flowed as I curled in my sheets. There was a light knock on the door. Barely audible, I said, "Come in."

"May I?" Tivon inquired.

He took my sitting up as an invitation and sat down on the edge of the bed.

"I'm sorry, Arie. That was brave of him. I would have never guessed he loved you that much. He truly was your other half."

"I'm sorry it took him dying for me for you to see that," I said bitterly.

"Yes, I do regret how I pushed River on you."

"Don't regret it. I love River. You saw the good in him and were right to want him for me." He turned to me. For the first time, he looked tired. The events had taken their toll on everyone. "How are River and Amary?"

"River is healing. He should be better by morning before he returns home."

Another notch to chisel in my heart. "He has to leave so soon?"

"He's already been here longer than he should have been. He's more like us than Star, but he still needs basic necessities that we can't provide, like food. His essence isn't strong enough to withstand the power here. It could kill him."

"There is so much I still don't know or understand about this place and myself."

"You will learn our ways again and your history here in time."

"How's Amary?"

"She's sleeping. We thought it would be best if her mother's death came from you."

As much as I didn't want to I knew he was right. I was the closest thing she had to a mother now. "How is Amary able to stay here if she hasn't ascended?"

"Because she is part of you and you are part of her. Your presence here sustains her until her ascension when she's eighteen."

"Why butterflies?" I asked.

"Butterflies have always signified long life, and they contain the essence of those that have passed on here. Essence is a part of the universe and can never truly die. It... *we* will always be here in some form or another. You should sleep now. Today will be another hard day on everyone."

He got up and left me alone with my thoughts once again. A hard day for sure. I would have to say goodbye to another loved one and tell Amary her mom was really gone this time. I couldn't go to sleep with all of this looming over me. I went to the window that looked exactly like mine at home except for the view.

The sun had started its ascent, and the rays glistened on the river like a million crushed diamonds. As I scanned the beautiful landscape, I saw River sitting on a large rock overlooking the water. The way he was slouched over told me he was in mourning, too. This would probably be my only chance to talk to him alone before he left.

Even though it was morning, the house was quiet. Everyone was recovering from the long night. Although we were victorious, there would be many hearts mourning the loss of their loved ones today. Many died last night to protect me. *They said I was special, but all I felt was cursed.* I scooted out of bed and went into the bathroom and splashed water on my face, hoping it would wash away some of the dull ache I felt. As I dried my face, I was shocked to see the eyes the mirror reflected were no longer blue. They had become a golden amber, a signature mark of the people of this reality. I had been permanently marked, and now every time I stared at my reflection, I would mourn the loss of the eyes my mother passed down to me. The pain I felt went deeper than the physical, emotional, or psychological. It burned to my core. All I had left were the memories that, as life went on, would fade and be forgotten in the pages of my past.

I tiptoed through the hall and out to the back. As soon as I stepped out of the shade of the patio, the sun found me as if it was searching since its first ray reached the horizon. It energized my body like a battery charged a car. I felt strong, but my heart still felt weak.

If only it could be that easy. I reluctantly wandered to the rock that River perched himself on. The rock was large enough for at least two people if not more, so I climbed up and sat quietly next to him. My presence didn't stir his attention, but we never needed to talk to feel the comfort of just being near each other.

The sparkling water hypnotized me into a welcoming catatonic state as I waited for him to be ready to talk about last night, to say goodbye. He finally broke the silence.

"I have to leave today," he said solemnly without looking over.

"I know." I could feel the tears start in my heart slowly making their way up.

"You know what hurts the most?"

I stayed silent to give him time to say what he needed to.

"Watching the way you broke when *he* died and wondering if that had been me if you would have felt the same way about losing me."

Just hearing that was a slap in the face that I deserved.

"River, my love for you might be different than my love for Ashe, but it's no less. I'm broken without him, but not lost because I still have you."

He finally turned and glanced at me. His eyes were red from crying, the only sign left of his wounds. The universe was able to heal the physical, but I would be the only one that could heal what bruised him deep inside.

"I'm thankful that he saved you, because I can go on living just knowing you're somewhere walking the earth, but I hate him for having the part of you I want the most."

His head hung low as he memorized my face. I put my hand on his temple and clenched at the locks falling in his face and forced his forehead to touch mine. "A part of my heart is yours, River, and that's all that matters. You might have survived last night, but I am still losing you today, and that hurts more than you will ever understand."

He backed away and grabbed my face intensely as he ravaged my lips with his. The desperation pushed us further as our hands fought for a place to hold onto and never release, knowing when they let go, we would be no more. The tears flowed freely as my passion took the place of the word I could never say to him, *goodbye*. He pulled away after what seemed like an eternity in heaven and hell at the same time.

"I love you, Arie Belle."

He was holding my head in both hands, not wanting to let go. I fell into his chest. "Can you please just hold me until you have to go?" His strong arms wrapped around me with a false promise of locking me there forever.

He embraced me for the last time as we watched the sun's rising seal the fate of our impending departure. I imagined us like this thirty years from now in the same place, our love as strong as it was today. That would be the only dream that would give me hope that one day we would be together again. It was only a matter of minutes before the sun would reach the high point in the sky.

"I have to go now."

"I know." I heard little footsteps trotting towards us.

"River! Arie!" shouted Amary.

She ran in front of us and climbed the rock, squeezing herself in between us. River took her in his arms and pulled her onto his lap.

"Hi, little bug."

"Tivon said you have to go back now."

Tivon was lurking a short distance away to give us time to say goodbye in private.

"I do and I'm going to miss you, but I need you to do me a favor and take care of Arie for me. I know it won't be easy, but do you think you could do that for me?"

I shot him a playful glare.

"I sure can. Will you take care of my mommy?"

I looked back at Tivon questioningly. He just nodded and gave me a condoning smile.

"Tivon said she had to go back last night, but that she loved me, and I would see her soon."

He rubbed the top of her hair playfully. "Of course, I'll take care of her. Did you want me to give her a message?"

She suddenly jumped up and wrapped her arms around his neck and hugged him tightly.

"Can you give her this?"

I put my hand over my mouth as if that would keep me from showing my pain for her loss.

"Sure thing, little bug."

Tivon gave her many more years of ignorant bliss, but the day she would finally learn the truth would shatter her perfect existence in this fairy-tale land. I would memorize every moment of her happiness to remind her when we lost her to the depth of darkness that I was now sinking into with every passing second.

Tivon approached us. "It's time."

We all slid off the rock, staying glued together until the very last second. Amary stayed between us, holding both of our hands tightly.

River touched her hand lightly as a sign to release. She did and he closed the distance to Tivon. Tivon placed his hand upon River's cheek, and Amary buried her face in my leg.

"Thank you for protecting my daughter all these years. You knew what you were giving up, and for that I am honored and grateful. In another life, my friend."

I wrapped my free arm around my stomach holding myself together as much as I could. A light filled Tivon's hand and spread like wildfire over River's body. I had to shield my eyes when the light was too strong to stare at anymore. Just like that, the light burnt out, and hundreds of butterflies swirled in the shape of River's body and flew over the river toward the sun. A beautiful lone butterfly fell behind and landed on my hand as I stretched it out. It was shades of blue with yellow stripes. It lingered for a moment and then jumped on Amary's hand before chasing after the other butterflies. That one gesture by the butterfly that carried River's essence back home lifted my spirits and solidified that we would one day see each other again.

Amary dropped my hand and ran after the butterflies, giggling along the way. Tivon stood next to me and we watched her prance around the grass. Several other kids joined her in the fun. "Thank you for that. I don't think I could have lied to her."

"I knew you couldn't, so I shall carry that burden for you."

"She'll be angry with you when she finds out."

"I know, but she too will learn to forgive me one day as you have."

He put his arm around my shoulder, and I willingly rested my head on his shoulder seeking all the warmth I could get now that the two I relied on most were gone. "So, what happened to Pyrrhus and the other shadow stalkers?"

"They were forced into the reality that holds the balance of darkness."

"How were there so many of them?" I inquired.

"I don't know. While we all have the ability to visit other realities, it is limited. Their lasting presence here is being looked into. We would have felt if that many had turned."

"We?"

"Yes, there is a group of us who keeps watch over the balance of nature."

"What happened to me in the ascension?"

"No one knows. You are the first so we learn together, but your essence is different from ours, and your energy is unparalleled. I have a feeling this is just the beginning of your true destiny, my child. The universe made you to be a protector and a savior, the likes of which we have never seen before, so we heed that as a sign of things to come. To ignore it would be ignorant, but we are hopeful, and we have peace for now."

He let go and strolled to the riverbed to watch the kids play. I felt empty, confused, and lonely. My destiny might not be fully realized yet, but this was Amary's and my home now. I had to find a way to start over and to make the best of what time we had together.

My personal destiny was to protect that little girl and to teach her the ways of the world as my mother had taught me. She was my life now, and nothing would take that from me.

Epilogue

The sun had set, but the yard was still bustling with people as the pinks and oranges of the sky reflected on the river. The curfew had been lifted, and many thanked me as I wandered quietly around getting acquainted with my new home. Tivon wanted to honor my mother's life and those that passed on last night by performing a ceremony much like a funeral. The riverbed was packed with hundreds of people that could have easily been over a thousand. Sage approached me with her head down.

"We are ready to begin," she said quietly.

"There are so many people. Where did they all come from?"

"This reality is just as big as your... as the other one. People love Tivon and are grateful for your mother's sacrifice. They came to show their love for all the souls that were lost."

"I had no idea."

"We're a small community here compared to the rest of the world. We like it that way."

"Thank you, Sage, for talking to me freely. Not many have."

"Please, don't be offended. They are cautious because of recent events. They remember you from before, but it will take time to get reacquainted. The last couple of decades have taken their toll on all of us. We never knew what darkness was until then. It was a shock on everybody. And now many are without their loved ones, which is a new feeling, as well. Everything will take time, but we are all hopeful."

She squeezed my arm gently and retreated to join the others. I took a deep breath and followed. All eyes focused their attention on me as I approached. A sea of people separated, making a path for me to reach my father. They bowed their heads solemnly as I went past them. I could feel everyone's pain. It bit at my skin, tearing me to pieces.

If I allowed it to, it would swallow me, but I would stand tall and be strong for them. I owed them that much. My father stood at the water's edge watching me. This moment could easily be mistaken for my wedding day with my father standing proudly to give me away to my essence's true match, but sadly, that would never happen for either one of us. We had both lost the only ones we could truly love with every fiber of our being.

There would be others who would help fill the void and stand by us admiringly, but we would never feel the bond created when our hearts beat as one. A close second would have to be good enough.

I thought of River. He would never be completely what my soul needed, but he would be enough for me.

I reached my father and took his outstretched hand. Amary broke from her group of new friends and latched on to my other side. The river was glorious. Flower petals of every shape and color covered the surface. Adorned on each one of them was a butterfly floating with the gentle current.

I turned to Tivon. "This is lovely."

"Every butterfly represents the essence of those that were lost and those who mourn for them."

The intention was beautiful, but the reality was heartbreaking. The true loss was laid out on the riverbed for all to see. I felt small. I was the root of all this pain. Had Pyrrhus not fallen in love with me and had I not rejected him, he would not have killed me, which in turn, started the chain of events to occur that led to this moment.

Tivon squeezed my hand and gave me an approving look. He heard what I was thinking. I looked back on the water as it slowed down and then stilled. All the sounds and movement had ceased. Tivon let go of my hand and turned to the crowd.

"We are here to honor the fallen, but not to say goodbye. They live on in the butterflies before you and will frolic amongst our land watching over us. Remember the light they brought to our lives and never forget they are with us always."

He turned back to the water. A butterfly flew off a petal and landed on Tivon's finger. Its wings were painted with splatters of every color imaginable. It jumped to my hand. Tears filled my eyes. "Is this...?"

"Yes, it carries your mother's essence."

I couldn't take my eyes off it. I could feel her life layer my skin with the familiar unconditional love of the past.

"Thank you," I said to the butterfly. It flew back toward the river above the other butterflies. They fluttered their wings and fell in line behind it. They spiraled around the air for a few moments and then headed toward the horizon. The river started to flow, and the sounds returned as they disappeared. I was, however, still paralyzed by emotion. I didn't want to leave.

I knew Tivon said this wasn't goodbye, but I felt like the moment I left this spot it would be. The crowd started to disperse around the yard. People congregated in clumps, and the kids played chase around the yard. Their laughter was much needed. Amary had left my side to join them. Someone had pulled Tivon away, and I was left alone still staring at the river as the last of the petals floated by.

"Are you okay?" asked Sage.

She stood next to me giving me personal space with a light coating of easiness.

"I don't know how to answer that right now."

"I understand," she whispered.

I couldn't help but feel like Sage was more than a passing presence. "There were times in the other reality that I would see fireflies when I was visited instead of butterflies."

"Fireflies are butterflies of the night. They are one in the same. They carry our essence from one reality to another."

"Can everyone visit other realities?"

"No, only those who can harness the energy of nature can do that. Your bloodline is extremely potent with this ability, as is Ashe's."

I was taken aback when she mentioned Ashe. No one spoke to me about him.

"I don't remember much from my other life, but from the few memories I have had, it seemed that Ashe was like the forbidden fruit."

She looked around cautiously and stepped closer to me.

"It is believed that if your two bloodlines mixed, the potency of your combined essence would kill both of you and cause an irreparable imbalance."

It made so much sense now. My dad pushing River on me, the intensity I felt when I was with Ashe, and the blackouts. My body wasn't strong enough to handle that kind of power, which was why he kept his distance.

"I'm not sure how much you know about my other life, but when I was human, it was as if certain things controlled mine and Ashe's essence when we were together. Like a certain place."

"The transfer of essence is complicated and dangerous. Your dad made a spot when he met your mom, so they could be together. You are truly unique, Arie."

We stood silently for a moment. "Were we friends in my other life?"

She looked at me, tears escaping down her beautiful long lashes. "The best."

I threw my arms around her and hugged her tight.

"I have missed you so much," she mumbled.

Flashes filled our embrace. Us running on the riverbed as little girls around Amary's age carrying bouquets of flowers we had just picked. Smiling and laughing.

Another flash of us several years later as we sat on the grass cross-legged giggling as we watched the boys kick a ball around an empty field. And then the flash of my ceremony after I was killed. It was much like my mom's, except there were no butterflies. Just a lot of somber and shocked faces.

Sage was in the front next to my dad, void of life. I could feel her sadness, her pain, her emptiness. She had become what I was after I lost my mom. I pulled away from her arms and locked eyes with her.

"I remember." I started to cry happy tears as she pulled me back into another hug. I wasn't alone here. I had my best friend again.

It was almost dark now, but the yard was still filled with many bodies floating from group to group.

"Can we talk more tomorrow?" she asked.

"I would like that very much."

She drifted to one of the groups.

I slipped away and strutted slowly through the forest, feeling all the plants along the way. With every touch, my fingers tingled, every piece of nature giving me something different. The moon was following its normal path, but like me, it was missing a piece of itself. It was no longer whole, and neither was I. I found myself in front of the waterfall sanctuary, so I climbed over the rocks remembering the last time I was here was with Ashe. It was the last time we kissed, and it was shrouded in pain and anger. I had said goodbye to him then, but didn't realize it would be forever. Had I known...

I stopped my thoughts short as I broke out from behind the waterfall. The view was even more magnificent at night.

The moon reflected in the water and the rays bounced off the hills of the valley. Stars covered every inch of the sky. They looked like a bed of sleeping fireflies. I sat down on the same rock Ashe and I had once shared and closed my eyes to remember our last happy moment together. I could feel his hand on my cheek and the taste of his lips on mine.

I opened my eyes, and an apparition of Ashe was kissing me. A faded memory my eyes were tricking me into believing in again. But then it pulled away and the gleam in his eyes and the warmth deep in my core made me think otherwise. I couldn't hear him, but his lips mouthed, *I am still here,* and then it disappeared and a single butterfly hovered in its place. It was the same one that had landed on the rock where Amary and I were first trapped. It had flown in and perched itself on a rock and then flew away just before Ashe had appeared to help us escape.

It was as beautiful as I remembered, covered in bright oranges and reds, like it was a flame burning with life, waiting for fuel to help it spread. It flew over and took its place by my side on the rock. I wasn't alone after all.

"Would you mind if I joined you?" Tivon asked over my shoulder. The butterfly flew away as he took a seat beside me. "I saw you sneak away."

"Yeah, I'm sorry. I just haven't had much time to process everything." I fidgeted with my ring. "I miss them."

"I know," he muttered as he looked out into the distance.

"I'm sorry I didn't save her for you."

"Arie, as much as I miss her, I would have done the same thing. I am just sorry *you* had to make that choice. You did the right thing."

"I wish I could say I would do it again, but I can't. Does that make me a bad person?"

"No, you have an unbelievable spirit, which is why nature trusted you to restore balance."

"It's not over, though, is it?" I looked at him alarmed.

"I don't think so. There were so many."

"Any ideas?"

"I have a theory. We have the ability to visit other realities, but we are limited on how long we can be there and how many times. I'm wondering if they somehow found a loop hole."

"Or a worm hole," I whispered.

"Exactly. The universe is magnificent, and there are so many untold stories buried in it that we are left with a lot of unknowns. Like with you, for instance. When I stole your essence to save you, I didn't know if it would work. I just had a feeling. As nature spirits, we make decisions based on our instincts, but like anything else. we can never be sure. Just a lot of faith and hope."

I didn't mean to, but a little sigh of frustration escaped me.

"I know that's hard for you, but it'll get easier for you to believe."

"There's something that you said that has been bugging me."

"And what would that be, my child?" His voice rose in curiosity.

I nervously twisted the ring on my finger, afraid of the answer to the question I was about to ask. "You said the dagger was life and death, and that it was nature's will what would happen to Ashe. Does that mean... is he not..." I couldn't find the right words to ask him.

"It would seem that not everything is set in stone, and you are proof of that, so it all comes back to hope and believing," he said as he stood up. "Come with me, my child."

I listened and followed him to the back of the waterfall. He stared into the cascading water, the mist covering him with a layer of moisture that glistened in the moonlight. He was so young and handsome it was still hard to believe he was my father. He could pass for an older brother, but definitely, not my father back home.

"This is your home now, Arie."

"Shoot. I forgot you can hear me. Sorry, I have only known this place for a little while, so it might take some time."

"I'm not offended. I'm only reminding you. Now, stand by me and look beyond the water. Tell me what you see."

I squinted to try to see anything but water, but no matter which way I contorted my face or turned my head, all I saw was the water. Tivon's contagious laughter filled the air.

"What are you laughing at?"

"You, my child. I didn't know someone could make that many faces."

"Funny, Dad." I sucked in a deep breath of air, trying to take back that last word. It just slipped out in the moment.

"Thank you," he said as he smiled from ear to ear.

We stood in unsettled silence, letting the moment absorb and pass.

"Look with your heart, not your eyes."

I was determined to understand what he wanted from me. If he would just tell me what to look for. I closed my eyes and let my mind go blank as if I was sitting in my meadow meditating. After a moment, I opened my eyes and gasped. It was River. He was running as he always did. He had fallen back into his routine. Then, his image disappeared, and Star was there.

She was sitting on her couch snuggling up to Donut Dan, eating popcorn while watching a movie. She was okay, and she had somebody. I wasn't sure how to feel. I was happy they were okay, but at the same time, I was sad. It was almost like they had already forgotten me.

"They haven't forgotten you, my child. They have hope that they will see you again, and that allows them to move forward and live."

The images washed away. "Thank you for showing me them."

"I didn't do anything. I only told you to look. Your heart showed you what you wanted to see."

"Will you show me how to visit them?"

"Yes, but not now. One thing at a time. I'm going to go back now."

"I think I'm going to stay for a little while, if you don't mind," I said.

"As you wish. Although it seems someone has followed me here," he said playfully.

I saw brown curls flying up from behind a rock. "Hmmm, I wonder who it could be," I said as I winked at Tivon. He smiled back and gracefully stepped over the rest of the slippery rocks and out of sight. Amary started giggling as Tivon passed her without a word.

I played along. "Who is that giggling over there?" Amary poked her head around and carefully hopped over to me, giggling the whole way. She fell into my legs with a big hug.

"This place is pretty," she said.

"This is our place now, Amary. Are you okay with that?"

"Yes, if you're staying."

"I'll never leave you, Amary. I promise." I squeezed her gently into my embrace. The butterfly flew back in and spun around us, lighting up like a perfectly orange flame. A flame that symbolized the fire that burned so brightly between Ashe and me. In that moment I felt it. I felt hope. I felt *him.*

READ THE LIFE BEFORE ARIE FOR FREE
http://www.danihartbooks.com

Arie's journey continues in...

Dreams

THE ARIE CHRONICLES
Volume 2

Available now

Acknowledgments

Writing and publishing my first novel was an amazing experience. From the first edition to the second edition there are many people to thank for making this the best piece of work possible.

Jennifer Pooley, development editor, is the magic behind the second edition helping guide me deeper into this fantastical world I have created, which is no easy feat in fantasy. I have so much respect for this woman and her particular eye for detail both physical and metaphysical. Such an amazing talent! Paige Smith, copy editor, is just as amazing as Jennifer with her attention to grammatical accuracy and syntax. Her ability to enrich the written word is a talent to worship.

Beta readers are an important piece of the puzzle and mine have been loyal and at times, hard on me which I appreciate and respect. Their honesty and feedback ensures that I am producing something all readers would want to read. A special thank you goes to Amanda Wooden, Natasha Burkowski, and Shasta Mosley.

Finally, I acknowledge all of my readers. Thank you for your support, encouragement, and feedback. I write for me, but I also write for you. This is only the beginning of Arie's journey and I hope you take it to the end.

About the Author

DANI HART graduated from the University of Southern California with a degree in Theatre and a concentration in Screenwriting. Dani also writes under the penname D. Hart. To find other books by this author, please visit her website.

Website: http://www.danihartbooks.com/

Facebook: https://www.facebook.com/authordanihart

Twitter: https://twitter.com/authordanihart